THE LAST RESORT

ALSO BY SUSI HOLLIDAY

Writing as SJI Holliday:

Black Wood

Willow Walk

The Damselfly

The Lingering

Violet

Writing as Susi Holliday:

The Deaths of December

THE LAST RESORT

SUSI HOLLIDAY

This is a work of fiction. Names, characters, organizations, places, events, and incidents are either products of the author's imagination or are used fictitiously. Any resemblance to actual persons, living or dead, or actual events is purely coincidental.

Published by Thomas & Mercer, Seattle

www.apub.com

ISBN-13: 9781542020015
ISBN-10: 1542020018

Cover design by The Brewster Project

Printed in the United States of America

To Granny Peggy and Papa Allan,
who never ran out of stories to tell

'Memory is the diary that we all carry about with us.'

Oscar Wilde

Summer 2000

Monstrous waves crash against the rocks, their white foam leaving a slow trail before retreating back into the murk of the sea.

Anne is standing just the right distance from the edge – close enough that she can see what's happening below, but far enough away that the sea spray and the whipping wind can't catch her and drag her over the cliff.

Her heart thumps hard and fast. She takes a deep breath. 'George!' she calls back over her shoulder. 'Help me. Please! We can't just leave him!'

Her voice is swallowed up by the cacophony. The wind, the waves, the gulls. And the other sounds too – the blood rushing to her head; the little voice inside, whimpering, telling her to *help him . . . help him.*

She blinks, trying to magic it all away.

He's not real.

She takes another step back, closer to safety. She can no longer see the little ledge that juts out below. She can no longer see the old man's hands gripping its edge, gnarly knuckles glowing white. Slipping. She can no longer hear his cries, desperate for help.

She feels herself drift away. Her mind floating off elsewhere, ignoring the horrors in front of her. *Not happening. This is not happening.*

She closes her eyes. Anne isn't even her name . . . and George is not her friend's name – her summer friend, just someone to while the time away with for the two boring weeks that she's stuck here. Her grandparents are too old to do anything exciting these days, so it was lucky she'd met George on her second day, before it became unbearable.

It was George's idea to give them both nicknames.

'You be Anne,' George had said that afternoon on the beach, when she was getting ready to head back to the cottage for another dreary dinner and another battle with the TV, trying to get reception while the wind howled outside and the windows rattled and shrieked their annoyance. The sun had been bright that day. A huge yellow beach ball, bouncing off the white sand, making the whole bay twinkle like diamonds. 'And I'll be George. Get it? Anne and George – from *The Famous Five*! We'll be friends now and friends forever.'

She hadn't read *The Famous Five* for years. Couldn't even remember if the George character was a girl or a boy. She didn't care anyway – she'd preferred Nancy Drew. But she'd agreed to this, deciding it was OK to do silly things with someone she'd never have to see again. Next year she would be telling her parents that she was *not* spending two weeks here on this godforsaken island, even if it did have water so blue it looked like something from a painting, and soft sandy beaches, and endless rocks to scramble over.

It's so *boring*! At least it was. Until now.

She licks her lips, tasting salt. Opens her eyes and blinks, remembering where she is. Wishing she was anywhere but here right now. With George . . . and this *man*.

The old man should not be here.

He has no business on this island. His small boat wasn't built for these deep, choppy seas. It's no wonder it crashed and splintered against the rocks.

She'd been gathering twigs, snapping the ends and inspecting them for sap. She'd wanted to build a fire. George had seen him first, called out to her, warning her. 'Anne! There's someone . . . a man . . . behind you. He's—'

She'd whirled round and found him there, looming over her. Hair blowing wild, a halo of gorse around his head. His beard thick and matted, coiled and dark like bladderwrack. His eyes red-rimmed, and his smell of the sea – rotted fish and wetness, and something old and terrifying bubbling under the surface. His face was scorched from the sun and the salt, his mouth had opened and he'd said something to her in a strange, guttural language . . . and she'd laughed.

She'd laughed, because she realised then that he wasn't real. He wasn't a man. He was a creature that she and George had cooked up in their imaginations, desperate for some excitement. Adventure.

Fun.

She'd laughed as she stood tall and walked towards him, thrust a hand against his chest and shouted into his ruined face – a face that she fully expected to crumble to dust in front of her eyes, maggots squirming from empty eye sockets, tiny, slithering snakes from what was left of his ears.

She'd pushed him, and for a moment she was shocked – because he didn't turn to dust or air, or disappear in front of her eyes. His chest was solid. Unyielding. But his legs were weak, and he'd tried to gurgle something else, some other words of nonsense, before they buckled beneath him and he stumbled back . . . and back.

And then he disappeared.

George's voice hits her as the wind changes direction – surging towards her, loud and clear. 'Come back from the edge, Anne. We can't help him.'

What?

Anne starts to shake, adrenaline coursing through her veins. He'd fallen right in front of her, down onto the ledge with a thump. Then over its edge with a throaty scream. And now he's hanging there, dangling above the rocks and the sea and the remains of his broken boat.

But they *can't* help him, can they? They are both too small. Too thin. Their arms are not strong enough to pull him back. Their skinny legs not fast enough to run down the hill to get help in time. He has no time. His fingers can't hold his weight for much longer.

No one knows that they are up here. 'It's my secret place,' George had told her.

No one knows that this man is here. This man from the sea, who has travelled from afar. Who has bloodied his hands and torn out his nails climbing up to a place of safety.

He doesn't belong here. Who is going to miss him?

She closes her eyes as the wind picks up, howling around her. Waves, gulls, blood rushing. Broken nails scraping on jagged rocks. The incessant hum inside her head: *Help him . . . help him . . .*

. . . and George's voice, flat. Determined. 'Leave him.'

She swallows a lump of fear. Takes another step away from the edge.

'Come on, you silly sausage,' George says, putting an arm around her shoulder. Gripping on to her just a little bit too tight. 'Let's go back to mine for tea . . .'

Amelia

T - 24

Amelia avoids eye contact with the other passengers as she boards the small plane and slides into the window seat of the last remaining row. There are six of them. Three men, three women. And now her, unbalancing the group. Potentially unbalancing the plane.

She knows about these planes. She's flown in them many times before, for work. Taking off and landing on runways that are nothing more than dirt tracks. Over parched soil, dense jungle, and everything in between. She's landed on water. She's had to parachute, more than once, when the plane hasn't been able to land at all.

She's worked in humanitarian aid programmes all across the world. She's dealt with fragile egos, misplaced do-gooders, corrupt officials, and many, many genuinely good people who have made it their life's work to help others. But none of the people on this plane look like aid workers, and as much as she's tried to avoid staring at them, she's felt their collective gaze on her, taking in her cotton khakis and bottle green T-shirt, her beige backpack that she's stuffed under her seat.

The others are dressed very differently to her.

The young woman in the seat directly behind her hasn't even glanced up from her phone. She's blonde, pretty and plugged into headphones, her plump, shiny lips set in a permanent pout. Amelia had only shot a quick glance at the others, but she swivels slightly in her seat now, trying to see them out of the corner of her eye. Sure, she could just turn and address them, but something about these people intimidates her more than any of the dangerous situations she's been placed in over the years. Besides, it's early. The taxi picked her up at 5am, and she dozed most of the way to the airfield. No one needs to be having conversations with strangers at this hour.

'Does anyone know where we're actually going?' a gruff American voice blurts out from the back.

Amelia turns round fully, relieved that someone else has taken the initiative. The voice belongs to a serious-looking guy in a smart, well-fitting suit. His hair is dark, parted neatly and greying at the temples. He might be attractive if he wasn't frowning, accentuating the long, vertical wrinkle that splits the middle of his forehead. He's wearing a headset with a microphone sticking out by his cheek.

'I don't think we're meant to know yet,' says the woman across the aisle from him, in the single seat. She's red-haired and bouncy, her eyes wide with excitement. 'But who's going to pass up one of these things? Isn't it exciting?'

'Pass up what things?' comes the bored voice of the man in front of her. He's the grungy one; mussed hair and two-day-old stubble. He's wearing a faded Ramones T-shirt and clutching a camera on his lap. 'I'm not sure what's so exciting—'

'We've been specially selected for this,' the redhead says. 'Or didn't you read your invite?'

'Ah, but did we all get the *same* invite?' This from the man-bunned hipster type sitting next to the plugged-in blonde, who is seemingly oblivious to the others talking. 'I doubt it.' He nudges his companion, but she ignores him, bopping her head to the beat of whatever it is she's listening to.

This is a good point, Amelia thinks. It was clearly stated that they weren't allowed to tell anyone what was in the invitation. Not even each other.

Especially not each other.

She'd been worried about that initially, but they'd explained why it all had to be kept hush-hush, and it had made sense in the end. You can't be too careful. She clears her throat. 'We're all here to provide feedback on a new luxury service. A unique island adventure, it said. I—'

'Oh, for goodness' sake. I have it right here.' An immaculate older woman in an expensive-looking blue linen dress loudly cuts her off. She pulls a piece of paper out of her oversized handbag and pushes her delicate-framed glasses up her nose. Her hair is styled into a helmet so smooth and neat it looks like it would prevent a head injury if she were to fall from a height. 'This is what *my* invitation says.

'*Congratulations on passing the selection process. The Directors of Timeo Technologies formally invite you to participate in an exclusive demonstration of their brand-new luxury concept island adventure. You have been chosen due to your potential fit with the brand and we would request that you do not share this information with anyone else at this time—*'

'Right. Yeah . . . that's the same as mine,' says Camera-guy, cutting the woman off. He widens his eyes, flashing Amelia a look.

Amelia clears her throat. 'Mine too,' she says, 'but that's the only part of it we're allowed to talk about, right?' They all stare at her, and she takes in their expressions.

It's not hard to recognise fear.

She gives them a small smile, surprised again at how out of place she feels here. Despite all she's achieved, she feels like that lost girl she was at school. Not fitting into one group or another. Everyone slightly bemused by her, although she could never really work out why. A creeping sense of dread washes over her, just for a moment. Then it's gone.

The older woman scowls, then drops the paper into her bag, saying nothing more.

The girl in the seat behind Amelia finally takes off her headphones. 'Anyone know where we're going then? This is such fun!' Her accent is pure *Made in Chelsea*, her smile full of perfect, too-white veneers.

'Nice of you to join us.' Her man-bunned companion pokes her in the ribs and she giggles.

Camera-guy sighs. 'Can't be going too far, in this thing. Right?' He addresses Amelia, and for a second she can't speak. Why would he assume she would know? Although as it happens, she does.

'This is a modified PAC Cresco. It's usually an agricultural plane, used for short distances. We can probably travel five hundred miles without refuelling, unless the wind is against us, in which case it's more like three hundred. I suppose that could take us to Guernsey or maybe France, at a push—'

'Wait,' the American says. 'Where'd all *that* come from? What are you, a pilot?'

Amelia shakes her head. 'No. I just have some experience getting flown around—'

'Well, damn. Impressive. But Guernsey – that's hardly a luxury retreat, is it?'

'Actually—' the helmet-haired woman starts, but she's cut off by a voice coming over the tannoy.

'Ladies and gentlemen, this is your captain speaking. Welcome to the start of your adventure . . .'

As he speaks, there's a mechanical whirr as the blinds come down. Amelia raises an eyebrow. All mod cons in this plane, then.

Most other times she's flown in one of these, seats were removed to make room for supplies, and the windows were filthy with ingrained grime. Certainly no automatic blinds.

'Please ensure your seatbelts are securely fastened,' the captain's voice continues.

'Oh, I hope we'll be getting some refreshments soon,' Headphone-girl's shrill voice comes from behind her. 'I'd *love* one of those miniature G&Ts!'

She's soon drowned out by the sound of the engine starting.

'Aren't we having a safety demonstration?' someone shouts from the back. It's harder to pick out the voices as the noise intensifies.

The plane starts to shudder, and then it moves. Slowly at first, taxiing along the runway. Amelia has flown during the small hours before, so it shouldn't be so disorienting, but she usually knows where it is she's flying *to*. All part of the adventure, though, she supposes. The plane picks up speed and she leans back in her seat, closing her eyes. Her hands grip the armrests on each side. It doesn't matter how many times she's flown, she still feels nervous. Still feels ridiculously relieved when the plane lands safely.

Her stomach flips as the plane lifts into the air. The whining of the engine is loud now, an angry screech, vibrating her whole body with its strength. She knows it'll calm down soon. Once they've reached their cruising altitude, the plane will level out, the noise will abate, and she'll be able to stop gripping the armrests quite so hard.

There's a click as the tannoy switches on once again. 'Please relax and enjoy your short flight.'

Odd, Amelia thinks. Odd that they've chosen such a small plane with no cabin crew, but the passengers are taking up all the available seats as it is. It's not the best way to put everyone at ease. The plane is steady now, the engine noise a drone rather than a screech. She takes her hands off the armrests.

'Is there even a toilet on this thing?'

She turns her head and sees that Helmet-hair near the back of the plane has removed her seatbelt and is in the process of standing up.

'Sit down, lady,' the American barks at her. 'No one said we could get out of our seats yet.'

The woman opens her mouth to respond, but she doesn't get a chance to speak.

The fasten seatbelt lights above each seat start flashing red. Then a pinging starts, and the plane lurches to the side. The woman falls back into her seat and swears under her breath.

'Told you,' the American mutters.

The plane lurches again, and the pinging gets faster, louder. The plane dips and tips, and Amelia grabs the armrests again, tighter than before.

'Wowee!' Man-bun shouts, his voice full of wonder rather than fear. 'Is this part of the adventure? Because you can consider me truly adventured. What d'you think, babe? Maybe they'll do a loop the loop!'

Amelia daren't look round. She feels a dull ache in her chest and a flurry of hot fear coursing through her veins. She tries to take a deep breath, but it sticks in her throat. A stabbing pain starts above her left eye. She knows what this is.

She looks up at the console above her head, with its flashing lights and constant pinging, and waits for the little door to open.

The tannoy screeches. 'Please remain calm. We're currently experiencing a temporary drop in cabin pressure . . .'

The little door opens and the oxygen mask drops in front of her face.

Behind her she can hear the sounds of chaos and confusion. Whimpers of fear mingling with the excited squeals of Man-bun, who still thinks this is part of the adventure. 'This is so cool,' he says.

Amelia pulls the mask onto her face and snaps the elastic over her head. *Too long*, she thinks. *The masks should've come down sooner*. Already she feels woozy from the pressure drop, the oxygen not kicking in as fast as usual.

'I feel weird,' Man-bun says, his voice trailing off.

Me too, Amelia thinks. Her head swims. The pain in her chest disappears. She feels calm, despite the plane bumping and lurching. A strange feeling that she's floating. As if the plane is descending, leaving her behind. Her eyes feel heavy and she lets them close. The choppy movements of the plane seem to stop, or maybe she just can't feel anything anymore.

The sounds around her fade, until there's nothing at all.

Amelia

T - 20

The door is wide open and a warm, gentle breeze drifts in, bringing a scent of engine oil and a hint of the sea. It wafts under her nose, making it twitch. But she has difficulty opening her eyes. They feel heavy, as if she's been in a deep sleep for a long time. Images swirl around, fragments of a dream. Or something else. Something more real.

Where am I?

She lifts her arms to her face and they feel heavy. Her whole body feels weighted down. She blinks. Rubs her face with her hands, trying to wake herself up properly.

Eventually, her surroundings swim into focus and she remembers where she is. The plane. She jerks awake fully. Remembers the turbulence. The pinging. The oxygen masks. She touches her face again, confused. Runs her hands over her forehead, then over her whole head, patting at her hair.

No mask.

She looks up at the console and the little door is closed. The mask safely inside, presumably.

Did she dream it?

She unfastens her seatbelt and swivels round in her seat. The other passengers are still there. The couple directly behind are still out of it, heads leant against one another.

No masks on their faces either.

The American is awake, rubbing at his eyes. The redhead is starting to stir.

Amelia's earlier feelings of being overwhelmed and inadequate are gone. She's been in situations like this before. Emergency landing. Or did they crash? The blinds are still down. The curtain at the front is wide open. The pilot's seat is empty.

What the . . . ?

The sound of footsteps on aluminium stairs makes her jump, and she turns just as Camera-guy appears in the open doorway, his face red. He runs a hand across his forehead and she can see that it's slicked with sweat.

He stops. Looks a little startled for a moment. 'Oh, at last . . . someone else is awake,' he says, composing himself. He gives her a fleeting smile before sitting down on the empty seat across the aisle. 'I . . . uh . . . I've had a look around, but there's no sign of anyone out there.'

'What happened?' The American unclips his seatbelt and stands up. 'Did we crash?'

Camera-guy shakes his head. 'Nope.'

'Where are we?' Redhead says. 'Did we turn back? What's happening?'

Camera-guy stands up again and heads towards the door. 'Probably better you come and see for yourselves.'

They leave the still-sleeping passengers and follow him. The smell of the sea hits her as she steps outside onto the top step, but what's out there is not what she expected.

She's not sure *what* she expected. But she'd thought at the very least they would be outside in the open air.

'See?' Camera-guy says. 'Didn't want to spoil the surprise.'

'So we *have* turned back?' Redhead says. 'We're back where we started. Is this some sort of elaborate stunt? I don't have time for this. I'm getting out of here.'

She marches down the steps and turns towards the nose of the plane. Then she stops dead. 'Woah.'

Camera-guy laughs. 'Woah indeed.'

Amelia knew they weren't still in the airfield they'd taken off from. The air feels different, and there's that distinctive briny smell of the sea. But she hadn't expected *this*.

They're in a hangar. A curved metal roof arches over them. At the rear end there's a wall. Various bits of machinery. Boxes. A small vehicle that looks like an electric golf cart, tilted slightly to one side due to its missing wheels. The smell of engine oil is stronger now that she's down the steps.

But it's what's at the front of the hangar that caused Redhead's 'woah'. The front of the hangar is wide open. And straight ahead is the sea. Sun glints off the bright turquoise water as rippling waves draw in to the golden sandy beach in front of them. The sky is clear and blue, almost mirroring the water below. The view, framed by the arch of the hangar, is breathtaking.

The four of them walk away from the plane towards the stunning vista in silence.

'Well,' the American says, 'I'm willing to forget about the chaotic bumpy hell-ride, if this is what it was all about.'

The creak of the aluminium stairs makes them all turn round, and the remaining passengers disembark.

'This is awesome,' Man-bun says, rubbing his eyes. 'The fake turbulence and the sleeping gas were excellent touches.'

'What?' Redhead says. 'No way.'

'Is that really what you think happened?' Helmet-hair says. 'Because I'm personally not one for gimmicks. What if one of us had a medical problem? What if the gas had reacted with someone's medication?'

'It didn't though, did it?' the American says. 'Gotta remember, we were selected for this. They musta checked us all out, right? Made sure there were no health issues . . .'

'Without our consent?' Headphone-girl says, her voice incredulous. 'I'm not sure that's legal, is it?'

Man-bun laughs and grabs her around the shoulder. 'Relax, babe. It's all part of the game, innit?' Then he leans in close to her ear and whispers, 'You *did* sign the consent, babe. Don't you remember?'

Amelia looks away. Pretends she hasn't heard. Just because she was told not to share anything about the selection process doesn't mean everyone was told the same. Maybe these two have some sort of joint agreement.

It doesn't matter right now.

She walks out to the edge of the hangar, breathes in the sea air. It's been a while since she was near the sea. Most of her work lately has been inland. In landlocked countries with dried-up rivers. She'd been surprised to receive the invitation, especially as it had come to an old email address that she didn't always check. But something had made her check it that day. She'd thought it was spam, at first. Then, that someone had hacked her old emails and dredged information – they knew so much about her and seemed to think she was the perfect candidate for this adventure. The money they'd offered had been hard to ignore too, especially in comparison to most other jobs – jobs that generally took a lot longer than a weekend. But presumably this is just the first weekend – to assess things on a high level. It was something she wanted to talk to them about at the end of the day, hopefully over a nice dinner with some decent wine.

She'd been wary, initially, about the non-disclosure agreement – secretive clauses have always made her nervous. But when they'd explained why – that what they were doing here was something that might one day help the many causes Amelia chose to fight for – it had all slotted into place . . . and she'd decided that yes, a little break from the norm might do her good. Besides, she was intrigued. Most of her jobs were pretty straightforward – organisations contacting her after seeing her on a news item, or reading an article about her work. Word of mouth too, of course. The world might be huge, but the network of aid workers was surprisingly small, and she was never one to shy away from a challenge.

All things considered – despite the turbulence, and that brief moment when she was sure they were going to crash – she's glad she decided to come.

Now they just have to figure out what happens next.

She steps outside the hangar and walks down the hard-packed mud road that leads to the beach. The others, with no reason to stay in the hangar, follow her out. Up ahead, there's a small stone building with a pitched glass roof. A path lined with smooth white pebbles leads to a white-painted door. As she gets closer she can read the sign bolted to the wall next to the door.

VISITOR ORIENTATION.

Camera-guy catches up with her and she gestures at the building ahead. 'So did you explore any further?'

'Nah. Just walked to the edge of the hangar and then went back. I was still feeling a bit woozy. Then I got a bit spooked, actually. It's so quiet here.' He raises his hands, palms up. 'Wherever *here* is. Besides . . . I didn't know if anyone else was going to wake up.'

'I am *so* thirsty,' Headphone-girl pipes up behind them. 'So much for our refreshments. I do hope we'll be getting something soon, because I need to stay hydrated, you know. I—'

She's cut off by the sound of the metal door rolling down on the open end of the hangar behind them. 'Wait, my bag!' she shouts. She starts to run back, but it's too late. The door slides down fast, shutting the plane and all their belongings inside with it.

'Neat,' says Man-bun. 'Now they're isolating us from our possessions.' He rubs his chin. 'Standard survival game protocol. Luckily I've got my phone in my pocket, but you know . . .' He takes out his phone and peers at it, then grins. 'Yep, as I thought. No reception. *Standard*.' He rocks back on his heels, pleased with himself.

'How come you know so much, buddy?' the American asks him.

Man-bun rolls his eyes. 'It's my business, man. I'm a games designer. Virtual reality, actual reality, survival, online treasure hunts. I'm Giles Horner. You might've seen my Insta?'

'Instagram?' Helmet-hair sniffs. 'Please. Such nonsense.'

'It's the way forward. I can give you some pointers if you like. Or Tiggy can help you, if you prefer the female perspective. She does travel, mostly. Don't you, Tigs?'

Headphone-girl grins and thrusts out a hand. 'Tiggy Ramona. At your service. What is it that *you* do?'

The older woman looks slightly horrified. 'Tiggy? What kind of name is that?'

Tiggy laughs. 'Oh, everyone asks me that. It's *so* funny! So my *full* name is—'

'Never mind that now, Tigs.' Giles raises an arm and everyone turns to see what he's pointing at. A golf cart, like the one in the hangar, is making its way silently down the hill towards them.

'Well . . .' Redhead says. 'Looks like we've got company.'

Amelia

The buggy stops in front of them and a man climbs out. He's dressed from head to toe in white. Trousers smooth, with a crease down the middle, polo shirt neatly tucked in and buttoned to the top. There's a gold logo on the right, with *Timeo* in a swirly embossed typeface.

'Hello!' He grins at them and his eyes crinkle at the sides. It's hard to put an age on him. His skin is smooth and tanned. He's in good shape. Late forties, maybe. *He fits the demographic for this type of company*, Amelia thinks.

He picks up a white plastic box from the back of the cart and walks towards them.

'Well, don't all talk at once,' he says, still grinning. He heads along the pebble-lined path to the visitor orientation centre. Amelia tries to catch Camera-guy's eye with a 'who's *this*?' look, but he doesn't notice; everyone is watching the newcomer with interest.

He holds his watch up to a sensor at the side of the door, and there's a small click as the door unlocks and swings open.

He turns round and gestures to the group with one hand, the other still clutching the white box.

'Come on in, then,' he says.

They follow him into the building. It was hard to judge from outside, but it's smaller than she expected. The glass pitched roof gives a feeling of space, but there are no windows. The walls are painted a pale lemon and lined with built-in sofas in the same colour. In the centre of the room there's a glossy white table, empty except for a pile of white plates and a row of glasses at one end. Underneath the table is what looks like a long, low fridge. As the last person enters, the door swings closed and the room is silent, but for the hum of the fridge and the mild static charge of anticipation in the air.

The American breaks the silence. 'So, are you going to tell us what's going on? Are you in charge of this thing? What the heck happened in that plane? Can we get a drink or something?' His words continue tumbling out on top of each other, his blurted frustration fuelled by the shock of what's happened so far, the confusion about what they're all doing here.

It's clear that none of them is used to being kept in the dark – relinquishing all control. The American's outburst has triggered that little niggle in her again. The NDA. The secrecy . . . and whatever it was that happened on the plane, it's not exactly normal to have them all panic like that. If the aim was to unsettle them, then they've succeeded. Amelia wonders if it's too late to back out. Ask to return to the plane. To her real life, where none of this stuff matters. Does she really care about this so-called luxury retreat? Not that there's been anything luxurious about it yet. A fleeting thought crosses her mind. She remembers a festival that was supposed to happen in America – something with proper, no-expense-spared luxury – except it was all a sham. Or a scam – the organiser had gone to prison for fraud, hadn't he? Hopefully this isn't what's happening here.

The American is still gabbling on, the anxiety clear in his voice. The man in white raises a hand, silencing him. 'All in good time, my friend.' He nods towards Tiggy. 'I think you were after a drink too, is that right?'

She wrinkles her nose. 'Yes. But how did you . . . ?'

He grins again and points to the fridge, ignoring her question. 'Maybe you'd like to hand out some water? Then we'll get started.'

She looks disappointed for a moment, then opens the fridge and sees the rows of designer mineral water, smiles as she hands one to each of them. 'This stuff has purified charcoal crystals in it,' she whispers as she hands a bottle to Amelia. 'It's a *complete* mind-and-body cleanser.'

Amelia smiles back, thinking of the filthy water she's had to boil up and purify with iodine, and wonders if this stuff is going to change her life, or just hydrate her like any other water. The consumerist world is bad enough at the best of times, but it seems even worse when you've lived in the places that she has. The places where people die because they don't have essential medicines. In Tiggy's world, people get stressed when the composition of their mineral water isn't to their liking, and excited by the prospect of an energy boost from purified charcoal. What a lot of nonsense.

Perhaps it *was* a mistake to come here. Her mind keeps flitting back and forth. It's not like her to do something so frivolous, and she's finding it hard to adjust. It's never been money that's attracted her to her job.

Low-level chatter has started now that everyone has had a drink and they're feeling more refreshed.

The man in white clears his throat. 'OK, guys. Let's get down to business.' He waves his watch across the side of the white box and there's a click as the top pops open. 'Right,' he says, taking a small device that looks like a Bluetooth headset out of the box. 'Who's first?' He holds it up for them to see, and Amelia notices a thin metal prong protruding from the back of the piece that hooks over your ear. She's about to ask about it when Giles stands up.

'Me?' He places his empty water bottle on the table.

The man in white nods, then runs a finger across the surface of his watch. 'Hmm . . . hang on.' He looks at Giles and grins again. 'Nope.'

Giles blows out a breath and sits back down. 'Right then,' he mutters under his breath, clearly annoyed at not getting his own way.

'Sorry,' the man in white continues. 'I'm afraid I'd forgotten that there's an order here.' He shrugs. 'I'm just following instructions.'

'Can you just tell us what's actually going on?' Redhead says. 'I'm sure I'm not the only one getting a bit impatient.'

'Yes. Of course. Sorry. Please bear with me. This is the first time we've had a group here and we're still working it all out.'

'So we're guinea pigs?' the American asks. 'I mean, that's fine . . . but we were promised luxury, right?' He stands up and turns to the group, raising his palms. 'We're not too impressed so far, buddy.'

There's a rumble of agreement from the group.

'Sorry. Sorry,' says the man in white, sounding a bit flustered now. 'OK, first up is . . . Lucy De Marco.' His eyes scan the group. 'Which one of you is Lucy?'

'That's me,' Redhead says with a grin. 'Go first for what?'

The man in white holds the device aloft. 'To get this set up. Once we—'

'What even *is* that?' Giles butts in. He steps forward to get a closer look, but the man pulls it back, covering it with his palm. 'Are you checking how far we walk around the island?' Giles continues. 'Assuming this *is* an island – which, by the way, is very Agatha Christie and all. But could you tell us what we're doing in here?' He surveys the room, lets his gaze land on Tiggy. 'We were kind of expecting a champagne reception. Weren't we, babe? Under the palm trees kind of thing—'

‘In fact,’ Helmet-hair says, ‘perhaps you could start with your name, and why you’re here? Are you in charge of this’ – she pauses, gesturing at his polo shirt – ‘Timeo? What is *Timeo*? This is all getting ridiculous, quite frankly. I don’t have time to sit about in here drinking foul-tasting mineral water with a group of strangers. I have work to be getting on with, and I was assured that coming here was going to be something I’d like to potentially invest in. But so far I’m not seeing anything particularly investable—’

‘Right,’ says the American, talking over her. ‘I had to fly from Los Angeles for this. I hadn’t planned a trip to the UK this month . . . are we still in the UK? The cloak-and-dagger is getting kinda wearing.’

The man in white lays the device down on the table, then raises his hands, trying to placate them all. ‘You’re right. Of course you’re right. I thought I had the script off pat, but it seems I have some work to do. My name is Harvey. I work for Timeo Technologies, and I’m here to facilitate your day. There will be a full presentation very soon, but first, I do need to allocate you all a tracker so that we can get started. It’ll all become clear once you’re plugged in.’

‘Plugged in?’ Amelia says. ‘What do you mean, exactly?’

Harvey nods at her. ‘Don’t worry, all will be explained. First, if I could just ask Lucy to come up here and then we can carry on with the demo. After which you’ll get a full itinerary, and then – of course – some proper refreshments. How does that sound?’

There are murmurs of assent. Then Lucy walks up to him and offers her wrist.

‘Oh no,’ Harvey says, shaking his head. He smiles. ‘Your devices aren’t quite the same as mine. We’ve been trialling a few different prototypes and we’re delighted to offer you our brand-new neuro-wearable device.’ He nods at Lucy. ‘If you could move your hair back at one side.’

She looks confused.

'May I?'

Harvey steps towards her, the device still in one hand. With the other, he lifts the hair above her left ear, holding it out of the way. Then he clips the device over her ear. 'You'll feel a small stinging sensation while it beds in.' He presses firmly on the back of the ear-clip.

'What the . . .' Lucy starts to say, and then 'Ow!' She pulls away and flings her hand up to her ear. Harvey steps back from her, alarmed. 'What did you do?' Lucy says. 'Take this thing off.'

Harvey shakes his head. 'I'm sorry, I'm afraid I can't do that.'

Lucy grabs at the device and tries to pull it off. She lets out a small squeal of pain. 'It's stuck. It's actually stuck *into* my head. I felt it pierce the skin!'

'Don't worry,' Harvey says. 'This is just how it works. We need to penetrate the skin slightly in order to access your neural pathways—'

'You need to do *what*?' Helmet-hair says. 'I most definitely didn't sign up for this. I've changed my mind. Take me back, please.'

No one speaks for a moment, all of them staring at Lucy, waiting to see what she's going to do next. Amelia takes a step towards her. 'Maybe I can help?'

Lucy blinks, her voice calmer now. 'It's fine,' she says. 'I'm up for this. I'm intrigued. After that little sting, it's nothing. I can't even feel it now.' She turns to Harvey. 'In fact, I'm feeling a wee bit trippy. Are you going to tell us what this thing actually does, Harv? Have you fired in something to calm me down?'

Harvey smiles at her. 'Yes, OK, you're right. But it's really nothing to worry about. I'll explain precisely how it all works, of course. But let's get you all kitted out first.' He runs a finger across the watch screen again. 'OK. So which one of you is James?'

Camera-guy shrugs. 'That's me,' he says. 'But hang on . . . can you tell me what it is you've injected her with, and why she needs it – because I'm not sure I'm 100 per cent on-board with this just yet.'

Harvey fixes him with a hard stare. 'I can assure you that anything we attach, administer or instruct is completely safe and for your own benefit as part of the day. Without getting all heavy on you, this was spelled out in your acceptance form. You've signed a waiver.' He turns round, making sure they're all paying attention. 'We wouldn't want any of you to jeopardise your *remunerations*, would we?'

Tiggy takes Giles's hand and he responds with a grimace. 'Sure, dude,' he says. 'We get it.'

Helmet-hair purses her lips, crosses her arms, but says nothing more.

James walks over to Harvey and tips his head towards him. 'Come on then. Let's get this done.'

Amelia

T - 19

After Lucy's shock at the attachment of the device, and Harvey's little admonishment, everyone seems to have calmed down. Each time Harvey has glanced at his watch, Amelia has expected it to be her. But she's last, it seems. After Lucy De Marco, the redhead, and James Devlin, the camera guy, had come Tiggy Ramona – which surely can't be her real name – and her boyfriend, the pushy games designer, Giles Horner. Then the American, Scott Williams, and finally Brenda Carter, the woman with the unmoving helmet of hair.

Apart from Tiggy and Giles, who have already revealed their jobs, and with it a suggestion of what they might be doing here, Amelia is still none the wiser about the others' roles, and her own part in this. But everyone seems to be much more relaxed with their devices attached behind their ears. Partly down to the drug, assuming they've all had the same thing. Amelia stands and walks towards Harvey, supposing that she's next.

Scott, the American, is chuckling to himself. 'I get it,' he says. 'I'm digging this sedative, by the way. So you're administering it via the metal sensor that's pierced the skin, right? A microlance of some sort? Is it something in the metal, or something you're firing through the hollow chamber?'

Harvey looks away and starts fiddling with his watch. 'Nothing like that—'

'Oh, sure,' Scott says, turning to Amelia and winking at her conspiratorially. 'I work in this field, you know. Nutraceuticals and all that. Our biggest thing at the moment is those vitamin infusions that're pumped in via a drip. All the rage. Anything you need – energy, calm, anti-anxiety . . . You name it.'

'Are you kidding?' Lucy interrupts. 'They're pumping drugs into us? I was joking earlier! This *cannot* be legal.'

'Of course it wouldn't be legal,' says James. 'But you RSVP'd, right? Did you read the non-disclosure agreement? Sign the waiver? Harvey literally just mentioned it five minutes ago.'

'I didn't see anything like that,' Giles says, his eyes scanning the room, looking for some backup, 'about giving us drugs . . .'

'You said we did, babe,' Tiggy stage-whispers to him. He ignores her.

'Well, I read it,' Brenda says. 'It's watertight. I just wasn't expecting this.'

'Shall we sort out your tracker?' Harvey says, turning to Amelia. He's still smiling, but there's uncertainty in his eyes now.

Amelia hesitates. 'Perhaps if someone could explain all this a bit more—'

'Look, lady,' Scott says. 'We've all got one now. Just embrace it. I mean, come on. It's not like they're trying to kill us.' He tries to laugh, but it sounds hollow.

'Maybe they are, though,' Tiggy says. 'Maybe this is one of those extreme reality TV shows or something. Oh God! Why didn't I think of this before?'

'What,' Scott says, 'a reality show where they *kill* the contestants? What kind of hardcore TV shows do you Brits go in for, for God's sake?'

Tiggy glares at him but doesn't say anything more.

Amelia sees Brenda and James exchange a glance. Then James shrugs and turns back to Amelia. 'It's fine,' he says. 'The rest of us are OK, right?' He flashes a look at Tiggy. 'No one is trying to kill us.'

Amelia swallows. Brenda and James seem to be the most level-headed. If they're OK with it . . . She turns back to Harvey, lifts her hair away from her ear, like she's seen the others do. Harvey leans in and places the loop of the tracker over the top of her ear. She braces, expecting the small sting that the others have mentioned. Expects to flinch. Imagines it's a bit like getting your ears pierced – that terrifying-looking gun that fires the earring post through the soft flesh of your ear. She stopped wearing earrings when she started to get a skin reaction, many years before. Hopes that the metal prong of the tracker – or whatever it is – doesn't do the same.

Harvey takes a step back, his face scrunched up in confusion. He taps his watch. Blows out a breath. He leans over and touches the device. 'You're Amelia, is that right?' She nods, letting him continue. 'Did you feel it? It would've just been a tiny pinprick, but you should definitely feel it. That area of skin is very thin.'

'I didn't feel it.' A small bead of worry slides across her chest, making her heart flutter.

Harvey presses on the tracker. Then looks at his watch. 'It's not registering.' He unclips the piece that hooks over her ear and pulls.

'What the . . . ?' Giles starts. 'How has hers come off like that?' He tugs on his own device, then winces. 'Ouch. Jeez.'

'Please,' Harvey says. He has two spots of red on his cheeks. Sweat is prickling on his forehead. 'Please don't try to remove the devices. As I explained, they're connected now, and they're calibrating. We need to remove them properly later on, or they could damage the skin, and—'

'Maybe try on my other ear?' Amelia suggests. She takes a deep breath, trying to swallow the bead of worry and dissolve it deep inside.

'No . . . no,' Harvey says. 'It has to be the left ear. It connects to . . .' He lets the words trail off. His watch beeps and he looks down at it again, reading a message that's flashed up. 'OK, right. We need to revert to Plan B for you. Just for now.' He sticks his hand back into the white box and pulls out a watch, similar to the one he's wearing. 'Left wrist,' he says, nodding at Amelia. 'The sensor isn't as advanced on this one – no skin penetration. This is Prototype II. The staff wear them, but we'd hoped that all of you would be able to wear the brand-new Prototype III. But not to worry, we're still in the testing phase. In fact, this might be a good thing. A mini clinical trial, I suppose. One of you having the standard device, the other six having the new one . . .'

'Oh, whatever,' Tiggy says. 'I'm bored now. When are we heading to the retreat?'

Harvey ignores her.

Amelia fastens the watch onto her wrist, and as the final clasp clicks into place, a green, wavy line starts to flow across its screen.

'It's your heart rate,' Harvey states. 'It'll go dark again once it's calibrated. Make sure you keep it fastened tight, so the sensor gets as much skin contact as possible.' He snaps the lid of the white box shut, then addresses them all. 'OK then. Here's what's going to happen. Your sensor is tapping into your neurological pathways as we speak. It is picking up your *vibe*. It is assessing your health. It is investigating your pleasure points, and your quirks and foibles, and all the things you don't like. After about ten minutes, your device will have completely mapped your body and mind, and it will provide you with a personal programme for the day. Everything you need will be individually transmitted – just for you.' He pauses, looks at his watch. Then he holds the screen towards them, letting them see what's on it. 'It's T minus 19. The device knew that I wanted to know the time, and that's what it's shown me.'

'Oh, please,' Lucy says, 'this is nonsense. There's no device that can read your mind.'

Harvey smiles. 'You don't know about Timeo yet.'

'We don't know anything yet, buddy,' says Scott. 'You've told us nothing about the company, or why we're here, and I guess now we're just supposed to believe that this device you've jammed into our skulls is going to tell us what to do for the rest of the day?'

'How does that even work?' James says. 'She's got a watch like yours – she can see what it says. How are we supposed to know what to do, if the thing's just attached to one of our ears?'

'T minus 19?' Tiggy blurts. 'What kind of time is that anyway?'

'You must've heard it like this before? It's a countdown. Like when they're about to launch a space rocket?'

She gives him a blank stare.

Harvey sighs. 'It's nineteen hours until the party, where all will be revealed. I'm going to leave you to it. If you need help, help will arrive. In the meantime, just decide when you want to start . . . and it will happen.' He makes a double-tapping gesture on the side of his head, then he picks up the box and disappears out of the door before they can ask him anything else.

'Right then,' Scott says. 'So, who's gonna go first?'

'We need to clear our minds,' James says, 'you know . . . like in *Ghostbusters*.'

'The Marshmallow Man,' Scott and James say together. They both laugh. 'Don't even think of that,' James says, his expression serious again. 'I think we need to be careful.'

'We need to do *something*,' Scott says, 'or we're going to be stuck in this room for nineteen hours.'

'Let's just go with it,' Giles says. 'I'll go first . . .'

Lucy

Lucy leans back into the soft cushions of the sofa and pretends that she's not taking in the other six people who are scattered around the small room. The girl in khakis – Amelia – looks relieved at not having the tracker stuck into that soft, thin skin above her ear, and Lucy feels a prickle of annoyance that she's got away with it. Maybe this is all part of the 'game'. That's what Giles seems to think it is. Maybe she's in cahoots with this 'Harvey' guy – if that's even his name.

Of course the 'tracker' thing has to be just a bit of fun. She'd laid it on a bit thick, saying she felt funny after it was attached to her. The feeling had passed soon enough; no way are they really firing drugs into her head. She wrote an article once on autosuggestion, after one of the celebs she was digging into said they were being hypnotised for an addiction and ended up acting all weird. It's easier to trick the mind than people realise.

She'd done a bit of digging on Timeo before she'd RSVP'd, but their website hadn't given anything away. It had a black background – making her think she'd crashed her laptop – then a single line of scrolling text appeared, saying 'Creators of the technology you didn't know existed', before ending with their simple logo, just like on Harvey's polo shirt. That was it. Nothing else in Google – every search link led straight back to the same place. Which – although frustrating for someone used to being able to find all the information required, in record time – was more than a little bit intriguing.

Lucy's whole online life is based on intrigue. Intrigue and cynicism, in fact. It's not as if you can write a high-profile gossip column and not experience both those things on a daily basis. She's heard of Tiggy and Giles – these so-called 'influencers' have become celebrities in their own right, and it's especially intriguing when they come as a pair. Lucy had done a piece on Giles Horner only a few months before, dredging some dirt on some of his previous work, before he became a YouTube sensation – sharing his bespoke games and his views on those developed by others. The virtual reality games are particularly popular, and her column had a lot more hits than usual when she'd hinted that it wasn't actually him who'd developed these but a silent partner – someone who wasn't quite so Instagrammable. It's just like those music scandals in the eighties and nineties. Milli Vanilli with their big hit 'Girl You Know It's True', and the two pretty boys with the braids who turned out to be nothing more than glorified dancers – the real singers not being photogenic enough to show to the world.

It's exactly this kind of thing that's wrong with the world, in Lucy's opinion. Hence her glee at exposing all the celebrity mistruths and cover-ups she can find. Most of it isn't meant to harm, though – she strongly believes that the majority of the celebrities out there are fully aware of the nonsense of it all. Except for the reality TV stars who truly believe their own hype. Still, let them have their fifteen minutes of fame. Their antics are what pay Lucy's exorbitant London rent. She can always move back to Scotland when she gets bored of it all.

But there *must* be some dirt on this Timeo set-up, and she'll do her best to uncover it – but obviously that's not really why she's here. She's been invited here to review the experience with a view to attracting the very celebrities she spends her days toying with. Well, there's that, and the promise of a significant sum of money to lure a couple of young royals onto the island, should the whole retreat thing end up going ahead. And of course, it's not like she had much of a choice, with those links she'd been sent. Self-preservation and financial gain are a potent combination – one that she's definitely not immune to.

'I'll go first,' Giles says. 'I reckon I can play this thing.'

Lucy glances over at Amelia and pulls a face. Amelia gives her a brief smile. She looks nervous and out of place, but she shouldn't worry about that. Everyone here is in the same boat right now. No one knows who anyone really is. It's going to be interesting to see how the dynamics shift as people start to come into their own. What Tiggy said about it being a reality TV show set-up was spot on. Before she'd started her own – anonymous – column, Lucy had worked for a couple of the overpriced glossy magazines. She'd been forced to go on a team-building weekend once – one of those adventure things with ropes and helmets and zip wires, except they'd adapted it for the company, added in shelter-building and fire-making, made them all camp out there overnight. Her sense of humour had got her through it, but her cynicism had been in overdrive – mixing creatives with sales and marketing and the high-level finance bods had been an interesting idea. It had shown her that people always show their true selves when under pressure. Mainly it had shown her that she hates climbing ladders, and has no patience for the timid. Who's going to be the timid one today? Her eyes are drawn to Tiggy, who's busy nibbling the skin on the side of one thumbnail, her eyes flitting from one person to the next, as if awaiting instruction.

Giles walks away from her into the middle of the room, taps the tracker twice, just as Harvey had indicated, and says, 'Who am I and what am I doing here?' Then he grins, pleased with himself. 'Got to follow the signals, right? You saw him tap—'

'Wow,' Tiggy says, cutting him off. 'Look!' She points behind him to the bare expanse of wall, which is not bare anymore but covered in green writing – more of it being added as it goes. Lucy turns round to look at another wall, and the writing follows.

'What the . . . ?' Scott puts a hand in front of his face, then takes it away. 'I can still see it when I cover my eyes. You guys—'

'I don't understand,' Lucy says, feeling a prickle of panic inching down her spine. 'Giles, can you . . .' She lets the sentence trail off. Everyone is standing still now, staring in different places, their expressions ranging from alarm to wonder.

All except Amelia, who is whirling around, looking from one wall to the next. Tapping at her watch. 'I don't see it,' she says, her voice rising in pitch. 'What are you all seeing?'

'It's bright green,' Tiggy says. 'How can you not see it?'

'What's bright green?' Amelia walks briskly over to Tiggy, stares in the same direction. 'I can't see it.'

'"Name – Giles Horner,"' James starts reading aloud. '"Age – twenty-eight. Nationality – British."'

Scott takes over. '"Current residence – Chelsea, London, UK. Marital status—"'

'"In a relationship,"' says Tiggy. She turns to Amelia. 'You really can't see this?' She pauses, her eyes widening. 'Woah. Now I can see it on your face.'

Amelia grabs her shoulder. 'See what? I don't understand!' Tiggy takes a small step back, and Amelia lets go of her. She jabs at her watch, her face pinched in annoyance.

Lucy takes a step towards her. 'There's writing,' she says. 'Green writing. It's written like a list of vital stats – like the kind of thing that pops up on a video game.'

'"Job – games designer, YouTuber, influencer,"' Giles reads. He's grinning. 'This is really cool. "Why you're here – to critically assess the components of the game."' He pauses, uses both hands to smooth his hair up to his bun. 'See, I told you guys it was some sort of game.'

Lucy keeps watching as the cursor blinks . . . waiting.

'This is *so* cool,' Tiggy says. 'Isn't it amazing that it's coming from our trackers? It's like some weird sci-fi thing. Or like that series, what's it called . . . ?'

'*Black Mirror*,' James says. 'Right? Although I can't believe it's coming from our trackers. It's some kind of trick. Has to be . . .'

'Amelia can't see it, though, can she?' Scott says, turning to face Amelia, who is silent now, her mouth etched into a tight line. She shakes her head, and Lucy thinks she can see her eyes start to fill with tears.

'This is because my stupid tracker doesn't work, isn't it?'

'Did you try tapping your watch? Maybe it just has to get transmitted a different way,' Lucy says.

'You saw me try that,' Amelia says, pressing on her watch again.

The cursor stops blinking at the base of Giles's list, and more green type appears.

> YOUR GREATEST FEAR: GROWING OLD
>
> YOUR LAST LIE: YOU TOLD TIGGY YOU WERE AT CAMERON HEALY'S 30TH BIRTHDAY PARTY LAST SATURDAY WHEN IN FACT YOU WERE WITH JULIA HUGHSON IN THE HILTON ON PARK LANE. ROOM 415. ROOM SERVICE CHAMPAGNE AND A BOWL OF CHIPS AT 23:47. CLASSY.

The cursor blinks again.

There's a smattering of awkward laughter, then Tiggy pulls her knees up to her chest and buries her face, wrapping her arms around her legs. Her hair falls down, concealing her face, but from the gentle shuddering of her shoulders it's obvious she is crying.

It's also obvious that this isn't the first time something like this has been revealed.

Amelia looks from Giles to Tiggy, confusion on her face. 'What does it say?'

Giles ignores her and turns to Tiggy. Lets out a bark of nervous laughter. 'This is nonsense, Tigs.' He raises his palms and glances around the room. 'You know it is. It's just a stupid game.' He turns to Amelia. 'Just some made-up bullshit.'

'Pretty specific though . . .' James mutters.

Giles's face flushes pink. 'What's this "fear" nonsense anyway?' His earlier bravado is long gone. 'Growing old? As if I'd say that.' He sits down beside Tiggy, whispers something Lucy can't hear.

Lucy watches him with interest. This is the kind of information she likes to dredge up for her column – and it's not that hard to find people to spill the beans, even on their friends. But she's never been there when someone's been directly affected. She knows Giles's type. He's definitely a boy-man who craves adoration and doesn't know when to say no. Tiggy probably just puts up with it because she likes to be associated with him. It's pathetic, but it's also a bit seedy, seeing it like this. It's at times like this she's glad her column anonymity is airtight. She's made sure of it.

No one knows that she is the voice behind *Real Celebrity Gossip UK*.

Not one person, other than herself.

Amelia

Scott breaks the awkward silence. 'Well,' he says, 'this is obviously all part of the game. I suggest we carry on. Get whatever it is they've got on us out into the open. The psychology here is clear enough. They're trying to rattle us, see how we react. It feels more like a corporate team-building event than something I thought was meant to be luxury . . . and fun . . . but I guess we need to get it going, then see where it takes us.' He scans the room. 'Who's in?'

There is a flurry of reluctant yeses, and Amelia feels like she has no choice but to join in, even though she can't read what is appearing to the others. Not that she has anything to hide, and she's actually quite interested in what 'fear' is going to come up for her. If someone was to ask her right now, she wouldn't be able to choose one for herself.

'Can you read it all out to me, please?' she says. 'Take it in turns, or whatever. I feel like I'm really missing out now without the proper tracker.'

'Giles is a naughty boy,' Scott says with a smirk. 'That's all you need to know about that one.'

Giles jumps up from his seat and takes a step towards Scott. 'Listen, mate—'

'Oh, for goodness' sake!' Brenda says, cutting him off. 'I'll go next. It's all rather ridiculous, but if we have to play along to get things going, then let's just go on with it.' She double-taps the device on her ear and says, with a small flourish, 'Reveal who I am.' Then she smiles and turns round to face the blank wall behind her. 'Ha!' she says. 'I knew it was a load of nonsense. I thought I'd try a different command to Giles, and look, it's not working . . .'

Her voice trails off as Lucy begins to read out what everyone but Amelia can apparently see before them.

NAME: BRENDA CARTER

AGE: 50

NATIONALITY: BRITISH

CURRENT RESIDENCE: SEVENOAKS, KENT, UK . . . DORDOGNE, FRANCE . . . UPPER MANHATTAN, NEW YORK, USA

MARITAL STATUS: DIVORCED. WIDOWED. MARRIED.

JOB: HEDGE FUNDER/VENTURE CAPITALIST

WHY YOU'RE HERE: TO EVALUATE THE FINANCES OF THE GAME.

Everyone stares straight ahead, unblinking. Amelia looks at each of them in turn, sees the minuscule left-to-right movements of their eyes as they read the text on their own projected screens.

Lucy clears her throat and continues.

YOUR GREATEST FEAR: SNAKES

YOUR LAST LIE: YOU TOLD YOUR LATE HUSBAND'S DAUGHTER THAT THE BONDS HE HELD IN TRUST FOR HER WERE NON-VIABLE AND SUGGESTED SHE SELL. YOU MADE A HEFTY PROFIT AND REINVESTED THE MONEY INTO YOUR OWN PORTFOLIO. DID YOU KNOW SHE HAS CANCER?

There is a collective, audible gasp from the room. Brenda's face is stony; the age lines she's taken great pains to cover with her carefully applied make-up and subtle use of fillers are harsh now against her pale skin.

'Absolute nonsense,' she says, but she won't meet anyone else's gaze.

'See, Tigs?' Giles says, seeing an opportunity. 'Hers isn't true, either. It's just cruel lies, put up there to unsettle us. Go on, you go next. Bet you it's a load of rubbish that they come up with for you too.'

Amelia glances over at Lucy, who is clenching and unclenching her hands. Lucy closes her eyes for a moment, then opens them and blows out a long slow breath through pursed lips. She looks rattled. And when Amelia turns her gaze towards Scott, he is frowning, the deep wrinkle between his eyebrows more visible than ever. Only James looks unperturbed, and she wonders if this is nonchalance, bravado, or if he really has no skeletons causing him any worry.

She leans back into the cushions and stares up at the ceiling. What might the game reveal about her? She doesn't have anything bad in her past. Nothing that immediately springs to mind. Giles's reveal – assuming from what Scott said and Tiggy's reaction that it was something about cheating – was fairly innocuous compared to Brenda's, so clearly there are levels. There will no doubt be something embarrassing that will come out, but it's not as if she's intentionally done anyone any harm. Has she? Certainly nothing that she can remember. But then memories are such a personal thing; everyone recalls events with a slightly different tinge.

Lucy breaks the silence. 'Perhaps we should get outside and start exploring this place,' she says, her voice wavering slightly. 'We can't just sit in here all day unleashing our dirty wee secrets.'

'Agreed,' says Giles. He marches over to the door.

Tiggy moves across the seat towards Brenda, who still looks ashen. 'It's all a lot of nonsense,' she whispers to her. 'We all know you'd never do something like that—'

'How do we know?' Scott says. 'None of us knows anything about anyone in here.'

'But it's so cruel,' Tiggy says. 'And what they said about Giles too—'

'Oh, for—' Giles swears and kicks at the door. He rattles the handle, then swears again. 'It's locked.' He turns round, his cheeks pink from the exertion. 'We're locked in.'

Amelia takes a deep breath. 'I don't think we're getting out until we finish these introductions. Let's just get it over with.'

'Fine,' Scott says, loud enough to make Tiggy jump. 'I'll go next, OK? Right . . . tell everyone who I am.' He stands back and crosses his arms. A moment later, he starts to read.

NAME: SCOTT WILLIAMS

AGE: 35

NATIONALITY: AMERICAN

He pauses. Mutters, 'Duh,' before continuing.

CURRENT RESIDENCE: VENICE, CALIFORNIA, USA

MARITAL STATUS: SINGLE

'. . . and ready to mingle.' He laughs, then when no one laughs with him, he carries on.

JOB: CEO OF NUTRICEUTICALS START-UP

WHY YOU'RE HERE: TO ASSESS THE HOLISTIC HEALTH BENEFITS OF THE GAME

YOUR GREATEST FEAR: EXTREME PAIN

YOUR LAST LIE: YOU PROMISED A WOMAN AT YOUR POP-UP HEALTH STALL IN THE AMERICAS MALL IN WEST LA THAT HER FERTILITY PROBLEMS WOULD BE CURED BY A SERIES OF YOUR NUTRIENT INFUSIONS. FALSE HOPE IS DANGEROUS, YOU KNOW. AS IS EATING TOO MUCH SATURATED FAT.

He shakes his head. 'Oh, for God's sake. I hand out leaflets listing the full ingredients. Anyone who wants to believe that these things are genuinely beneficial is just asking for it.'

'Proud to be a snake-oil salesman, are you?' James says, raising his eyebrows.

'Wow. Just wow,' Scott says. 'You think I'm worse than her?' He points at Brenda. 'Duping her own dying stepdaughter?'

She gives him a hard stare. 'Don't start on me. At least I'm not a hypocrite. I set out to make money and that's what I do. You sell people cures for conditions they don't know they have, or convince them you can make all their worries disappear with an overdose of vitamin C that will only get pissed out the next time they go to the toilet . . . and your greatest fear is extreme pain? Don't you have some kind of pseudo-pharmaceutical *drip* for that?'

'Guys, guys . . . come on.' Giles stands between them and holds a palm out to each of them. 'Like we said, we don't know if any of this is true. It's clearly all being set up to cause friction here – and guess what? It's working. Right then,' he says, turning to Tiggy. 'Tigs, you go next.'

Tiggy gives him a quick smile, then stands up. 'What've you got on me, then?' she says. She smiles nervously, lays a hand on Giles's arm, giving his biceps a quick squeeze. 'Babes, can you read mine out?'

Amelia is surprised that Tiggy has seemingly forgiven Giles so quickly – but she doesn't know these people, or what their relationship is all about, so who is she to judge?

Giles grins, then leans in and kisses his girlfriend on the forehead. 'Course I can, babes. Right . . .'

NAME: THERESA 'TIGGY' RAMONA

He puts an arm around her. 'Theresa. That always makes me laugh. My little nun, aren't you, babes?' She smiles at him, and he carries on.

AGE: 25

NATIONALITY: BRITISH

CURRENT RESIDENCE: CHELSEA, LONDON, UK

MARITAL STATUS: IN A RELATIONSHIP

JOB: TRAVEL AND DESIGNER CLOTHING BRAND INFLUENCER

He pauses again. 'Doing well too, ain't she?' No one reacts.

WHY YOU'RE HERE: TO VALIDATE THE BRAND-SELLABILITY OF THE GAME

YOUR GREATEST FEAR: BEING ALONE

He stops, pulling her closer. 'Is it, babes?'

She nods, casts her eyes down.

'What, even more than spiders in the bath?' He prods her on the shoulder. 'And getting fat?' He laughs, but she doesn't look at him. He turns to Amelia and rolls his eyes. 'Only kidding. Anyway . . .'

YOUR LAST LIE: YOU TOLD THE MANAGER OF A WELL-KNOWN HOTEL CHAIN THAT HIS LATEST HOTEL IN PARIS IS THE BEST HOTEL YOU'VE EVER STAYED IN. YOU TOLD YOUR BROTHER THAT THE BEDS WERE TOO HARD AND THE BREAKFAST WAS 'NO BETTER THAN A PREMIER INN'. IS ANYTHING YOU PROMOTE AS GOOD AS YOU SAY IT IS?

Giles starts laughing. 'To be fair, Tigs, despite this being the most lame lie I have ever heard, it's spot on. You do tell a few porkies when it comes to your reviews.'

Tiggy frowns. 'Just because I don't always like a place doesn't mean someone else won't love it.'

'You lie, then,' James says. 'They give you a free stay and you give them a good review? No doubt they ply you with other freebies too.'

'So what if they do?' Tiggy says. 'It's all fake, isn't it? Surely everyone knows that?'

'God, this is depressing,' Lucy says. 'I suppose I'll go next.'

James stands up. 'No, let me. Reveal all,' he says, tapping his device. 'You can read it out if you like?'

Lucy looks startled for a moment, at the cheek of him. Then she huffs out a breath and starts to read aloud.

NAME: JAMES DEVLIN

AGE: 31

NATIONALITY: BRITISH

CURRENT RESIDENCE: HACKNEY, LONDON, UK

MARITAL STATUS: SINGLE

JOB: FREELANCE PHOTOGRAPHER

WHY YOU'RE HERE: TO TAKE PROMOTIONAL SHOTS

YOUR GREATEST FEAR: BEING BURIED ALIVE

Lucy pauses. 'Interesting—'

'Just finish it,' James says.

She huffs again, then continues.

YOUR LAST LIE: YOU SOLD A PHOTOGRAPH OF A WELL-KNOWN GIRL-BAND MEMBER TO A TABLOID FOR SEVERAL THOUSAND POUNDS – A PHOTOGRAPH THAT NOT ONLY REVEALED THE SUBJECT IN A CAREER-JEOPARDISING SITUATION, BUT THAT YOU DIDN'T ACTUALLY TAKE. YOU STOLE THIS PHOTOGRAPH FROM THE PERSON WHO DID TAKE IT, WHO SENT IT TO YOU FOR ADVICE – YOU TOLD THEM NOT TO USE IT, BUT TOOK CREDIT FOR IT YOURSELF. NOT ONLY UNSCRUPULOUS, YOU'RE TOO LAZY TO DO YOUR OWN WORK.

Lucy sneers. 'Nice.'

'Ha,' Brenda says. 'A lazy, unscrupulous paparazzo. What a shocker.'

'Whatever,' James says. 'We all need to pay the bills.'

Lucy bites her lip, then stands up. 'OK,' she says, 'tell them who I am.' She looks around at the group. 'And before any of you start, I'll read my own.'

She puts her hands on her hips and begins to read.

NAME: LUCY DE MARCO

AGE: 38

NATIONALITY: SCOTTISH ITALIAN

'Italian? With that hair?' Scott looks her up and down, fixing his gaze on her with a barely disguised leer. 'Does the carpet match the drapes?'

'You're a pig,' Lucy says, her face wrinkling with distaste. 'Anyway . . .' She continues:

> CURRENT RESIDENCE: SOUTHEND, ESSEX, UK
>
> MARITAL STATUS: SINGLE
>
> JOB: CELEBRITY GOSSIP COLUMNIST

'Oh yeah,' Scott butts in again. 'A paparazzo and now a hack. Great group we've got here.'

Lucy glares at him before continuing once more.

> WHY YOU'RE HERE: TO SPIN A GOOD STORY
>
> YOUR GREATEST FEAR: BEING FOUND OUT

Her voice breaks. 'I, um . . . can someone else finish this, please?'

Amelia glances across at Lucy, taking in her expression. Whatever her 'lie' is, it's obviously something that's rattled her.

Brenda nods. 'I'll read it.'

> YOUR LAST LIE: YOU SHARED FABRICATED INFORMATION ABOUT AN AFFAIR, WHICH LED TO A VERY AWKWARD WEDDING DAY SHOOT BY *HELLO!* MAGAZINE AND A SUBSEQUENT SUICIDE ATTEMPT BY THE BRIDE WHILE ON HONEYMOON IN THE SEYCHELLES. NO COINCIDENCE THAT THE GROOM WAS YOUR EX?

Lucy sits down, her expression stony.

'Ouch,' says Tiggy. 'I guess he must've really hurt you, then?'

'Are you serious?' says Scott. 'What *she* did is hardly fair play.'

Lucy says nothing, but she turns to Amelia, catching her eye – and Amelia is sure for a moment that she looks relieved. As if she'd been expecting something far worse to be revealed, and she's got away with it.

For now, at least.

Brenda

Brenda is furious, but she tries hard to keep her anger in check. She doesn't want any of the others to see how much the revelations have rattled her. It's lies, of course. Investment professionals are always getting this sort of misinformed treatment. It's not like she hasn't heard it all before. But dragging her family into it was a low blow. Yes, she had suggested that Maggie get rid of those bonds, and yes, maybe it had been partially in her own interests – but Brenda was the one taking the big risks. She was the one entitled to the big pay-offs. Besides, it wasn't actually *cancer* that her stepdaughter was diagnosed with. She had a dodgy-looking mole, and it was being removed. No big deal.

The thing that bothers her most about all this, though – ridiculous sensationalism aside – is where the information came from. The company had made it clear through what they'd sent over with the invitation that they had significant knowledge of her business *and* family dealings that Brenda wouldn't want leaked. And the offer of some serious insider-trading deals in exchange for her co-operation had of course piqued her interest. But Brenda is stringent about her privacy, both professional and personal. As soon as she gets off this island and back home, she'll be getting her assistant to launch a proper inquiry. The last thing she needs in her line of work is indiscretion.

None of the others' so-called lies had been particularly shocking, but just like anything else, it's all relative. That pathetic Tiggy girl looks forlorn now, sitting there nibbling at the edges of her nails. Her boyfriend is obviously a player – Brenda can spot the type a mile off – and the girl's own lie was so obviously fuelled by self-loathing and an excruciating desire to please that Brenda can't help but feel sorry for her. Normally she'd be telling her to sort herself out, but it's obvious that she's so downtrodden – so acquiescent and used to putting on her fake smile – that goading her would be worse than kicking a puppy.

Anyway, the main thing for now is to get out of this stifling little room and on with the next stage – whatever that might be. And right now, it's not Tiggy that's causing the delay. It's the other girl, the one whose ear-clip tracker didn't work and who had to be given a wrist-version instead. Brenda is keeping an eye on that one. She can't be the only person to think this lack of a proper tracker is all a bit convenient. If they really do tap into their neurological pathways, then this girl is going to be exempt – and Brenda is not sure yet what that might mean for the rest of them.

'Are you doing this, then?' she snaps, addressing Amelia, who seems to have lost herself in a trance, gazing at the door as if expecting it to magically open.

The girl blinks. 'Yes, sorry. Gosh, I was miles away there. It's all a bit surreal, isn't it?'

'She's right,' Scott says. 'We're waiting on you, lady.'

Amelia takes a deep breath. 'OK,' she says, then taps the tracker on her wrist. 'My turn to share.'

The words appear on the ceiling in the familiar green, stuttering script. She directs her wrist towards one of the walls, quickly realises that the text is now upside down, then flips her wrist to project it to the other wall. 'Can you all see this?' she says. 'I guess it's because of the different sort of tracker . . .'

'Yes,' Lucy says. 'I can see it.' The others nod.

Amelia doesn't bother to read the words out loud.

NAME: AMELIA LAWRENCE

AGE: 30

NATIONALITY: BRITISH

CURRENT RESIDENCE: WOKING, SURREY, UK

MARITAL STATUS: SINGLE

JOB: HUMANITARIAN AID WORKER

WHY YOU'RE HERE: THAT'S FOR YOU TO FIGURE OUT

The words stop flowing; the cursor blinks. Then stops.

'Well,' Giles says. 'That's different.'

'Maybe it's because of the different device,' Lucy says. 'Harvey did say that the little prong in our ear-versions was connecting to our neural pathways.'

Scott laughs. 'That's complete bull though, right? It's a trick. Has to be. There's no device that can do that.'

'How do you know?' James says. 'None of us knows what Timeo actually does. Maybe this is what they do. Maybe we're trialling these tech prototypes, not just messing about playing a game on a random island.' He pauses. 'Talking of which, does anyone know where we are? Did any of you recognise that bay outside?'

'We didn't get much of a chance,' Giles says. 'The sooner we get out of here, the sooner we can work out what's going on.' He frowns and tugs at his device. 'Interesting theory though, about the device. The technology in wearable trackers is a lot more sophisticated than most people realise, you know. There's a tech guy in Sweden who's been firing nanochips into humans for the last few years – the chips are just like the ones in your bank card, except even more minuscule. You think all that near-future sci-fi you watch on Netflix is still years away, but it's not . . . it's the next big thing in gaming. Virtual reality is just the start. This biometric tracking stuff is almost old news.'

Brenda shudders. 'I'm no dinosaur, but I hate all that stuff. It scares me. Artificial intelligence is going to cancel out the human race one day. I know it.'

'But what would be the point in that?' James says. 'Who'd be around to benefit from the machines?'

Brenda wants to say more, but she holds herself back. She's scared that all this tracker stuff might be real after all.

Tiggy giggles, but when she speaks her voice wavers. 'You're all getting a bit carried away . . . let's just get on with the game, shall we? Because this is totally a game. I think we must've signed something saying they can do what they want . . . and I think they're watching us right now. We're probably being live-streamed on TV.' She pauses, turns round and flicks her hair. Pouts. 'I can't see any cameras, but that's the whole point, isn't it? And if we're live right now, then they want us to fight . . . and it's working! We haven't even got properly started yet and everyone's driving each other mad.'

'I, um . . . I think we need my information thing to finish first.' Amelia taps her tracker again. 'Continue?'

She taps her wrist-device once more, and the text recommences scrolling.

YOUR GREATEST FEAR: INFORMATION NOT AVAILABLE

YOUR LAST LIE: INFORMATION NOT AVAILABLE

'Not available? What the hell is this crap?' Scott strides over to Amelia and grabs her wrist.

'Hey,' she says, pulling away from him. 'Don't grab at me.'

'That's enough now.' Giles steps towards them and Scott holds his hands up in surrender, muttering a quiet 'sorry' under his breath before sitting back down.

'This is all because she's got the wrong tracker,' Lucy says.

'Or,' Tiggy says, pausing for effect, 'it's because she's the wrong person.' She glances around the room again, winks. Brenda observes her little performance as she plays to the cameras she's clearly sure must exist.

'Huh?' says James. The others gather round.

'Amelia Lawrence, right?' Tiggy says, emboldened now, addressing the girl. 'Humanitarian aid worker?'

'That's right,' Amelia says. 'I've been doing it since I left university.'

'And why would *you* be needed here?' Tiggy says. 'This is supposed to be a luxury *game*.' She curls her fingers into air quotes as she says the last word. Then she pouts again and raises her hands, gesturing towards the others. 'We've got a games designer, a gossip columnist, a photographer. We've got finance and medical. And there's me – a well-known influencer. All of these things hang together. But then there's you.'

'She's right,' Brenda says, impressed by Tiggy now that she's come out of her shell and made these deductions. Not such a pathetic little creature after all.

'So where do *you* think you fit into this, Amelia?' James says gently.

Amelia shakes her head. 'I don't know . . . I thought maybe it was something to do with the infrastructure. I've worked on all sorts of projects. Maybe they want my advice on the logistics of it all . . .' Her voice trails off when she notices the sceptical faces.

'You know what I think?' Tiggy says. 'I think you're not meant to be here at all—'

'But, I—'

Tiggy holds up a hand. 'There's a high-profile marketing agency run by *Amy* Lawrence. She's about the same age as you. She works with start-ups, and she knows everything there is to know about social media marketing. She was behind the orange square campaign for Fyre Festival, although they didn't credit her with it – which is just as well, as that whole thing changed the landscape for influencers . . .' She pauses. 'Anyway, my point is – I think it's *her* who's meant to be here, not you.'

Everyone stares at Amelia, and she seems to shrink into herself. She opens her mouth to speak, but changes her mind.

Tiggy smiles sweetly, obviously pleased with herself. She walks over to the door and tries the handle. There's a small click as the lock releases. 'Let's get out of here,' she says, and everyone follows, casting glances at Amelia, who holds back to the end. James waits for her, beckons her to follow, and after a moment she does. Brenda watches as he leans in and whispers something to her, and then Amelia nods and gives him a smile.

Outside, the sun is fierce. Seven small backpacks are lined up on the path, each with a name attached. The group make their way towards the bags, each picking up their own and flipping open the top to see what's inside. James and Amelia are close together, and he whispers to her again.

Brenda picks up her bag and sidles closer to the pair. She wants to know what he's said to her, and whether this is yet another little nugget dropped on them to try and unsettle them – or if she really is here by mistake. And if she is – how is that going to affect the rest of them?

A screech of static, then a tannoy announcement stops her from having any more time to think about it.

'Welcome to The Island, everyone. Please take your kitbag and follow the instructions according to your devices. There's a change of clothes in there for anyone who might need it. Have a wonderful day, and we'll see you soon for the end-of-day party. It is now T minus 18.' It screeches again, and then stops.

Brenda looks around at the others. Lucy and James are already picking up their bags. James hands Amelia hers. Tiggy and Giles are cuddled up, leaning against the wall of the visitor centre; his head is dipped, so Brenda can't see if he's whispering to his girlfriend or if they're kissing. Scott is standing on the rough path that leads to the beach, hands on hips, looking out at the sea. No one seems bothered about Tiggy's outburst. No one seems bothered about whether Amelia is meant to be here or not.

No one seems bothered that they might be getting streamed on some TV show, all around the world.

Money, she thinks. It's the only explanation. This is why they're bound by the NDA, even among themselves. *Everyone here has been offered a lot of money.*

But what for?

'Right then,' she mutters to herself. It's only a day . . . and who knows what it might bring? She squints into the harsh brightness of the sun.

'Best get on with it.'

Tiggy

T - 18

Once everyone has collected their bag and sorted themselves with sunscreen, hats and sunglasses, they head off together as a group. Tiggy had assumed that they would each be following the instructions from their own trackers, but inside their bags they'd all had one piece of paper, telling them to follow the arrows for clues. Paper! How retro.

The first arrow – painted onto a flag like you usually see on the holes at a golf course – is to the side of the visitor centre, pointing up a sandy track. The track is overgrown in places, and the plants and brush growing either side are not like anything she has seen before. She's not much of a hiker, and she's never been anywhere like this. Not that she can recall anyway. The landscape is a mix of sand dunes and luscious green foliage, and as the path gently inclines, the vastness of the sea comes into focus. A deep blue with sparkling diamonds of sunlight bouncing off the waves.

'I think we're somewhere in the Med,' she announces. 'Look at the colour of the sea.' Giles murmurs something she can't hear. The others look out towards the sea.

Scott cups his hands around his face as if it will help him see further. 'It's kinda weird not knowing where we are,' he says, 'but I don't mind it. You're probably right about the Med though. Aren't there a bunch of small islands off the Spanish coast?'

James veers closer to the edge, peering over. 'We're pretty much on a rock. Has anyone here been to the Channel Islands? I'm thinking it might be one of those . . . one of the smaller ones that no one goes to.'

'It's pretty, wherever it is,' Lucy says. 'Have you seen these?' She bends down and lifts the rose-shaped head of a bright green plant poking out from a gap in between some rocks. 'It's a succulent, I think. I don't know what the species is. I have one like this in a little pot on my desk. I've never seen them growing wild.'

'Kind of tropical-looking, isn't it?' Brenda says, leaning over and inspecting the plant. She stands up and pushes her sunglasses up her nose. 'We can't be anywhere tropical though, can we?' She turns to address Amelia. 'Five hundred miles, you said, didn't you? We can't even be in the Med, can we?'

Amelia shakes her head. 'No. I don't think so.'

'So when does it start being customised to what we actually want?' Tiggy asks. 'Because if it's meant to be tapping into my brain to pull out my ideas of luxury, then something has gone seriously wrong there.' She marches past Amelia and James and stops when the path levels out, widening into a clearing. It looks as if the shrubs and brush have been removed on purpose, rather than normal erosion from people walking by. *But how many people do walk by*, she wonders. She turns round slowly, taking it in. She's about to say more when the tracker vibrates above her ear. 'Oh,' she says. 'Something's happening, I think.'

'What?' Giles bounds up the hill towards her like an excited puppy. 'Has Big Brother spoken?'

'Ha,' Tiggy says. 'No. But my tracker vibrated.'

The others join them at the clearing.

'Mine hasn't done anything yet,' Brenda says, disappointed. 'Did you do anything to it?'

Tiggy shakes her head. 'Nope. But I did say I thought it wasn't working. Perhaps we have to speak what we want out loud, rather than just think it. Maybe it's just not that sophisticated yet?'

'Oh, please,' Scott says. 'I thought we covered this. It's not *really* connected to your brain. It might be measuring your heart rate or something, but don't be fooled that it's any more than that.'

'We don't know that,' James says, folding his arms.

'We actually don't know anything,' Lucy agrees.

Tiggy turns away from them and puts her hands on her hips, stares at the path winding to the right up ahead. A narrow track disappears off to the left, to a place she can't see. She's too hot already, and this is not her idea of a fun activity to do in the blazing sun. 'I would *love* a cocktail and a sunbed right now,' she mutters. 'And a big umbrella. And something else to wear. I already feel sweaty. But I am *not* wearing those shorts and T-shirt they've put in the bag.' She wrinkles her nose in disgust. 'Do they think I want to dress like I'm part of a cut-price tour group?' The tracker vibrates again.

'Take the path to the left,' a voice whispers in her ear. 'Tell the others to keep going up to the right.'

She whirls round. 'What the . . . ? Who said that?'

'Who said what?' Giles is at her side now. 'Oh wait, my tracker just vibrated too.'

Tiggy's eyes widen, and her heart starts to beat faster. The tracker pings above her ear, making her flinch, like she's been flicked with an elastic band.

'Chill out,' the voice says. 'It's a transmitter. What did you think it was?'

She raises a hand to her ear and touches the tracker. She feels calmer now, but she doesn't know why.

'We've just targeted one of your pressure points. Don't be alarmed. You'll get exactly what you're looking for in just a moment.'

'Wow,' she says, turning back to the group. 'It's doing some sort of acupressure thing now. Is anyone else getting anything?'

Brenda nods. 'Mine is kicking in too. I've been given some instructions and then there was a little sort of shock, and I feel—'

'Relaxed?' Lucy says. 'Me too. I suppose this is where we all start to get our tailored programmes then?'

The group murmurs its assent. Everyone seems slightly dreamy, or maybe that's just how she's seeing them all. She walks away from them now, taking the path to the left, as instructed. It stays level, heads across and inland instead of up and hugging the coastline. 'You guys should keep going that way,' she says. She doesn't bother to wait for Giles, assuming that he's following behind her and not trailing off with the rest of the group.

She feels hot and slightly shaky, and wonders for a moment if she might have sunstroke. But she hasn't been exposed to the sun for long enough, has she? She walks for a few more minutes and then stops. Ahead of her, a piece of land has been cut away, recessing down into a dip. There are stone steps and a couple of large white umbrellas. Just visible are the ends of what look like two sunloungers.

She grins. *Now this is more like it.*

She walks down the steps and the loungers come into full view. Thick, padded beds with cushions and soft blankets folded neatly across the middle. Between them, a round white table, on top of which sits a small tray with two martini glasses. Inside, something pink, topped with white foam. Condensation running down the outsides. In front of the glasses, a bowl of green olives. Underneath the table, an ice bucket with a few bottles of the fancy water from before. Nestled in beside them, a bottle of sun cream.

Laid out neatly on one of the beds is a thin, strappy sundress. Pale yellow with abstract dark flowers. And on the other, a pair of turquoise shorts and a soft white T-shirt. Under each bed is a pair of towelling-covered flip-flops, like the kind you get in spas.

Music is being pumped from somewhere unseen. An old chill-out tune, something that's always on those Ibiza compilation playlists but no one can ever remember the name of.

She barely notices Giles as he comes down the steps behind her. 'Babe,' he says, 'this is just what we need.' She feels his hands on her shoulders, and her earlier anger melts away.

Yes, she thinks. *This is perfect.*

Lucy

Lucy follows behind Giles as far as the top of the steps before she realises that this little scene is meant for two only. 'Oh, right,' she says, laughing to herself at the boring cliché that is Tiggy and Giles's luxury fantasy. 'Have fun, guys.' She turns back and heads towards the others, who are still standing in the clearing despite Tiggy's instructions for them to go on ahead.

Brenda is smiling for the first time since they arrived, and it makes her look younger. That harsh hairstyle is what ages her the most, Lucy thinks. Not to mention the M&S Classic range clothing. She glances around at the rest of the group. Isn't it interesting how people can come from a similar age bracket and yet look and act so completely different? She's often thought this about the celebs she's massacred in her column. They try so hard to stay young that their whole perception of age gets lost. Poor, unsuspecting members of the public have no chance of keeping up, although plenty seem to try it – Botox and fillers, dressing too young for their age. Brenda has managed to do the opposite of this, despite probably having more disposable income than any of them.

Then take James, the kind of man who looks like he's lucky to remember to clean his teeth every day, never mind using any sort of grooming products. Yet he looks younger than any of them.

There's a chance, of course, that the ages that showed up on their holographic bios weren't accurate. Like Scott, Lucy is still not convinced that there's a biometric element to the trackers, other than the basics.

Brenda is still smiling, but she's nodding too now, as if in response to someone. But she's standing alone, a few steps away from Amelia, who is repeatedly tapping her watch, her face scrunched in concentration. Scott is sitting on a rock, eyes closed, head tilted back like a sunflower.

'Who're you talking to, Brenda?' Lucy asks.

James is sitting on the ground, cross-legged, fiddling with the lens on his camera. He looks up when Lucy speaks, and his eyes flit towards Brenda, awaiting her reply.

Brenda blinks. Frowns. 'I wasn't talking to anyone. I was listening – but it's stopped now. What did you do that for?'

'What's stopped?' Lucy says.

'It was an audio play. *The House on the Strand*. It was just getting to a good part. I was remembering . . .'

It's Lucy's turn to frown. 'You're listening to an audio drama? Now?'

'It's the tracker,' Scott says, without opening his eyes. 'Hasn't yours kicked in yet?'

Lucy taps her tracker, but it stays silent. 'I don't understand.'

'It's a transmitter, and an acupressure device . . . as well as all the other stuff it's apparently meant to do,' James says. He shrugs. 'All mine said was "wait for instructions".'

'Mine too,' Amelia says. 'It scrolled over the screen. Vibrated on my wrist. I keep tapping it, thinking it's going to tell me something else, but it's been quiet ever since.'

'But Brenda's got an audio drama?'

They all turn to Brenda, who is sitting down on a rock now, her back to them. She doesn't respond, so Lucy assumes her audio has kicked in again.

She's about to walk over and tap Brenda on the shoulder when there's a crackling in her ear, and a voice says, 'Leave the ones who want to relax, they'll be taken care of. The rest of you should start exploring. Head to the brow of the hill and await further instructions. You like mysteries, don't you? Well, keep your eyes peeled and your ears open.' It crackles again, then stops.

'Oh, right,' she says. 'Now I get it.'

'You got instructions?' James says. He uncrosses his legs and stands up. 'Lead the way.'

Lucy doesn't know why she's become the leader now, or how the voice – whoever it might belong to – knows she likes mysteries, and that Brenda likes audio dramas, and that Tiggy and Giles like to lie on loungers and drink cocktails; but she's glad that they have a plan. Even if it is only getting to the brow of the hill. Maybe that's where the house is, where the party is being held. That would make the game a bit short, but that's all right. So far it's not proving to be particularly exciting.

She marches off up the hill, and hears the crunch of footsteps as the others follow behind.

'Can't say I'm impressed so far,' Scott huffs behind her. 'Can you slow down a bit?'

She glances back, slowing slightly. Scott is already red-faced, from the sun and the incline.

'Thought you were the health guy,' James says, sliding past Scott. Amelia follows and the two of them fall into stride together. Scott slows even more and falls further back. He doesn't reply, focusing his energies on getting up the hill instead.

Lucy turns back to the front and keeps walking. She's a keen walker – racking up miles every day while she dictates her column into her phone. Easiest way to keep in shape, and always a good way to shake off the fuzzy head that seems to greet her more mornings than not. As they climb higher, the path arcs to the right and a rocky cliff face comes into view. She stops, letting the others catch up. An idyllic turquoise cove lies a long way down below, with rippling white horses lapping into the shore, breaking as they reach soft white sand. A bamboo-topped tiki hut sits back from the water's edge, with what looks like bar stools lined up beside it. Next to that, a pile of single-person kayaks and a couple of paddleboards.

'Now that's more like it,' she says. It's a long way down, but there must be a reasonably easy path. She looks back at the current path; the top of the hill is not quite in view, but it can't be far now. They hadn't been screened for fitness, and it looks like James and Amelia are fine, but Scott is struggling. He's almost bent double by the time he reaches them, his breath coming in short, heavy puffs.

'Jeez,' he says, forcing the word out with a breath. 'I think they misread my preferences by quite a long shot.'

'Have you got some kind of problem, mate?' James says. 'Because you seem particularly unfit for someone who promotes health products.'

Scott wheezes, puts his hands on his hips. 'Screw you, buddy.'

'Maybe you should stay here,' Amelia says, reasonably. 'Maybe you could tell the tracker . . .'

'The tracker . . . is . . . nonsense,' he says, shaking his head. He takes his backpack off and yanks the zip open, grabs the water and gulps it down greedily. 'I told you already about the trackers.'

'Well, they're clearly working for some people,' Lucy says. 'The other three back there have got what they want. Maybe you need to ask more nicely.'

'Brenda told me she'd asked for "me time",' Amelia says. 'I guess that's what she's getting right now.'

'And what did you ask for?' Lucy says.

Amelia shrugs. 'Nothing. Not yet. I'm still trying to figure this thing out.'

Scott shoves his arms through the straps of his backpack and barges past, marching off ahead. 'Come on then, Miss Leader Lucy. Let's go.'

James rolls his eyes. 'He'll be huffing again in a minute.'

They follow Scott up the hill, and thankfully it's not too much further to the top. Lucy has hiked many hills like this, and she'd half expected it to be a false summit. It wouldn't be the first time she'd eagerly marched to the top, only to find that there was a much bigger peak hidden behind. They're here now, though. They made it to the top.

The landscape has changed from sandy scrub to lush green leaves. The path is soil and stone. And there are trees that weren't visible at all from further down the hill, their trunks slim and bent over like willows by the wind. The island is proving to be quite the roving landscape, and all the while the sun beats down, and they still haven't found any refreshments, except for the one bottle per bag – which, as Lucy discovers when she takes hers out for a sip, is not just water. There is a slight metallic taste to the clear liquid, and judging by the new spring in Scott's step, it contains something to keep them going until they figure out what they're actually doing here. She's not madly into drugs. The occasional recreational smoke or pill now and again. But she decides to go with this. Just like the sedative they were given earlier, it can only help them – right? Thirst taking precedence over the potential risk, she downs half the bottle.

James and Amelia watch her, and then follow her lead.

Soon they're all smiling, enjoying the sun and the mild buzz from whatever is in that water. Then an alarm sounds – a single high-pitched screech – and as they turn to face the direction of the sound, the familiar green holographic writing starts to scroll out in front of them.

WELCOME.

YOU MADE IT TO THE STARTING POINT.

THE OTHERS WILL JOIN YOU SOON.

FOR NOW, PLEASE THINK OF YOUR FAVOURITE DRINK . . .

IT WILL BE SERVED TO YOU SOON.

AND THE ARROWS WILL GUIDE YOU DOWN TO THE BAY.

WHERE THE FUN WILL REALLY BEGIN.

. . .

. . .

AND EVERYONE WILL FIND OUT WHO YOU ALL REALLY ARE.

Summer 2000

There's a low roar from below them. Something between a scream and a howl. But George doesn't look, just keeps staring at Anne, with a grin so rigid it hurts. *It's OK*, the grin says. *We just need to stay calm. We can get past this.*

Anne's eyes are wild. 'George . . .' she tries but can't get any more words out. She yanks herself away and flees down the hill, dark braids whipping behind her like reins.

'Wait!' George cries after her, but Anne doesn't wait. It only takes a moment before she's gone from sight.

George turns slowly back towards the cliff edge. The wind is howling now, waves crashing against the rocks. George takes a careful step forward, peers over.

The boat is in pieces, but there's something much worse than that down there now.

A wave of nausea. Knees hitting the ground, then retching and retching until there's nothing left but bile. Stomach constricting in waves of pain.

Purge the sin! Let it all out! Repent!

It's hard to tell that it's a man at all. His jacket has puffed up with air, but it hadn't made much of a parachute. He's face down, half on the rocks, half in the sea, his hair swirling back and forth as the waves hit his broken body, each retreat pulling him further and further away.

His hand slides off a rock. *Dear God – is he still alive? Still trying to claw himself up to safety?*

But no one could survive that fall.

The wind whips and whirls.

What have we done?

A moment of madness. Bravado. Something they'll replay over and over in their minds for the rest of their lives. Memories tarnished forever.

And what about Anne? Will she already have made it to the bottom? Will she have gone straight to the police?

Perhaps they're already on their way . . . with Father. *No! Repent! For all your sins will consume you!*

George takes a deep breath and another step closer to the edge.

'Please.' The voice comes from behind. 'Don't jump.'

It's not Anne. She's not coming back.

George turns round. '*You* . . . Go away! I've told you before. You need to stay away from here. Go back home. Now!'

Amelia

They fall silent for a moment as the writing scrolls away. Then Scott begins to laugh. It starts off as a giggle, but before long he is hysterical.

'Oh, this is the best,' he says, leaning forward, hands on his thighs as he tries to catch a breath. 'They really are trying to mess with us now.' He stands up straight again, and his face is streaked with tears. 'Well done, Big Brother,' he shouts up to the sky. 'You got me.' He starts a slow handclap, but no one joins in. Everyone is staring at him with various expressions of amusement and alarm.

'Scott, mate' – James steps forward and lays a hand on his shoulder – 'are you . . . ?'

Scott shrugs him off. 'Pina colada for me, please.' He glances around. 'Are you listening? Did you get that?' He makes off down the hill at a pace.

'Jeez, Scott. Wait up,' Lucy says, marching off behind him. She looks back at them, eyes wide and questioning.

Amelia stares at James, not quite sure what to say. He holds her gaze, and she feels a connection forming deep inside. So far, he seems the most normal of the group and she wants to build on that. Things are already starting to get weird, and she needs an ally. Maybe this is intentional. Whether Tiggy was right or not about it feeling like a reality TV set-up, there are group dynamics at work. Is she just playing into their hands?

'I guess we'd better follow them,' Amelia says.

She and James head off down the hill after them as the track winds and twists towards the bay.

'Those two need to go slower,' James says. 'This path is too unstable to be running so fast.'

'Especially someone like Scott. It's not long ago that he was huffing his way up the hill.'

James kicks a stone and it hurtles off the path, disappearing over the edge, somewhere into the rocks below. 'I'd like to know what's in this water,' he says. He holds his bottle up.

'You haven't touched it?'

'Not yet . . . I'm waiting to see if Scott keels over first.'

'Wise. Although Lucy seems OK on it. Besides, I took a sip and I feel fine.'

He mutters what might be a 'Hmm.'

They keep walking, and as the decline increases she starts to feel the burn in the front of her thighs. 'What drink are you hoping for down there?'

'Well . . . I think Scott's choice is a good one, but a bit obvious. I mean, it's a tiki hut. It looks like the set of *Cocktail*.' He pauses, looks at her. 'You probably don't even know what that is.'

'Eighties film. Tom Cruise. The Beach Boys sang the theme song.'

'"Kokomo"! What. A. Tune,' he says. He starts humming it. 'Sometimes I think I'm the only eighties movie fan I know. And far too many people dismiss Tom these days . . .'

'Oh, come on. Tom Cruise is excellent. He might have a questionable personal life – although I'm not one to judge – but he is the perfect action hero. Did you see that stunt he did on the wing of a plane for one of the *MI* movies?'

'Legend. Only surpassed by him smashing his ankle when he jumped across a rooftop for—'

His sentence is cut short when they hear a piercing scream from somewhere below them. They both speak at the same time.

'Scott.'

'Guys, can you hurry?' Lucy's voice now, yelling up at them from further down the path. They can't see her, but she can't be too far ahead.

They pick up the pace, marching faster but trying not to step on any loose stones and staying as far from the edge as they can. Her thighs are burning now, but she ignores it – adrenaline kicking in. Their march turns into a jog, until Amelia slips on the path. Stumbles.

'Careful,' James says, grabbing her arm. 'We don't need another casualty.'

They slow down, and soon the path dips and they can see the others. Lucy is crouching next to Scott, who is lying across the path, one leg dangling over the cliff edge, the other bent at the knee, his foot turned inward. He is shaking and blubbering and, despite his earlier histrionics, clearly in real pain.

'What happened?' Amelia hurries around to the other side of him, keeping close to the inside of the path.

'Tripped over that, I think.' Lucy nods towards what looks like a gnarled tree root pushing out from the side of the bank. The tree is some kind of shrub – scratchy with thorns and bent from the wind. But the roots are wiry, and she can see it would have been easy to dismiss them. He's lucky too, where he's landed. He could have gone right over the side. The footpath is perilously close to the edge here.

James walks over and tugs at the clump. 'Hard as nails and bedded in tight.' He turns to Scott. 'Unlucky, mate.'

'You're telling me,' Scott says between groans. 'I wish I'd brought some of my new painkiller formula with me. I could sure use it right now.'

Amelia leans in towards his foot. 'May I?'

Scott lets loose a burst of expletives, ending with, 'Don't touch it!'

She leans away from him. 'I won't hurt you, I promise. I've dealt with this kind of thing before. I know how to set it, so that you'll be able to walk on it.'

'First aid training?' Lucy says, crouching down beside them.

'A little.' She takes Scott's hand. 'Please? Otherwise I'm not sure what we're going to do. I don't think any of us can carry you.'

'They'll send someone, won't they?' Lucy says. 'They know we're here. Scott, tell your tracker you need some assistance.'

Scott groans again.

'You know,' Lucy says, 'there was a wee flash of light, just before he fell. Like it came out of the bushes or something.'

'It flashed right in my goddamn eyes,' Scott says. 'Coulda blinded me.'

James flinches. 'Maybe a bit of broken glass or something. Sun just caught it. Like I said . . . unlucky.' He goes back to the offending bush and rummages around underneath it. 'Can't see anything.'

'Never mind that now.' Amelia drops from a crouch to her knees. 'James? Could you try and get a straight piece of wood for me? And maybe something flat . . .' She looks around at the landscape. Frowns. 'Whatever you can find.'

'Roger that.' James turns away and starts to hike back up the hill, stopping now and again to pull at various plants, looking for something suitable to take back.

Scott is breathing heavily now, but he's stopped whimpering. Lucy hands him a bottle of water and he gulps it down. Then he lies back into the bank and closes his eyes.

Amelia is still trying to work out what to do with his foot. In the jungle, she'd once used banana leaves and twine to strap up one of her fellow workers' ankles. But this place has nothing so obvious at hand. She tries to think back to the bushcraft course she took in Australia. There has to be a way to fix this, if she could only remember how. It's funny what the mind can lock away from you when you need it most.

'So,' Lucy says to her, 'what's *your* story? We didn't get to hear it back at base. Is Tiggy right to wonder why you're really here?'

Amelia's head snaps up. 'I'm trying to fix Scott's foot, and you're questioning why I'm here?'

'Jeez, OK. Chill out. I was just making conversation.'

'In a bit of a confrontational way, don't you think?'

Lucy blinks. 'Not really. Don't you think you're overreacting? I only asked . . .'

Amelia wipes a hand across her brow. Is it her imagination or is it hotter now? They're quite exposed to the elements, and the sun has definitely changed position. She sighs. 'Look . . . I'm sorry, OK? I just get a bit flustered when people talk to me when I'm trying to concentrate. Let's sort out Scott, then you can interrogate me all you like. Deal?' She gives Lucy a smile.

'Deal.' Lucy raises a hand and gives Amelia the peace sign.

They both turn back to Scott, who seems to be fast asleep.

They look at each other. That water. There's definitely something in that water.

Lucy lays a hand on his shoulder. 'Scott—'

James comes bounding down the hill, panting. He has something in each hand, but Amelia can't see what it is yet. Something whitish and straight. She stands up, ready to greet him.

'Brilliant, you found something . . .' Her voice trails off when she sees what he's carrying. Sees the expression on his face. He holds his hands out towards her, and she can see they're shaking.

'Woah,' Lucy says. 'Are those . . . ?'

'Yep,' says Amelia. 'Unless I'm mistaken, those look very much like bones.'

Tiggy

'Come on, Tigs. No one's going to see us.'

He pokes her in the ribs and slides a hand up her T-shirt. She bats his hand away and pouts.

'They could come back any minute. We don't even know them yet. I'd rather not be caught *in flagrante* by a bunch of randoms, thank you very much.' She flips over onto her side and pulls the blanket up to her neck.

She's grinning, but he can't see her face.

'Tiggy . . . Mrs Tiggywinkle . . . you know I'm not going to fall for that crap. You're not telling me you knew all those people on the train that time. Or those people walking back from the club via the park bench you were joyfully grinding me into.'

She rolls over onto her back and lets the blanket slide off. Her T-shirt is halfway up her stomach and the warmth of the sun feels good against her bare skin.

'That was different. They were total strangers.' She reaches down and pulls off a sock, throws it at him. 'Just go back onto the path and make sure they've gone, OK? I don't want that Scott seeing me half dressed. He gives me the creeps.'

Giles gives her a look of despair but says nothing. Just disappears up the path. If there's one thing she knows how to do, it's getting him to do what she wants. She runs a hand along her bare stomach, pushing her shorts down. He does what she asks, and he does it well. She groans, remembering the last time they were at a beach resort together. Their own cabana on a private beach, sheer white curtains billowing in the breeze. She'd lain back into the sumptuous pillows, looking down at Giles's head, and the perfect azure water lapping into the shore behind him. He'd looked up at her and grinned and she'd disappeared to another place, somewhere far, far away. Somewhere floating on a cloud, blissful and beautiful and rapturous. She was almost there now. He'd better hurry up.

'Giles, baby . . . where are you?' Her voice is hoarse, almost breathless.

He comes bounding back down the sandy path towards her, his face flushed. He sees her, and he knows. Oh yes, he knows.

He pulls his T-shirt over his head and she sees the sleek sheen of sweat defining his perfect biceps as he leans down, putting his hands on either side of her head and moving in for a long, slow kiss.

He pulls back, trails his hand gently over her bare skin. She shudders. So close.

'I see you started without me . . .' He pulls down his shorts and lies on top of her.

The weight of him alone is almost enough.

'Oh, Giles . . .'

His lifts one hand off the lounger, ready to guide himself in. His breath is fast and hard, and she's ready for him. So ready.

A high-pitched beep sounds somewhere close by and she flinches as her tracker vibrates against her ear. Giles collapses on top of her.

'Babe.' He nudges her. 'Turn over.'

But she can't. She's seen it now. In front of her own eyes.

It flickers. Pixelated. Then it clears.

Porn? They don't need porn. She almost laughs, but then she sees what it is.

'Babe?' He tries again, but she wriggles out from under him. Pushes him off. All feelings of desire have gone. 'Oh, shit . . .'

Of course it was too good to be true.

The volume is low, but not too low that she can't hear the sounds coming from the sordid little scene that's being projected, somehow, from her tracker.

'Babe,' he says, 'I can see it too. I don't want you to watch this. Please . . . close your eyes. Maybe if we close our eyes it'll stop.'

But she can't stop it. Doesn't want to. She's inside his head. Seeing the projection in front of her as if she's him. She stares at the white fabric above her, the image sharpening, slightly curved with the shape of the umbrella.

In the projection, her eyes – Giles's eyes – flit from one girl to the other.

Same dark hair. Deep blue eyes, huge dilated pupils. Girl one. Girl two. Plumped-up lips, high cheekbones. Massive fake tits. Jeez, are they twins? On top of one, and a side glance to the other, and she's grinning, rubbing herself. Bending down to kiss the other girl. Tiggy can almost feel the force as he thrusts himself so hard that the padded gold fabric headboard thumps against the wall. Feels like she's fucking that girl herself. It would be comical if it wasn't so utterly tragic.

She closes her eyes, and this time the image disappears.

As she opens them, a treacherous tear slides down her face and she wipes it angrily away while trying to find the sock that she'd thrown off the lounger only a few minutes earlier.

'You utter shit.'

Giles yanks his shorts up and tries to vault over the lounger towards her but gets tangled in the blanket. He swears. 'Tigs . . . wait. I can explain. It's not what it looks like, I promise.'

Tiggy snorts. She can't quite believe that he's trying to weasel his way out of this, with the evidence playing right in front of them.

She has literally seen it with her own eyes. Exactly what he's done. And yet . . . somehow, she understands.

Because she's good at denial. It's something she's had to deal with her whole life. It's easy to paint a picture of happiness on your social media channels, when in reality you're dying inside. Of course she'd known Giles was cheating. But she loves him. In her own way.

Perhaps it's just the *idea* of him she loves. The idea of them. The Golden Couple. Love's Young Dream. Is there any such thing? All the high-profile couples that people worship are a sham. Everyone buying into it, because the reality – the cold, hard reality – is that everyone is alone.

'I'm done with this.' She grabs hold of her tracker, tries to twist it off, but it won't budge. She means the performance, but she means Giles too. She should never have listened to him when he said they should tell each other everything about their invitations. Is this her punishment for violating the NDA? He said it'd be better if they shared information. Worked as a team. None of the others had to know. But now this.

This was *not* meant to happen. And now her ear hurts. She rubs the skin behind the tracker, trying to soothe it.

'Tigs . . .'

She ignores him. She picks up the martini glass and tips the pink drink down her throat. It's sharp, strong. But it's just what she needs. She picks up the other glass and does the same. Then she lets out a long, slow breath of satisfaction. Smacking her lips together exaggeratedly at the end.

Giles is looking at her with an expression of fear and panic. His shock emboldens her. Just enough.

'I'm going back to the others,' she says, trying hard to keep her voice level. 'Don't bother following me.' As she walks away, she turns back to him one last time. Her voice shaking, she says, 'I *despise* you, Giles. Right now, I wish you were dead.'

She makes it up the path, past the small clearing and over the other side of the hill before she bursts into tears. Huge, hot tears of pain and humiliation.

What an idiot she's been.

There's a small beep in her ear from the tracker. Presumably that signifies the end of her request. What a waste of time that was. She should have wished for something just for her. Giles has probably done that. He didn't even say what his wish was. So much for collaborating. The utterly selfish shit.

'Babe!' She hears the pleading in his voice from behind her. He's not close, he hasn't run to grab her. He can't be bothered, can he? She ignores him.

She sighs. Wipes away her tears. Smooths her hair back. She's finally got herself together, when she hears the scream.

Brenda

She hadn't even noticed the others leaving. Just sitting there, leaning against a rock, the sun on her face. The soothing voice of the narrator coming in through the earpiece from her tracker. Bliss. Goodness knows how they do it, but the sound seems to be coming in through both ears. Some sort of audio trickery, but not something she's complaining about. She moves now only to stretch her legs.

The audio goes off.

'Ah, come on,' she says, assuming that they are listening. Whoever *they* are. 'I was enjoying that.' She frowns. Does a few bends and stretches, hearing something in her neck make a little cracking sound as she tips her head from side to side.

She doesn't stretch enough. Doesn't relax enough. She's a victim of her own success with the business she's built up. The London Stock Exchange might rest for a few hours, but then it's overlapped by New York and the Dow Jones . . . and Tokyo. There's a two-hour window where nothing happens, and this is when she rests, or tries to. Margaret Thatcher famously ran the country on four hours' sleep a night, so surely Brenda can run her own empire with only two?

It's always an intense two hours. As though her body goes into complete shutdown, desperately trying to regenerate the things that would take seven or eight hours for anyone else. But she is not anyone else. That's the point.

She takes a few steps towards the edge of the cliff, looks down. The sea is smacking gently against the rocks below. She looks up and around at the vast blue sky. Clear and cloudless. The shriek of a gull before it lands on a rock partway down the cliff face. Someone once said to her that there is no such thing as a 'seagull' – there are several different types and the generic term shouldn't be used to describe any particular bird. What a load of nonsense. She has no idea what kind of gull is sitting on the rock. It's white and grey with an angry-looking black beak. It swivels its head and looks up at her. It's probably wondering what she's staring at.

It squawks loudly, its beak opening wide. Then it flies off. Shrieking, squawking, flying high until she can't see it anymore.

There's a rustling sound in the bushes somewhere behind her. She turns back to the clearing where she's been sitting, squinting, trying to focus on the shrubbery. Some sort of small animal. She decides not to investigate.

She might be in the great outdoors for a day, but it doesn't mean she has to find a sudden interest in the flora and fauna.

'Ready for your lunch?' The voice comes through the earpiece. 'Take a look behind that bush.'

She hadn't even thought about lunch yet, but her stomach rumbles at the mention of it. 'I assumed I'd be joining the others for lunch,' she says. She'd felt self-conscious at first, talking to someone who wasn't there. But it's not really any different to an audio Skype call, and she has plenty of those. She's used to having an earpiece stuck to the side of her head. Not quite like this one, but still. The other difference is that she usually knows who it is she's talking to.

'This is your moment, Brenda,' the voice says. 'You wanted relaxation. You don't need the others bothering you. Am I right? That irritating Instagrammer and her full-of-it boyfriend? The stupid American with his pseudoscientific nonsense? You're better than them, Brenda. You're a captain of industry. You're Queen of the jungle. You eat these people for breakfast.'

There is a pause and Brenda smiles to herself, enjoying the praise even as she steels herself against it. It would be hard to overstate her wariness of this situation she's unaccountably volunteered for. Whoever is behind all this is moving them around like chess pieces, and Brenda is accustomed to being the player, not the played. But she'll go with it. For now. There's bound to be an angle here she can exploit, if she gives it a little time.

'Have you ever watched one of those videos on YouTube, Brenda? A snake eating a mouse. Whole. Doesn't even need to bite it. Just opens its mouth wide and grabs hold of that little critter. Swallows it whole and lets it dissolve slowly in its stomach juices. What a painful, protracted death that must be. Don't you think, Brenda? The ultimate in control.'

'No,' she snaps. 'That's not who I am.'

The voice chuckles. 'I'll let you ponder that for a while. Enjoy your lunch.'

Brenda balls her hands into fists. They've got her wrong. She's strong, yes. She's determined. She can be ruthless. Yes, she's a control freak – what successful person isn't these days?

But she's not a monster.

Her appetite has gone, but her traitorous stomach disagrees with a rumble. It *has* been a while since she last ate. Maybe she could have a nibble of something? Then she's going to ask to rejoin the group. There's a reason why she doesn't have time for solitary relaxation. It's because she can't relax. And being on her own here is leaving her vulnerable to attack. They can play their little games – she knows what those reality shows are like. Because that is what it is, whether it's being filmed or not. Throw a bunch of disparate characters together, put them under some sort of pressure, and see how quickly they turn on each other.

It's not unlike banking.

She's bored now anyway. Wants to know what the others are doing. Maybe she can put the lunch in her backpack and take it with her. She'd been into listening to that audio drama for a while; she'd needed to recharge. But she's lost interest now. She's had quite enough 'me time'.

Behind the bush is a wicker picnic hamper, laid on top of a red-and-white chequered tablecloth. A collection of thick, puffy floor cushions is arranged around the space, leaning against the side of the hill to form a makeshift sofa. There's a tray with napkins and a glass, and next to that an ice bucket with a variety of bottled drinks. She flips open the lid of the hamper, and her stomach rumbles again.

Inside, a selection of mouth-watering treats. Sandwiches cut into triangles, with the crusts cut off – laid out like a pyramid, and with various fillings. A cheese and ham quiche with cherry tomatoes pressed into the top. Slices of smoked salmon arranged like flowers and entwined with dill. She picks up a sandwich and takes a small bite. Cream cheese and cucumber. Her favourite. She finishes the sandwich, then picks up a piece of quiche and pops it into her mouth.

Now this is *the life*, she thinks, eyeing the ice bucket filled with drinks and trying to decide what to have. Elderflower pressé? Champagne? She leans down to pick up a small plate from a pocket on the inside lid of the hamper and notices a container of strawberries in the corner. She takes one out and is about to place it on her plate – then realises it's chocolate-dipped and shoves it into her mouth instead. It's plump and juicy, and a dribble of liquid seeps out of her mouth and down her chin. She grabs another one, then a sandwich, and plops them on her plate while also grabbing a napkin – red-and-white, to match the tablecloth. Then she looks down at her chest to where she is sure she's dribbled strawberry juice.

And that's when she sees it.

For a split second, she thinks she's mistaken. It's just a broken branch. It has been there all the time, but she hasn't noticed it. She blinks. It's still there, and it has moved. It is dark brown with barely visible markings. She wants to believe that it's merely an adder, and that there are probably thousands of them on this island, slinking around in the undergrowth. She's frozen to the spot. Plate in one hand, napkin in the other. The snake slithers closer, too close now to her foot, her bare ankle. Too close for her to step away. Her hands start to shake, and the strawberry rolls off the plate and hits the ground, causing a small cloud of dust to puff into the air. The snake flinches, pulls away from her and raises its head. It begins to coil itself upward. Its mouth opens wide – a strangely white mouth contrasting against the dark of its body.

She thinks about the voice earlier on, telling her about the snake and the mouse, and she thinks about the serpents in the Bible – always representing something bad. Evil. Is this a message? Was the earlier voice giving her some sort of warning?

Her greatest fear, of course – as was starkly laid out in the visitor centre for all to see. They've orchestrated this, somehow. Her mind tries to take her back to that afternoon in the woods as a child, when the snake had wrapped itself around her . . . but how could they know about that? She's still struggling to believe that the technology linked to the tracker can dredge up real memories. It's incredible, if it's true. But if it's a game, it's a cruel one.

She holds her breath, her body frozen stiff as the snake slithers over her foot and begins to wind itself upwards, slowly coiling its way around her bare leg.

Lucy

Lucy steps back, stumbling over a rock and landing on her behind. The thud gives her a jolt, but she doesn't cry out. She just wants to be as far away as she can from any of this weirdness.

James drops the bones on the ground. He's flushed from running and lets out a long sigh, then sucks in a deep breath. 'There was a whole pile of them . . . under a bush. I saw something white sticking out, and I' – he pauses, takes another deep breath – 'I thought maybe it was a branch. You know, when you see them bleached white from the salt and the sun? I was thinking it might be something we could use . . .'

His voice trails off.

Amelia clears her throat. 'I'm guessing they're animal bones. Probably a sheep or something. They're stripped clean. Could've been there for years.'

Lucy jumps up from the rock. 'A sheep? What, are you a veterinary expert now too?' She steps over Scott, who has woken up and is staring at them all in horror, as if he's forgotten who they are and where he is. She nudges one of the bones with her foot. 'These look too long to come from an animal. They look like thigh bones—'

'Forensic anthropologist, are you?' Amelia says. She's smiling.

'Touché,' Lucy says. She doesn't bother to explain her reasoning, but she's watched enough true crime programmes on TV to know what human bones look like. Bit of a coincidence though. James just happening to stumble over them like that.

James crouches down beside Scott. 'How you doing, mate?'

Scott groans. 'I think maybe I can stand, if you can all help me? I don't want to be a burden. We need to get down to the bay, right?'

James and Amelia glance at each other. Lucy doesn't know what their look means. They seem to have buddied up without her noticing. Great. This means she's stuck with Scott, does it? Although that might not be a bad thing. She thinks about the angles. Scott's line of business is one that must be very popular with celebrities. It's been a while since she's had a scoop on any big star from the US.

Scott tries to sit up, wincing as his foot flops over from its unnatural position.

'You know,' Amelia says, gently lifting his foot and leaning in to inspect it, 'I think maybe it's just a bad sprain. Can we take your shoe off so I can have a proper look?'

Scott nods. His face is pained, but Lucy thinks he might be putting it on a bit now. If the pain was that bad, he'd have squealed like a pig when Amelia lifted it. Lucy's not denying it was a bad fall, and it's obviously caused him some serious discomfort, but she can't be bothered with people who milk their situations for sympathy.

She's covered too many stories like that. Celeb does something bad, with no thought to the consequences. Celeb gets caught out. Celeb goes on TV and gives interviews, crying and begging for forgiveness. Not just celebs, either. Her ex had tried the same crap, but she's become immune to it. The more time she spends as a gossip columnist, the greater her lack of sympathy, and empathy. Hazard of the job. And the longer people try to manipulate you, the harsher a cynic you become.

Sometimes she has to remind herself why she got into the job. She'd had a perfectly nice life in Edinburgh, but the city is small and that meant opportunities for exciting news were limited. London gave her that, but it hardened her too.

Maybe Scott's not such a bad lad. Full of crap, maybe, but not bad. She should use this time away from the city to try and take advantage of the things she used to enjoy. Fresh air and friends being just two of them. She used to be a good laugh too. *Jesus, Lucy . . . what happened to you?*

Amelia has Scott's shoe and sock off now, and his foot is exposed in all its glory. A purple bruise is already beginning to flower. But there are no protruding bones, thankfully. That kind of thing is fine on TV shows, but she's not sure she could stomach it in real life. Looks like he wasn't putting it on after all.

'Can you wiggle your toes, Scott?' Amelia is asking.

Scott stares down at his foot as if he doesn't recognise it. Lucy looks at his face. His eyes. The pupils are dilated. Does shock do that? Or is it because of that water he's been guzzling? It doesn't seem to have had much effect on her, except making her overthink her life choices. She looks at his foot and sees his big toe move, just a little. Then the other toes.

'Well done,' Amelia says. 'I think you're going to be OK. I mean, it will be really tender for a while, and you'll have some fantastic bruising. But I think we can carry on. What do you think?'

'Can I have some more water?'

His voice is a little slurred, and something pings into Lucy's memory from earlier on. When they picked up their backpacks Scott had taken his water out immediately, and he'd turned away from them all. Something from his pocket . . . him looking around furtively. And then he'd screwed the cap back on and put the water in his bag. He hadn't drunk any of it. She looks again at his eyes, and at the vaguely blank expression on his face. Nutraceuticals? Is that what he calls them?

He's spiked his own drink.

Interesting, she thinks. She pulls out her bottle from her bag and takes a swig. There's something in this water, for sure, but it's probably electrolytes and vitamins – like they put in sports drinks – to keep them well hydrated in this heat. Maybe a bit too much caffeine, or that guarana stuff to keep them going. That's why it's only one bottle – because it's some sort of smart water. Tiggy had blethered on about minerals of some sort, hadn't she?

Speak of the devil.

'Guys . . . Oh my God, I'm so glad I found you!' Tiggy comes bounding down the hill like a puppy, a big grin plastered on her face. But there's something not right. Her eyes are red-rimmed, her hair mussed. She stops. Looks down at Scott, who now has his sock and shoe back on and is propped up against a large rock. 'What happened?'

James says, 'Scott tripped, and—'

'Oh my God, are these bones? Where did you find bones?'

'James brought them to us,' Lucy says. 'I think he's trying to freak us out.' She wants to deflect. Maybe they *are* just sheep bones.

'Where's your man anyway?' James says. 'Did you have a nice time?'

With that, Tiggy bursts into tears. 'I . . . I . . .' She glances around. 'I thought he'd have caught up with you before me.'

'Lovers' tiff, was it?' Lucy says. She hopes that's all it was. She could do without any more drama right now. He's definitely a player, that one. Tiggy probably deserves better, but she seems to live in a happy bubble of naivety. 'I'm sure he'll be back with his tail between his legs soon enough.'

Scott is standing now, leaning against the side of the hill. He's picked up one of the bones and is turning it over and over, an odd expression on his face. 'You know, guys . . . I definitely think these are human.'

Goosebumps shoot down Lucy's arms. 'I knew it,' she says, turning to James. 'Maybe you should take us to where you found them?'

James sighs. 'You know what? I'm getting fed up with this. I thought we'd be drinking tequila on the beach by now. But we've got Scott hobbling around, Tiggy's upset, Giles has gone AWOL . . . and Brenda is . . .'

'You're right,' Amelia says. 'Where *is* Brenda?'

Amelia

'OK,' Amelia says, trying to put as much authority into her voice as she can. 'We need to go and find Brenda. But we can't *all* go. The others need to stay here to look after Scott, and wait for Giles.'

Lucy shrugs. 'I suppose I need to stay with Scott. Right, Scott?'

'I'm *fine*, you guys. No one needs to babysit me. I'm not going anywhere.'

'I think I should come with you,' James says. 'Tiggy needs to wait for Giles, but she shouldn't be on her own.' He smiles at her and Tiggy smiles back, but it's forced.

Amelia wonders what it was that Tiggy and Giles fell out about. She feels protective of Tiggy. Something about her feels vulnerable. Tiggy still seems wary of her, after her outburst at the visitor centre about this marketing person she thinks is meant to be here instead of Amelia. But maybe she'll confide in Lucy instead. It's obvious now, after Scott's accident, that Amelia *is* meant to be here. To help the others deal with the outdoor environment. She looks over at Lucy, who has an arm around Tiggy.

'You sure you're OK, Tiggy? Maybe Lucy and James could—'

'She's fine here with me,' Lucy says. 'Off you go and find Brenda.'

Amelia wants to say more, but she's cut off by the sound of a high-pitched scream coming from the hill.

'Oh, that's just *great,*' Scott says. 'Something's happened to *Brenda* now. Any of you getting the distinct impression that we aren't going to make it down to that darn tiki hut? I thought the mind games were bad enough, but now—'

'Scott,' Lucy says, laying a hand on his good leg. 'Shush now. You need to rest.'

James grabs Amelia by the elbow. 'Come on, let's go. I think we should hurry.'

Amelia nods. 'Stay here, please,' she says to the others. 'We'll be as quick as we can.'

They march off together up the hill, and from behind she hears Scott muttering, 'Who died and put her in charge?'

'Ignore him,' James says. 'You're right to take control. Someone has to. I suppose this is the kind of thing you do in your job?'

'Not really. It's more about infrastructure. Transporting supplies to remote areas. Helping to lay pipes. Digging wells. Distributing food parcels . . .' She trails off as the hill inclines. 'Sorry,' she says, gasping for air. 'Need my breath for this hill. I'd thought I was quite fit—'

'You *are* fit,' he says. 'You didn't see me earlier when you sent me on the lookout for sticks. I was panting like a dog chasing a rabbit. You've barely broken a sweat—'

'Come on,' Amelia says. 'We need to conserve our energy for this hill.'

There's another scream. Louder now. Closer. Then a 'Help!' coming from somewhere not too far away.

Amelia marches faster. She can't run at this gradient, and she's already far too hot from the sun beating down on her. When did she last have a drink?

James catches her up. 'I think she's still in the clearing where we left her.'

Amelia swears under her breath. They're nearly there, but when they reach Brenda they'll have to get her back down to the others . . . and then further still, down to the bay. Assuming that she's hurt herself, judging by the screams. Amelia hopes that all this physical exertion has been forced on them to make them appreciate the luxury they all signed up for – because so far, there's been no sign of anything of the sort. She doesn't know what James has asked for, or Lucy, or Scott. She doesn't even know what she wants for herself. But surely they all have to get it soon – or else what is the point of this?

She makes it to the clearing a moment before James. She sees it a split second before he does. Just long enough for an ice-cold shiver to slide down her hot back. 'Stop,' she whispers.

James thumps into her. 'What the . . . ? Oh.'

Brenda is standing still, next to a red-and-white tablecloth with a picnic hamper on top of it. A plate of food lies at her feet, and she has her arms spread out to the sides, like a scarecrow. Her face is colourless, except for two red spots high on her cheeks. Sweat is beaded across her brow, glinting in the sunlight.

Wound around her left leg is a darkly patterned snake with its head turned towards them, watching them. Trying to decide on its next move. Its tongue slithers out of its arrow-shaped head, then it opens its mouth and makes a strange, breathy hiss.

Brenda's eyes are closed tight.

'It's Amelia . . . and James,' Amelia says to her. 'Has it bitten you? Open your eyes for yes, keep them closed for no.'

Her eyes remain shut.

'You're doing good there, Brenda,' James says. 'It's probably harmless. Just fancied a bite of your sandwich.'

Brenda lets out a small whimper. 'Please,' she says. 'Please get it off me. I . . . I have such a phobia of snakes.'

Amelia takes in the scene in front of her. Has a good look at the snake. She hopes it's just an adder, but she's never heard of an adder coiling itself onto a human like this.

'Do you know what to do?' James speaks quietly, close to her ear. She doesn't know much about snakes, and clearly he doesn't either, but all three of them have the sense to assume that no sudden movements and no loud noises might be the way forward.

Amelia shakes her head. 'I've come across snakes in the jungle, but I had a guide. A local. Someone who knew what to do.' She's annoyed with herself again. Why doesn't she know what to do? This must have been covered in that bushcraft course, but ever since she arrived on this island it's as if all the things she took for granted inside her head have become dimmed, out of focus. She hadn't wanted to voice her concerns before, but she's now sure of it. But she doesn't even have one of the embedded trackers. If something is trying to make her mind fuzzy, it's not via that route.

James places a hand on her shoulder, giving her a little shake. 'Amelia?'

She blinks. Brenda is staring at them, wide-eyed. 'I'm sorry,' Amelia whispers. 'I zoned out for a second.'

He ignores her. He's looking at Brenda. 'Listen to me,' he says, keeping his voice low. 'I'm going to do something now. It's all I can think of. I'll be quick, and then it will be over. Can you stay still there for me? You're doing a great job.'

Brenda nods. Her face is wet with tears.

'OK then,' James says.

He takes a slow, careful step, gently nudging Amelia out of the way. He keeps his eyes locked on Brenda the whole time.

'It's OK,' he says, inching forward again.

The snake is still staring at them, and Amelia looks away – a memory of a childhood movie; a snake's hypnotic gaze.

James takes one more step towards Brenda, then slides his hand into his pocket, removes something that Amelia can't see. Then, in one deft move he tosses the object to the ground with his left hand, lurches forward and grabs the snake around the middle with his right. The snake's head has turned to track what he's thrown and its body seems to have relaxed just enough for him to get a grip around it and yank it from Brenda's leg. It whips off like an elastic band, and he tosses it as far as he can, sending it pinwheeling away from them. Then he drops forward onto his knees and lets out a long, slow breath.

Amelia makes it just in time to catch Brenda as she faints, veering towards the picnic basket. James stands up and takes Brenda's other arm, and they lead her away from the clearing. From the food and the cushions and all the things that had been laid out for her relaxation.

'It didn't bite you, did it?' James whispers in Brenda's ear.

She gives a small shake of her head, but something feels false about the gesture. Though why would she lie about having been bitten? Amelia puts the thought away. 'Well done,' she says to her as they walk slowly away from the clearing.

She glances over at James, takes in his pallor. *He's in shock*, she thinks. 'How did you know what to do?' She needs to keep him talking. Brenda too.

'I saw a documentary . . .' His voice trails off, his strength gone. They are all suffering from the post-adrenaline slump.

As they pass the entrance to Tiggy and Giles's love nest, Amelia says, 'We should go and get Giles. Tell him he needs to come back with us.'

'What happened?' Brenda says, her voice shaking slightly as she valiantly attempts to get over her trauma. 'Isn't he with Tiggy?'

Amelia shakes her head. 'We don't know yet. An argument of some sort.'

James lets go of Brenda's arm and she falls into Amelia, before righting herself. 'I'm OK,' she says, giving Amelia a small smile. 'I'll be fine in a minute. Thank you.'

James disappears down the little path, and they stop to wait for him.

He arrives back barely a minute later, shaking his head. 'Well, I guess he's already got bored and headed down to meet the others.'

'He's not there?' Amelia says. She's surprised. She imagined him to be a bit of a sulker. Waiting there until someone came to beg him to come back.

'Nope. No sign of him.'

'OK then,' she says. 'Let's get back to the others.' As they start to walk something occurs to her that she'd meant to ask straight away, but it slipped her mind. 'Just wondering . . . what was it you threw?'

James gives her a puzzled look.

'You know . . . to distract the snake?'

He looks away. 'Ah, that. Nothing. Just some crap I had in my pocket.'

Just as with Brenda, Amelia feels sure he's lying, but she doesn't know why. She decides not to push it. If it's relevant, she's sure he'll tell her later. And if it's not, well, she'll just have to trust him.

Tiggy

'So,' Lucy says, 'are you going to tell us what happened with Giles?'

Tiggy sighs. 'It's such a mess. I just . . . No doubt everyone who's ever met Giles would say "I told you so", but I honestly thought he loved me.'

'How old are you again?'

'Twenty-five. Why?'

'And how long have you been dating . . . ? I mean, properly. Not like the buck-toothed eleven-year-old who gave you a Valentine's card and asked if you wanted to come to his weekender in the country and play with his ponies.'

Tiggy bristles. 'I don't know people like that. You're hearing the way I speak and making assumptions. I wouldn't do that to you.'

'Wouldn't you?' Lucy kicks a stone off the path and it disappears over the edge. 'You're right, sorry.'

Scott coughs, reminding them he's there. 'You both have lovely accents, if you ask me. I can't really tell the difference between the two, but—'

'Oh, come on,' Lucy says. 'We sound nothing alike. You damn Americans think we all speak like the Queen.'

He chuckles. 'You do.'

'My Italian grandmother would be turning in her grave,' Lucy says, 'except she's still alive and kicking and making the best pizza dough in central Scotland.'

'Don't start on that "Italians invented pizza" nonsense with me.'

'We did. And ice cream. Don't even go there.'

Tiggy ignores them both, switching back to Lucy's question. 'I started dating properly when I was fifteen. I haven't had many boyfriends. I don't do one-night stands, or anything . . .' She pauses, trying to find the right word. She wants to say 'seedy' but that sounds judgemental, and she doesn't quite know what Lucy is getting at – she feels that Lucy wants to use her dating history to prove some sort of point, and Tiggy doesn't want to be sucked into that negativity. Whenever she spends time around negative people, she feels her energy being drained, like a car battery when the lights and radio have been left on all night. She needs to replenish herself with happiness and sunshine and vitamins. She tips her head back, letting the sun soak into her face. Hoping that the vitamin D is getting through her sunscreen.

'You don't do one-night stands or anything . . . what?' Lucy says, leaning in closer.

'I'm not going to let you goad me. You're enjoying picking on me, but it won't be much fun if I ignore you.'

'Jeez, don't ignore her,' Scott chimes in. 'Then she'll start on me.'

Lucy grabs her water bottle from her bag and takes a swig. 'Ah, come on. I wasn't picking on you. All I was trying to say was, maybe you're being a bit naive about relationships. I can guess what Giles has been up to, based on what happened in the visitor centre when he got his tracker – that lie he spun you about the girl in the hotel room . . . and also from what I've heard about him before. Did you have a big row about him cheating on you? But then again, it was Giles who said this was all just a game—'

'Oh, wait,' Tiggy says. 'I knew I recognised your name. You were the one who wrote that horrible piece about Giles in *eXite* magazine last year.' She slaps herself on the forehead. 'I get it now. You're a nasty piece of work.'

Lucy tuts. 'Look, I'm not proud of every single thing I've written, but someone gave me the lead and I needed the cash. We don't all have the Bank of Mummy and Daddy to get us through the lean times.'

Tiggy crosses her arms. 'There you go again with your assumptions! And you actually want me to *confide* in you? Tell you about Giles?' She feels tears prick at her eyes and tries to blink them away. She doesn't want to let this woman see that she's upset. 'If this is a game, it's not very much fun. It's like Big Brother is some kind of psychopath!'

'Um, Big Brother *is*—'

'Ladies, ladies,' Scott says. 'How about we take a breath? Tear into *me* for a minute. I'm stuck here with this bum ankle. I'm not going anywhere. Take your best shot.'

'Sorry,' Lucy says. 'I think the sun is getting to me. Besides, I don't think there's anything I could say to you that would offend you, and to be honest, that's not much fun.' She picks up a small stone and throws it at him.

Scott shakes his head. 'You're warped, lady. There's something wrong with you.'

'No shit,' she mutters, wandering over to the bones that James has left in the clearing. 'Anyway, what do we think of these?' She picks up the largest and runs a finger over each end, peers down its length as if she's trying to read the grain.

'Anthropologist now, are we?' Tiggy says.

'Look at this,' Lucy says, ignoring her jibe. 'This end. It looks too . . . I dunno, smooth.'

'It's probably been worn away by rain and salt and wind and whatever else,' Tiggy says. 'It's not like it's been left here recently, is it? Some animal died. It doesn't look like there have been animals here for a while, so . . .' She shrugs. 'Look, it's just an animal bone. It doesn't matter.' She slumps inwards, plonks herself down on a rock. She has no more strength to argue. She's already feeling bad about what she said to Giles as she stormed off. He might be an absolute pig, but she does still love him. She certainly doesn't want him dead. She needs to pull herself together and show herself in a better light to have any chance of winning the prize money they promised her. She wonders if the others have been offered the same.

There's a beep in her ear and she flinches, looks around to see if anyone else heard it. Lucy is still inspecting the ends of the bone. Scott has his eyes closed again. The voice in her ear says, 'Thank you. Your preferences have been updated.'

She slaps the tracker angrily. 'What preferences? What are you talking about?'

Lucy looks up, raises her eyebrows.

Tiggy shakes her head and turns away. She's trying to decide how much she wants to say, with the others listening. Lucy is desperate for something juicy, and Scott is only feigning sleep – but then the sound of other voices, getting closer, stops her from asking the tracker anything else at all.

The others are back.

'Ah, the wanderers return,' Lucy says. She lifts a hand to her forehead, squinting into the sun. 'Brenda . . . you're looking a bit peaky. Dodgy prawn sandwich at the country club?'

'Something like that,' Brenda says.

Tiggy takes a good look at her. She does look pale, and something else. Like all her previous bluster has blown away. She looks smaller, somehow. More vulnerable. 'What happened? Was that you we heard screaming?'

Brenda nods. 'I just need to sit down for a minute.'

Scott has opened his eyes and pulled himself upright. 'You need to come and join invalids' corner, by the look of you. Care for a drink?' He offers his water, although there is barely a sip left.

Brenda shakes her head but sits down next to him.

It looks to Tiggy like she might have hurt her leg. She seems a little fragile in her movements.

'There was a small incident with a snake in a picnic basket,' James says. He grins, and it's clear he's trying to lighten the mood. 'It's fine though, I used an incredible technique I saw on TV. Distract, grab and toss. I think I might patent the terminology.'

'Jeez,' Scott says, turning to inspect Brenda. 'Was it poisonous? It didn't bite you, did it?'

Brenda shakes her head, but it's odd – she won't look him in the eye. 'Let's get down to the beach. I could really do with a drink.'

Amelia

T - 14

'Brenda's right. We're wasting time.' Amelia taps her watch. It's already T minus 14. 'We've wasted hours sitting around here. We're meant to be at the beach!' She gathers the bones from the ground and shoves them into her bag. 'We'll look at these again down at the bar. Maybe Harvey can tell us where they came from. He's surely due to check in on us again soon? He might already be there, and I'm sure he has medical supplies' – she looks at Scott and Brenda, who are leaning against each other, still propped up against a rock – 'for anyone who needs them.'

'Yes, let's go.' James offers a hand to Scott. 'Ready?'

'Ready.'

He pulls Scott up, while Lucy does the same with Brenda. Tiggy picks up everyone's backpacks and hands them around, helping Brenda on with hers. For a moment, no one is bickering. No one is complaining. They've become the group that they are supposed to be. Six strangers on an island – none of them with any real clue what they are doing there, but all ready and willing to accept the challenge.

The fact that there are *seven* of them has not escaped Amelia, but she's certain Giles will be joining them soon, once he's finished licking his wounds. She glances over at Tiggy and gives her a smile, and to her relief Tiggy smiles back. They haven't quite clashed as such, but she hasn't found a way to bond with her yet.

Hopefully a few drinks will help.

Lucy has taken the role of supporting Scott, who, after wincing a bit and a few muttered grumbles, is managing to walk down the uneven path – albeit slowly. Tiggy has linked arms with Brenda, and they both seem happy enough for the time being. Amelia takes the lead, with James following close behind, and as she looks down at the rocks, the waves gently lapping, leaving a slow trickle of foam, she can't help but wonder if this is the calm before the storm. She hasn't forgotten Tiggy's words from earlier, about this all being some sort of reality TV thing. Because if it is, there will surely be another curveball for them to deal with soon.

James taps her on the elbow. 'Let's walk a little faster,' he says, keeping his voice low.

Intrigued, Amelia picks up the pace and they walk together. 'What's on your mind?'

'That snake,' James says, still talking quietly. 'I know I made a thing of it with Brenda, telling her it wasn't poisonous and all. But I think it was. That documentary I mentioned? It was about the Florida cottonmouth. Not the most venomous snake in the world, but if its bite is left untreated, depending on the amount of venom released, and the size of the victim . . .' He pauses. 'Well, let's just say it can have pretty nasty consequences.'

Amelia frowns. 'But it didn't bite her, right?'

'So she says. But I don't believe her. I know she's in shock from it all, but she's been acting weird since we brought her away from that place. Did you notice how she sat down next to Scott? She didn't look comfortable.'

'Why would she lie though? If she *has* been bitten, we need to call for help.'

'I don't know. Either she doesn't want to make a fuss, or else she thinks it's not a big deal – if it wasn't a dangerous venom, maybe she thinks it'll just itch a bit then go away.'

'And it won't?'

'Not if it's a cottonmouth bite, no.'

'What would a snake like that be doing here, though?'

'The only way it could be here is if someone put it here. On purpose.'

'Oh God . . . and put it near where Brenda was having her little relaxation time. Hoping it would—'

'Yeah. You don't need to say it. I get the feeling that someone is messing with us.'

'But it doesn't make sense. We're meant to be here for fun, not some sort of test, aren't we? But Tiggy and Giles think it's a game, don't they? Maybe they're right.'

James reaches up and pushes away an overhanging branch from a bent, withered tree. 'I don't know about that. I'm starting to think that some sort of test is *exactly* why we're here. You know, there's something else I didn't tell you.'

Amelia turns, making sure the others are still far enough away. They are making progress, seemingly oblivious to her and James's whispered conversation in front. 'Go on,' she says.

'That thing I threw – to distract the snake? It was a bone. A small one, about seven centimetres long. With joints.'

'What kind of animal . . . ?' Her voice trails off. She already knows.

James shakes his head. 'It wasn't from an animal. I can't be 100 per cent sure, but I'm pretty certain it was a finger.'

'A human finger?'

'Well, yes. Unless it was a chimpanzee, which is even less likely.'

Amelia tries to work this through in her head. The thought of human remains scattered around the island is odd, of course, but is it any more than that? 'They could've been here for years,' she says. 'Maybe an old burial site was disturbed while they were setting things up for us to come here.'

James frowns. 'What *have* they set up for us, exactly? The whole place seems pretty untouched. The bones were on the edge of the track. It's not like there was an area nearby that looked like an old burial site.'

'You don't know what was here before. You don't know anything about this place. None of us do.' As she says it, a splinter of a memory pricks at her. An island she went to, long ago. Where was it? She massages her temples, as if trying to encourage the memory to resurface. She's been to lots of islands for her work. She's been told countless tales by the locals about the places she's visited. Sometimes she can't remember who said what and where, and there have been plenty of talks about burial practices in countries where people have very little money but plenty of land. In some of the African plains, there are more burial sites than villages. She blinks, and the splinter forces itself in deeper, the memory embedded inside, along with countless others. If it's relevant, it will work its way out sooner or later.

'OK,' James says, with a small sigh. He's obviously decided not to push it. Perhaps it's best not to think about other possibilities why there might be human remains on an island that none of them know the location of.

All the talk of snakes and bones has been a welcome distraction. Amelia barely noticed the burning in her thighs as they descended the final part of the hill into the bay, and now they've arrived at the beach, and the sun has crept around to find them. The sea sparkles like sprinkled gem stones, greens and blues and yellow and white. The sand is soft under her feet after the hard-packed mud of the path with stones and roots pushing through. She leans down and unties her boots, then pulls them off, followed by her socks. Her feet are hot and sticky, lined from where the socks have wrinkled and dug into her flesh. The warm sand between her toes is a welcome relief, and she flexes and curls them, letting the sand trickle through. 'Now this is more like it,' she says. James follows her lead, and then the others – with Tiggy helping Scott get the boot off his injured foot.

Then they are all smiling and relaxed – and the bar is there, waiting for them. Amelia had thought there might be a barman. Maybe Harvey. But there is no one.

'Self-service, is it?' Lucy says, catching up with her. 'I used to work in the students' union for a while, when I was doing my journalism degree—'

'You actually got trained to write that crap, did you?' Tiggy says, the sneer evident in her voice.

'Now, now, ladies,' Scott says. 'Keep your claws in for a bit longer, will you? At least until we get a drink.'

Amelia doesn't know what Tiggy is referring to, but decides not to ask. 'Well, if you fancy serving us, Lucy, that'd be great.'

'Or we can take turns,' James says.

Lucy ignores all of them and keeps walking towards the bar. When she gets there, she lifts up the section that serves as the door and slips inside. She bends down and disappears behind the bar, then reappears, grinning. 'They've got everything in here. But there's already a load of stuff made up in the fridge. And our names are on them.'

'Did you actually say what drink you wanted?' James says.

Amelia shakes her head. 'Although one of the instructions back at the start said *think* of it, didn't it? I *did* do that.'

'Me too,' Tiggy says. 'I thought of a bottomless Kir Royale, like they do in the Mambo Club in Mayfair. Made with Bolly, of course.'

'Expensive tastes, eh? I thought of a pina colada,' Scott says, with a small shrug. 'Not had one in years.'

'You didn't *think* that, Scott,' Lucy says. 'You said it loud and clear.'

He rolls his eyes. 'Whatever.'

'What about you, Brenda?' Lucy asks.

'White wine spritzer,' she says. 'I know, not very exciting. It's my summer drink. It automatically slotted into my head as soon as the question was put to us. If I was asked again now, I'd probably go for something stronger.' She winces, and Amelia notices her scratching her leg.

Maybe James was right about her being bitten. As though he's read Amelia's thoughts, he says, 'Brenda, are you sure you're OK? You've looked a bit uncomfortable since we brought you back, and I'm worried you're not telling us the whole truth about that snake . . . I might be wrong, but if it's the type I think it is, the venom could be pretty potent. Maybe we should get you some help, just in case . . .'

His sentence trails off as Brenda glares at him. 'I told you already. I'm fine.'

The group falls silent.

'I thought of a tequila sunrise,' Amelia says, trying to cut the tension. 'About as current as your pina colada, Scott.'

Scott doffs an imaginary cap. 'Nothing wrong with the classics.'

James climbs onto a bar stool. 'I asked for a bottle of Coke. A glass bottle. Real, not diet.'

'You can have anything you want and you ask for Coke?' Scott says. 'What – you an alcoholic or something?'

James fixes him with a hard stare. 'Only alcoholics drink soft drinks, is that it?'

'Alcoholics, pregnant women and children,' Scott says, pleased with himself.

'What about your vitamin-loving extremist health nuts, hmm?' Lucy says, pulling some glasses off the hooks above her head and placing them on the bar.

Scott snorts. 'Those people are the worst. Don't you think vitamin-loving extremist health nuts doth protest too much? They are among the biggest hypocrites I've ever met – and I include law enforcement personnel and bankers in the swathes of humanity I've had the misfortune to meet.'

'Wow,' James says. 'Cynical snake-oil salesman reveals true colours.' He turns to Lucy. 'How does that work for a headline?'

'Boring. Because he's right: it's all the evangelistic green juice yoga monsters you need to be wary of. Usually the biggest coke fiends in the business . . . and I don't mean the stuff you like in a glass bottle. Of course, there's always the possibility that you're drinking the soft stuff to keep a clear head . . . keep an eye on us, maybe.' She winks at Amelia, then delves under the counter again and brings out a series of metal flasks. She swivels them round; each one has a label. Seven flasks, one for each of them. Including Giles, who hasn't made it down yet.

Tiggy walks over and runs a finger along Giles's flask. 'I'm getting a bit worried about him now.'

'Oh, he'll be back soon enough,' Scott says. He reaches for his own flask, but Lucy pulls it away.

'I'll serve, OK? I've got all the correct glasses.' She starts to unscrew the flasks, sniffing the contents before pouring them into various shapes and sizes of glass, depending on the drink.

'I'm guessing they didn't psychically magic up my bottle of Coke then . . .'

'Ta-da,' Lucy says, tipping the head of the flask towards him. Then she sticks her fingers into the top and pulls out a bottle of Coke. 'Guess again, sunshine.'

She pours Scott's foamy pina colada into a long-stemmed goblet, garnishing it with a slice of pineapple. Scott grins. 'No biggie. You all heard me ask for this.'

'The Coke, though . . .' Amelia says.

Lucy pours the contents of Amelia's flask into a wine glass. It's mostly orange, but there's an unmistakable streak of red as the last of the dregs slide into the glass.

'Woah,' Scott says. 'None of us heard you ask for that.'

'So these trackers . . .' James starts to say.

'I don't even have the proper one, though. I only have the wrist sensor.'

'You can't all still be thinking that these trackers are tapping into your neurons or whatever,' Scott says, shaking his head. 'You know it's some kind of trick . . . or they looked up an interview with you online and got lucky.'

Amelia knows she's never mentioned tequila sunrises in any interview she's done, but she can't be sure she hasn't mentioned it somewhere. Social media, maybe. It wouldn't be any surprise that the host had researched them all thoroughly. They're some sort of tech company, after all. Maybe they've hacked their accounts.

'I bet Giles's is vodka Red Bull,' Tiggy says. 'He's such a commoner when it comes to drinks.' She pulls her phone out of her pocket and starts tapping away.

'There's no signal on that, is there?' James says. He's holding his Coke but he hasn't taken a sip yet.

Tiggy nods. 'No phone signal, but I seem to be connected to a Wi-Fi network. My calls go through that when there's no reception.'

'Have you tried ringing lover boy then?' Lucy says, unscrewing the lid of Giles's flask.

'No. I don't want to talk to him yet. I've just sent him an angry message instead.'

Lucy sniffs. 'Urgh, you're right about the drink. I hate the smell of that stuff.' She screws the lid on and goes back to pouring the remaining drinks – all of them correctly guessed.

They are still pondering that when Tiggy's phone pings.

'"See you soon, babe,"' she reads off the screen for them. '"Sorry. You know I can explain." Three kisses.' She scowls. 'Right, well, now that I know he's OK, he can bloody well stay away. I'm having a drink.'

'Cheers to that,' Scott says. They all raise their glasses.

Amelia takes a long gulp, savouring the orange and the tequila kick, and the sweet tang of the syrup. She instantly feels more relaxed. The others are quiet now, all enjoying their drinks. Amelia looks around at the bay – sunloungers, paddleboards, a rolled-up net next to a couple of bats and balls. The sand is deep, the water clear. On the other side, another path snakes its way up a hill lined with long grass. Finally, everyone seems content.

'Well,' Tiggy says, draining her drink, 'I wonder how long we'll be allowed to enjoy this place before the next part of the game?'

Summer 2000

She stops running when she reaches the bay. Her lungs and her leg muscles burn, and she has to put a hand on the wall of the shop to stop herself from collapsing. After a few moments, her breath starts to return to normal. But her face still feels hot and her heart is still thumping too hard.

She's meant to be back for dinner soon. But how is she going to eat after what she's just done? She steps away from the wall and walks around to the door of the shop. She knows what to do. She was told the first time she came here without her parents that if there was ever a problem of any kind, she was to go to the shop and they would help her.

The shop door is open, stands filled with buckets and spades lining the route inside. She takes a few tentative steps, spots the nice lady behind the counter who always adds an extra piece of fudge or an extra couple of Fruit Salad chews when she goes in for a mixed bag. The lady has a kind face. The lady will help.

She's almost at the counter when a man knocks into her as he passes. 'Get out of the way, girl,' he says, angrily pushing a bag of bread rolls across the counter.

She stands behind him, shaking. She doesn't like this man. Something about him gives her a bad feeling. She doesn't wait for him to turn round. She just walks out of the shop. Outside, she smacks right into a pale, skinny boy and he springs back from her, a terrified look on his face.

'Sorry . . .' she mutters, wondering for a moment why he looks so spooked, but not caring enough to stop and find out.

She walks quickly back to her grandparents' cottage, bursts in the door, hot-faced and sweating, and says, 'Please, I'm too homesick. I don't want to stay here for another week. I feel sick. I want my mum. *Please*, can I go back home?'

Brenda

Brenda tries to get comfortable on one of the sunloungers, but it's either too upright or too flat, and every time she swings her legs over the side to twist around and adjust it, a shooting pain travels up her thigh. She makes one final attempt to get the lounger to stay where she wants it, then, realising it's the best she can do without drawing attention to herself, she swings her legs back one final time and picks up her drink.

She's already on her second glass. It doesn't taste too strong – in fact, there's maybe a little too much soda for her liking – but she can already feel it going to her head. If she was at home, she'd probably stop now, but after the day she's had, and being stuck here with these strangers, she decides that another glass or two won't do any harm. Besides, it's taking her mind off her leg.

She doesn't think the snake properly bit her. It didn't really feel like a bite, as such. More like being stung by nettles, or the sharp scratch of a needle inserted in a vein to take blood. Do snakes even have teeth? She doesn't have time to watch wildlife programmes. How is she supposed to know how snakebites work? James had been extremely concerned when he'd asked if she'd been bitten, and for reasons she can't quite fathom now, she'd decided to lie.

Maybe it was just a drama she didn't want to be part of. Or maybe she's trying to convince herself that it didn't really happen.

She makes sure that the others are fully distracted before rolling up the leg of her shorts and taking a look. There's a swollen red bump that itches a little, and only seems to hurt when she moves her leg or touches it.

She rolls her shorts back down and takes another sip of her drink.

Best not to touch it then, she decides. Anyway – it's not as if it can be that bad, can it? They can't have put a potentially deadly snake in a place where she was sure to disturb it – that would be absurd. They invited her here to ask for her advice, and to offer her potential investment. She's hardly going to be interested if she ends up hospitalised.

She leans back into the lounger. James and Amelia are inspecting the sports equipment that's been left for them all. Lucy is rattling a cocktail shaker, leaning forwards and laughing at something Scott is saying to her at the bar. Brenda doesn't know what to make of her yet, but then she hasn't really spent much time talking to her. She'd helped Scott all the way down to the bay and Brenda had been more concerned with her own footing to pay much attention to what they were saying. Tiggy had walked with her, holding her elbow as if she were an old woman. She *is* an old woman to Tiggy though, isn't she? Sometimes she forgets what it's like to be so young and invincible. Tiggy had rabbited on the whole way, chattering about what a pig Giles is, but how he's such a genius and it's not surprising that he needs so many people around him – to stimulate his mind. She'd tried to explain her Instagram life, and how it made her money, and what she could do to help Brenda grow her 'online presence'. Brenda hadn't been able to get a word in to tell the girl that her business doesn't work like that. That discretion is the key to her investments, not shiny pictures of king-size beds with vases of artfully arranged flowers by the side and luxury robes laid out at the bottom, with pretty cotton slippers on the thick carpet. Towels fashioned into swans and hearts. Ice bucket on the bedside cabinet with a bottle of expensive champagne draped in a starched linen napkin.

Tiggy had explained all this with such passion that Brenda couldn't be bothered to tell her that she couldn't care less – that her assistant always booked her hotels for her, and that she wasn't particularly impressed by origami towels.

She takes another drink. Tiggy is down by the water's edge, glass in hand, taking small steps into the sea then flicking her feet up, spraying water across the sand. Giggling to herself. Not too bothered about Giles now, is she?

There's a beep. Not too loud at first but rising. She sits up straighter, glances across at the others. They are all looking around, trying to see where the sound is coming from. It beeps again, and then the sky seems to shimmer, moving lines flickering across her vision.

Tiggy's head snaps up and she whirls round to face them all. 'This is what happened earlier,' she says. 'When I was with Giles.' Her eyes are wide, and the fear is evident in her voice. 'It's . . . it's kind of . . . a video. Can you all see it? I—'

The swirling stops and the image comes into focus, slowly depixelating. It's above Tiggy's head, seemingly floating over the sea. Brenda blinks. When she refocuses her eyes, the image reappears. She turns her head and it moves with her.

It's not floating on some unseen screen – it's being projected from her own head. How can this be? Her heart starts to beat faster. A strange tingling comes over her. She blinks again, but the image keeps coming back.

She doesn't like this. It's a horrible, disembodying experience. But through the transparent projection she can still see the others, circling, holding hands to their foreheads as sun visors. They are seeing it too. Tiggy starts walking slowly backwards, away from the sea. She keeps batting a hand across the empty space in front of her, as if she's trying to get the screen to disappear. Brenda assumes that's what she's doing. She can only see her own projection, and Tiggy through the other side. She looks up again at the sky. If she's going to be shown something, she might as well make sure she can see it clearly. Tiggy's right. It is a video, of sorts. A streaming projection. It starts to play, and Tiggy gasps, falling back onto the sand.

'I thought . . . I thought this would be about Giles.' She stops talking.

It's not Giles in the scene that Brenda is viewing. Not yet anyway. It's Tiggy herself – her face reflected in her phone screen, by way of some sort of mirror app, maybe. So what Brenda is seeing is what *Tiggy* is seeing as this projection unfolds. It's all terrifically disorienting. She's living this scene *as* Tiggy. She has to accept that, or she might just be sick.

Tiggy lays the phone on the table in front of her, and through her eyes Brenda sees bare legs poking out from the bottom of a short red skirt. She glances around, taking in the plump green sofa in the corner of a stark room. Music is playing – something you might hear in a nightclub, no real words, just thumping bass notes and the occasional breathy moan. Something repeated, over and over again. There are other girls in the room. Chatting to each other, huddled together. An expensively bleached blonde throws her head back and laughs as two scowling brunettes turn to her – Tiggy on the sofa – and they say something, then they laugh again. Brenda feels a fresh wave of nausea. She wants to turn away, but she can't. The scene is still projecting. Trapped in this awful moment with Tiggy, *as* Tiggy, Brenda looks down at Tiggy's hands, watches as they clench tight into fists. Brenda can feel the tension in her own body as Tiggy's knuckles glow slightly white when she grips harder onto her drink.

'No. Please. Turn this off.'

Brenda looks down from the clear sky to Tiggy, here and now, where she is curled up on the sand. She can still see her through the projection. The effect sends her mind and stomach reeling in a new way.

Brenda turns to the bar, and then to the piled-up paddleboards. Everyone is watching, living through the 'on-screen' Tiggy at a party. Everyone is experiencing this.

Except Amelia.

Amelia is tapping her watch. 'Come on,' she says. 'This isn't fair.' She turns to Brenda, as though feeling her gaze. 'Please. Tell me what you can see?'

Then the real Tiggy, sitting on the sand, curled into herself, rocking gently – just as she did in the visitor centre when the text feed exposed Giles for the cheat he is – sobs, 'No. Stop watching it. Don't tell her . . .'

Brenda closes her eyes and the image vanishes. She could keep them closed. Ignore it. But would it still be there when she opened them? Is this what happened earlier? Did Tiggy get shown a projection like this of Giles? Some sort of memory feed?

She needs to see.

'Close your eyes, Tiggy,' James calls over from the paddleboards.

Amelia gets up off her knees and walks over and lays a hand on Tiggy's shoulder. 'It doesn't matter, Tiggy. I can't see it. Try not to get upset. It's just a game, remember?'

'Those bitches,' Tiggy says, just loud enough for them all to hear. 'This is *not* a game.'

Amelia crouches down beside her. 'Tell me then, Tiggy. Talk me through it.'

Brenda tips her head back up to the sky. She's Tiggy again, on-screen. Still pretending she can't hear what the other girls are saying, but the volume has been turned up loud enough for her to hear them now.

'Silly little cow. No matter what he does, she stays. Too pathetic to make a name for herself on her own merits.'

'Did you hear what he did with Cressida and Lorena? Talk about filth . . .'

'She's not that pretty, is she? She does all that contouring, but if you actually look at her face . . .'

'Shut up!' Tiggy on the beach says, clamping her hands over her ears.

Tiggy on-screen says nothing.

Feeling another wave of swooning dizziness, Brenda leans back into the lounger, closes her eyes. It was a mistake to have that third glass of wine. She never drinks this much, and with the heat . . . and . . . her leg itches again. A vision swims in front of her, as though it's imprinted on her eyelids. A fresh one; not Tiggy's. A small scene replays itself. An island, a long time ago. Waves crashing against rocks. A voice carried on the wind. 'No!'

Her eyes fly open again.

Brenda is back inside Tiggy's vision, just as she gets up slowly from the sofa, the glass still held tight in her hand. She catches a glimpse of herself in a mirrored pillar, and her face – Tiggy's face – is completely devoid of expression as she smashes the champagne flute against the high glass table where the three women stand, their faces fixed in horror as she raises a hand above her head, then thrusts the stem hard and fast towards the blonde woman's face.

Lucy

'Woah,' Lucy says, laying one of the flasks on the bar. 'That was quite . . . unexpected.' She's gazing out at the sea, still not sure what's just happened. Did she really experience a woman being glassed, through the eyes of sweet, naive little Tiggy?

'You're telling me,' Scott says. He swivels round on the bar stool. 'Hey, where'd she go?' He swipes a hand in front of his face. 'That was *so* weird, right?'

Lucy turns, and the projection remains in her vision – a horrible freeze-frame of Tiggy's hand clutching the broken flute, the woman's face etched with pain and terror.

Tiggy is no longer on the sand, where she'd fallen back in shock when the scene started to play. Brenda is sitting up on her lounger, mouth wide open in a stunned 'O'. James and Amelia are running towards the rocks in pursuit of Tiggy, who has fled the scene.

Lucy closes her eyes for a moment, but when she opens them the projection remains paused, hanging there above the calm sea like an angry, mocking cloud. It's been left on the still of the blonde woman's face as she reels backwards from the high glass table, a jet of dark red blood frozen in the air as though someone has shaken a bottle of ketchup with the lid off and caught it on time-lapse photography. Reflected in one of the club's many mirrors, Tiggy's face is fierce – mouth open, teeth bared in a silent warrior's cry.

The two brunettes have simultaneously thrown their hands over their faces, either in shock or as protection, or possibly both. It is a stunning visceral image – mainly because it shows a scene that is so unexpected in its horror that it takes a while for the brain to absorb it. And just like that, it flickers, then disappears.

'That can't be real,' Scott says, shaking his head. 'No way was that real.'

'What? The technology, or our Tiggy?' Lucy asks.

Scott blinks at her. 'What? Both, I guess. But yeah, Tiggy.'

'She's a dark horse, that's for sure. I had her pegged as pretty but vacant. Would never have thought she had that in her.' Lucy pours herself a drink and tops up Scott's. If this image is true – and at the moment she can't see how it isn't, as it's been revealed as if through Tiggy's own memory – then this could be the scoop of the century. She'd thought Cheryl Tweedy punching a toilet attendant at the height of her Girls Aloud fame had been a good one – but Cheryl had somehow bounced back from that to become the unthinking nation's sweetheart. There's no way Tiggy can come back from this. If this is leaked, she will be destroyed.

'I'll bet she just about broke the Bank of Mom and Pop to make *that* go away, huh?' Scott says.

'I'll drink to that,' Lucy says, and Scott swivels back round to chink her glass. He raises his eyebrows at her, and she shakes her head. 'Wow. Just . . . wow.'

A light breeze has started up, fluttering the coloured bunting that hangs around the hut. A gull circles overhead. Across the bay, near the rocks, she sees that Amelia and James have found Tiggy and are trying to coax her into coming back to the bar. She's shaking her head, gesticulating wildly. James tries to take her by the arm, but she shakes him off. 'It's bullshit!' She's screaming, and her words are being carried towards them on the wind, like the distant screech of the gulls. 'It's not real. Someone's made this, to make me look bad.'

Scott sniffs. 'It's not completely ridiculous. You must've heard of all this deep fake stuff they can do these days. If a bunch of amateur nerds can do it with actors' faces on YouTube, think what anyone with half a brain is doing. The CIA use it to trick people during interrogations. Make it look like someone they love is being tortured.'

'I think you've been watching too much TV.' Lucy rips open a packet of peanuts and pours them into a bowl. 'You don't really believe any of that, do you?'

'Are you serious? You've no idea . . .' His voice trails off and he shakes his head. 'Though you never know, do you? She seems like a sweet girl, but—'

'Got to watch the quiet ones.'

They take a drink, complicit now in their solidarity.

'Still,' Lucy says, 'it's the tech that's weirding me out as much as anything.' She taps the tracker, but nothing happens. 'It's incredible how it works – how we all see it through our own eyes . . . but we were seeing it as if we were Tiggy.'

'I agree, for once.' Scott sips his drink. 'Deep fake or not, having my own personal video stream is seriously whack.'

Lucy spies Brenda leaving her sunlounger, and as she starts walking towards them she seems to be limping slightly. Interesting. What with her and Scott, they'll be abandoning the injured left, right and centre.

'So maybe she did something to Giles . . .' Scott says, just as Brenda arrives back at the bar.

'Don't say that.' Brenda shakes her head. 'Don't even think it. She's a lovely girl. She was perfect company on the walk down here. When I first met her today I thought she was nothing more than a giggling airhead, but there's a lot more to her. She's got a savvy business brain, especially for marketing and branding. She's not going to do something to jeopardise what she's built.'

'She's got you convinced anyway,' Lucy says. She gestures at Brenda's glass. 'Need a top-up?'

'You know . . . could you maybe mix me something else? A fruit punch or something? I don't know if it's the heat or the walk or what, but I'm feeling a little woozy.'

'Three glasses of wine will do that.'

'It was a spritzer though, and not too strong. I'm sure my alcohol tolerance isn't that low.'

'You know what?' Scott says. 'This has only just occurred to me, but I've been drinking water all day, and now I've had two pina coladas, and I still don't need to go to the bathroom.'

'Just as well,' Lucy says, surveying the beach. 'I think our options are limited.'

'Oh, sure. I mean, al fresco is the way, obviously. But I haven't felt the urge, and I haven't seen anyone else disappear off into the bushes either.'

'You haven't been with everyone all day though, have you? Brenda was off on her own. James and Amelia went to find her. Giles and Tiggy were away—'

'Right. But I've been with you all day, and you haven't gone. Unless you've—'

'No, I have *not* peed my pants, if that's where you're going. But actually, you're right. I didn't drink as much of that water as you did, but since we've been down here I've had several cocktails . . . and alcohol usually does it. You know that's one of the reasons all the kids are drinking shots these days? Less volume. Less need to find a toilet.'

'I'm sure that's not true,' Brenda says. 'They'd just rather knock their drinks back and get on with whatever else they're doing.'

Scott sighs. 'Well, whatever. I'm just saying it's odd. I wonder if there's something in the drinks to stop us from going. Something else they're testing, maybe. For clubbers or something . . .'

Lucy shakes her head. 'You know what? I think we must be in shock or something. I can't believe we're banging on about our bladder habits when we've just watched what may well be an attempted murder, via some weird sci-fi technology that shouldn't even exist. Aren't you two completely disturbed by this? I keep looking around and expecting to see someone jump out like we've been tricked by Ant and Dec . . . or Punk'd, like they used to show on MTV, or something. None of this is normal, guys. Maybe we need to think about what the hell is going on here.'

'You're right,' Scott says. 'That's twice I've agreed with you now. I think I must have heatstroke.'

'What are you suggesting we do?' Brenda says. 'We all want to get to the end, don't we . . . ? We all want this thing to have been worth our while.'

'True,' Lucy says. 'I suppose we all have our own reasons for being here. We know why we accepted the invitation. So maybe we just go with it . . . whatever they throw at us.'

'We've made it this far . . .' Scott agrees.

'Fine,' Brenda says. 'That's settled then.'

While Lucy, Brenda and Scott have been sitting around the bar, James and Amelia have managed to get hold of Tiggy and walk with her across the rocks back into the sandy cove. Her face is flushed, her eyes puffy from crying, but by the time they arrive at the bar she's calmed down. The sun has slid behind a cloud, dropping the temperature just a notch. Tiggy is rubbing at her bare arms.

'Here, take this.' Scott unties his sweater from around his shoulders and passes it to her.

'Thank you,' she says, her voice a small croak.

'There's a coffee machine under the counter,' Lucy says. 'Let me make you a warm drink. Drop of brandy, maybe? You've had a shock.'

Tiggy nods, and Amelia leads her round to the other side of the bar, where there are two more comfortable-looking stools with cushions and proper backs on them. Lucy watches, impressed by Amelia's calm way of dealing with the girl. She saw what Tiggy was like over at the rocks – a wild animal, shouting and waving her arms about.

Lucy turns back to where the other three are gathered, and notices that James has a scratch on his cheek. It's not bleeding heavily, but there is a trickle of blood snaking down his face. She pulls a wad of paper towels from the dispenser.

'Here, let me help.' She gestures at his face and he looks confused for a moment, then puts his hand up and inspects it.

'I'm bleeding? I didn't even realise.' He takes the paper towels and dabs his face.

'Hold it tight for a bit. I'll get you something to rinse it with.' Lucy turns to the small sink and finds a first aid kit under it. She takes out some antiseptic wipes and a couple of different-sized dressings.

Amelia and Tiggy are huddled together at the bar, talking in hushed voices.

Lucy hands the kit to Brenda. 'Maybe look for something in there for Scott's foot too.'

'My foot is fine.'

'No,' James says, 'you just think it's fine because of the alcohol.'

'I'll get some more ice,' Lucy says, taking the bucket off the bar. It's still half full, but the ice dispenser is on the other side, nearer to Amelia and Tiggy. She wants to hear what they're saying. She's dying to know more about what really happened with Tiggy at that party, and given that Amelia couldn't see it, she wonders what Tiggy has told her. Non-disclosure aside, she needs to get something juicy out of this trip. Revealing Tiggy's secret would be gold dust, but given that Tiggy was the first one to mention that this could be a reality TV show, can they really trust her? Right now she's crying again, and Amelia has handed her some napkins.

'. . . I suppose it's not impossible that these . . . *scenes* we're all seeing could be fabricated,' Amelia is saying.

'And I'm telling you it *was* faked.' Tiggy sniffs.

'I'm sorry. I don't mean to sound like I doubt you. Can you think why someone would want to make a fake . . . video, or whatever, of you like that?'

'Well, if they released it as a video – and why couldn't they? – yes, absolutely. There are lots of people who'd want to hurt me. People who are jealous of me and Giles. I think it's all connected, you see. I . . .' She pauses, blows her nose. 'That's what happened earlier. With Giles.'

'There was a video of Giles?' Amelia says.

Lucy is crouched down, fiddling with the ice dispenser. They know she's there, but they're too engrossed to care.

'It was Giles and . . . this is so hard.'

'Take your time, Tiggy. There's no rush.'

Tiggy takes a deep breath. 'It was Giles and two girls. It was . . . pretty graphic.'

Lucy should start scooping the ice, but she wants to hear this. If she's here to get something to use in her column, she needs as much gossip as she can get.

'I thought it was porn at first,' Tiggy continues. 'You know. For our little love nest.' She tries to laugh. 'I thought that whoever is doing this hasn't done their research, because me and Giles . . . well, let's just say we don't need any help to get going.'

Lucy scoops the ice and throws it into the bucket. *Lucky little bitch.* She can't remember the last time she had a decent sexual encounter where the other participant gave more than a passing glance at her bits before trying to ram himself in. Tiggy's recall of Giles's memory feed sounds completely legit, based on what she's heard about him. And if that scene is real, then there's a pretty good chance that Tiggy's is too. The thought makes her feel sick. She stands up quickly, ready to speak, but she is instantly disarmed as Tiggy smiles at her.

'Hey,' she says. 'I'd really love that coffee now.'

'Coming right up.' Lucy takes the ice bucket back to the other side of the bar. She wants to kick herself for distracting them just as Tiggy was getting to the good stuff.

'The sun's out again,' Amelia says, climbing off the stool. 'We're going to sit on the loungers for a bit. Maybe someone could bring our drinks over?'

Lucy smiles sweetly. She'll get more out of Tiggy if she's nice to her.

'Sure,' James says. He has a gauze dressing on his cheek; the area around it is scrubbed clean. 'I'll bring them.'

Brenda closes the lid of the first aid box and tries to catch Lucy's eye. *We need to watch her*, the look seems to say. Lucy agrees.

Because Lucy's real mission here is to uncover someone's big secret – which, if she achieves it, will not only land her a scoop (ever and always a goal) but conveniently overshadow whatever might yet be mined from her own dark past.

Amelia

'How are you feeling now?' Amelia asks Tiggy, after giving her a few moments to relax on the sunlounger.

Tiggy offers her a weak smile. 'I'm OK. Thank you.' She glances over at the bar, where the others are chatting and pretending not to look their way. 'I'm glad you suggested we come over here. Everyone was being very kind, but, well . . . it's all just a bit overwhelming. Everyone seeing that memory, in their heads. I can't begin to understand how that works . . .'

'Memory?' Amelia frowns. 'It wasn't you though, was it? That's what you said. Someone's faked the scene, and they've managed to implant it in anyone who's wearing one of those ear things. Just like the one of Giles at the visitor centre.'

Tiggy is silent. She won't make eye contact. 'Look, I didn't want to say anything over there, with all the others. I . . .' She hesitates, trying to find the words. 'I'm not sure who to trust yet. I mean, I had a nice chat with Brenda earlier, but I know I was the one doing all the talking. James seems nice. I'm just not sure yet about Scott. And as for Lucy . . .'

Amelia looks at the bar again. Lucy is putting two cups onto a tray. She obviously senses Amelia's gaze, and quickly turns away. The others seem to be engrossed in something that Scott is saying. He's explaining something, pointing at things. James is nodding.

'What's wrong with Lucy?' she says.

Tiggy groans. 'Where do I start? She's a gossip columnist. If there can be any more of a low-life profession than that . . . although, hang on, isn't James a paparazzo?' Tiggy glares at the two of them. 'God, they probably know each other, don't they? They're both here to soak up our grubby little secrets. Urgh. I want to go home now.' She shouts up to the sky. 'If you're listening, Big Brother, can you come out of your secret hidey-hole and get me the hell out of here, please?' She puffs out a breath and crosses her arms over her chest, bringing her knees up and burrowing her face down in the same way she's done every time she's been upset before.

'I'm not sure James is a paparazzo as such,' Amelia says. 'He hasn't really spoken about it. And you know, I haven't seen him take one single photograph.'

Tiggy's head flips up. 'Well, you wouldn't, would you? He'll wait until you take your top off or something. Bloody leeches, the lot of them.'

'I've really no plans to take my top off,' Amelia says, puzzled. 'Listen. Why don't you just tell me about this party. These girls. The scene that was projected might not be real, but I have a feeling that you *were* there . . . that *something* might've happened.'

Tiggy drops her legs over the edge of the lounger and twists round to face her. 'What, you don't believe me now? You think I hurt her? You think I'm capable of pushing a champagne flute into someone's face? Some awful bitch's face? Some awful bitch who, along with her hideous bitch friends, had been taunting me, bullying me, goading me – about Giles, about his behaviour, about me, about my job, my family . . . my looks. Telling me all the time that I'm ugly, I'm not good enough?' Her face is bright red now, and the words come out in a stream of angry spittle. 'You actually think I did that?'

Amelia looks at the others, who are all watching with interest now. 'Did you?' she asks quietly. 'You didn't tell me about the glass before. You said there was an angry scuffle . . . I mean, I knew you were holding something back, but what you describe – the glass in her face – seems . . . extreme.'

There is a long silence, and Amelia starts to feel she's gone too far. Her heart flutters, waiting.

Tiggy drops her head into her hands. 'Yes,' she says. 'I did do that. I did glass her. It was this moment of pure rage. That thing people say about the red mist descending? It's true. It's actually true.'

Amelia swallows. Although she'd started to suspect it, she's still struggling to believe that this small, vulnerable girl could be capable of such a violent act. She glances across and sees that James has picked up the tray and is about to bring their coffees over. Their eyes meet and she gives him a small shake of her head, and he stops, setting the tray down on the bar. 'Let's go back to the others, shall we?' A shiver passes over her. Suddenly she is desperate not to be alone with Tiggy.

Tiggy shrugs. 'Are you going to tell them?'

The vulnerability is here again, and it's hard to compute. Maybe it was a one-off. Amelia shakes her head. 'Not right now. I don't think it would help anything, would it?'

Tiggy whispers a 'thanks' as they walk across the sand.

'Hey, you're back,' Scott says, swivelling round on his stool. 'We were just chatting about this place, trying to work out what we're doing here. It's not really what anyone expected, right? Any more word from Giles yet?'

Tiggy shakes her head.

James opens his mouth to speak as Scott swivels round again, and then stops. 'Hey, did you hear that?' He peers at the corner of the hut. 'I thought I heard it before, but then I convinced myself I'd imagined it.'

'Heard what?' Lucy says. She's looking at Tiggy with an expression that's part intrigue, part fear. She knows. They probably all know. They saw the projection, Amelia reminds herself. She's the only one who's had to hear it second-hand.

'It was a little click, and a whirr . . . electronic. I've heard it a few times now.' He walks over to the corner of the hut and lifts up a triangle of yellow bunting. Then he pokes about in the straw where the roof meets the side support.

'What is it?' Brenda says. She's rubbing at her leg distractedly, like someone shooing a fly.

'Hang on . . .' James roots around a little longer, then there's a small cracking sound and he steps back, a triumphant grin on his face. '*Et voilà*,' he says, turning and holding the thing out in his hand.

'What is . . . oh,' Scott says. 'Well, I suppose I'm not really surprised.'

Tiggy pushes forward, close to James. 'What is it?'

'It's a camera.' James holds it up. 'They're watching us. Listening too, presumably.'

Tiggy shrugs. 'Well, of course they are. I tried to tell you all this from the start.'

'Sneaky bastards,' Lucy says. 'I was kind of hoping that wasn't true. I wonder how many others there are?' She leans over the bar and grabs the small camera from James's hand, then she drops it on the floor and stamps on it. 'Right. Well, that's one angle they're going to miss out on from now.'

'I'm sure there are plenty of—' James starts to say, but he is cut off by a high-pitched screech, like the one that preceded the appearance of Tiggy's projection.

'Uh-oh,' Scott says. 'You're in trouble now, Lucy. Bet that thing cost a bunch.'

'I don't really give a shit,' she says. 'I don't remember consenting—'

'Good afternoon, everyone,' a booming voice says. 'Please tap your ear or wrist devices to start the film. The best viewing platform is the clear blue sky, as you have no doubt realised from your earlier entertainment.'

Amelia looks around the group; everyone raises an eyebrow or shrugs or nods – all seemingly happy enough to go along with this. But is *she* happy? On the one hand, she feels like she's missing out, having the wrist-tracker – not being able to experience the exciting, disorienting view of the memory feeds like the others. Maybe she should request a new tracker. Maybe that's what they want her to do . . . But on the other hand, she's freer than the others. The wrist-tracker is not clamped onto her skin. She's not being forced to endure what is transmitted. On balance, it's better that she keeps her mouth shut.

'You still with us, Amelia?' Lucy calls over to her, snapping her back to the present. 'On three . . . One, two . . . three.'

They turn in unison and tap their trackers. Amelia's holographic screen appears, hovering over the beach. It's pixelated at the beginning, and it takes a moment to come into focus.

'It's Harvey,' Amelia says, unnecessarily. She blows out a sigh of relief. She was expecting it to be one of them . . . maybe even her. After Tiggy's public shaming, it's obvious that they are all expecting the worst.

'Firstly, a little piece of housekeeping . . . we do understand that you might have been somewhat shocked to find the camera there, and you're right in thinking that it's not the only one. But I'd like to assure you that it is there for your own safety. This little beach is quite perfect right now, but most of it will disappear very shortly, when the tide comes in. I realise that none of you have thought of this yet, no doubt caught up in the moment . . . considering what to do about the revelations you've had about a couple of your colleagues. But I'm afraid that despite our many abilities here at Timeo, we can't yet control the tides.'

Harvey smiles, turns to face a screen positioned behind him and clicks his hand-held pointer. The screen changes from green to black, and the Timeo logo slides across it, followed by the tagline 'Creators of the technology you didn't know existed'.

'I'm going to step out of the way for a few moments, and let you enjoy the presentation.' With that, he clicks the pointer again and disappears from the screen – which is now fully taken up by the screen from behind, with the logo and the scrolling tagline.

'This had better be good,' Scott says.

'Welcome to Nirrik Island.' An unseen voice narrates as a drone-filmed aerial view of the island comes into shot. 'This special place is the realisation of a childhood dream, for your host – the founder of Timeo Technologies.' The image pans in, then tilts as the view of the bay where they are currently sitting fills the screen. The tiki bar is gone, as are the loungers and the sports equipment, and the beach looks calm and peaceful – and very, very isolated. Amelia shifts in her seat, not finding the stool particularly comfortable. The island looks vaguely familiar, but the aerial shot hadn't stayed on-screen long enough for her to work out why.

'Despite the various invitations you have all received, and the array of benefits and rewards you have agreed to, none of that is the true reason for your presence today on Nirrik. Your host has invited you here to showcase a series of products that are not yet available anywhere else in the world. The many, *many* exciting things that Timeo creates are *not* sold by Timeo. Although you have never heard of our company, you will have certainly heard of, and made use of, many of its ground-breaking technologies. Due to confidentiality laws, we are unable to reveal these technologies – but rest assured, many if not the majority of the companies that you believe to be the most innovative in the world have been made so by the products that Timeo has created, manufactured and developed – passing over full copyright and patents to the client companies involved.

'Timeo *is* modern technology . . . and what we *can* reveal is that memory-mining and neural pathway programming are at the very forefront of our research . . . and now you specially selected few are part of this exciting research and development pipeline.

'Congratulations! You are here to help make history. Please enjoy the rest of your day. Your host looks forward to welcoming you tonight to a party that none of you will ever forget . . . Oh, and please – don't destroy any more of our technology. As I said before, the cameras are there for your own safety . . . And finally, do not attempt to remove your ear-tracker. The next image will demonstrate this in more detail.'

An image fills the screen: an enlarged animated diagram of the earpiece tracker and the side of a head, showing the ear. The display is schematic, so they can see both inside and out, and the image rotates slowly, showing what happens as the prong of the tracker is inserted, and how it butterflies open inside, fixing it in place.

Amelia gasps. They don't need to see what happens if someone attempts to pull the tracker off. She looks at the others. They're silent, their mouths open in shock.

The image disappears and the aerial shot of the island returns briefly, before it pans out once more. The screen vanishes and Amelia stares at the blank space, swivels in her seat to take in the bay. So they've been duped. Brought here under false pretences to guinea-pig some newfangled neurology gizmos. Her first reaction is a wave of relief that her tracker couldn't be made to latch onto – *into* – her ear back at the visitor centre. But in the next moment, the feeling is replaced by a tickle of unease as she wonders if maybe it was a ruse. If there's a reason she's not getting access to the test device.

And that tickle is joined by another deeper, creeping feeling that she knows exactly where this place is – but her memory is keeping it tightly locked away from her . . . and she has no idea why.

Tiggy

Tiggy has heard enough. She's bored of this trip. There's no opportunity to build her brand. No opportunity to network with anyone of actual use to her. What has she gained, aside from a humiliating reveal of a night she'd much rather forget? It's all Giles's fault. If he hadn't been with those two sluts, if he hadn't apparently bragged about it, like it was something to be proud of, then those bitches would never have known. He convinced her to come here, and now she hasn't even got him here to get through it with. She's sick of these people.

She's also sick of these people asking her where Giles is.

At first, she'd played the worried girlfriend card – despite the horrible projection of his filthy threesome that she really didn't need to see, and his protestations that she'd got it all wrong. Yeah, it was all wrong – wrong because Giles is a filthy cheating scumbag, and apart from anything else, his attractiveness as a partner is very much on the wane. His late-night drug-taking is starting to take its toll, not to mention his business starting to slide down the chute of 'has been'. At least Tiggy is able to adapt her own brand and stay on trend. So what if those bitches say she's ugly? She knows she's not. She sorted them out anyway, didn't she?

They're just jealous.

She ignores Amelia's calls for her to come back, to stay with the group. All that crap about tides and rocks and whatever else. She can see the way out of here, and she'll head there herself. The aerial shot of the island hadn't been up for long, but she'd seen it, mapped it and spotted where they're all meant to be heading: the big house.

There was a lighthouse at the top end of the island, and the house wasn't far from there. The others might have come to the conclusion that she was stupid, but what they don't know is that she has both a photographic memory and an extremely good sense of direction. She excelled at geography at school, understood how to read terrain on a map and how to deal with it.

Yes, the tide is coming in soon. The position of the sun tells her what she needs to know. She'll be out of here and on a flight back to the mainland before the rest of them have even worked out where she's gone.

She's pretty sure she recognises this island, from a trip long ago. Something she hasn't thought about in years. Something she'd rather forget.

But that doesn't matter now.

She wants to find this 'host'. This person in charge of Timeo. She wants to know why she is here. Why her, when there are plenty of other brand experts and influencers they could have chosen? They'd told her it would be worth it. They'd told her it would clean her slate. Her 'slate' being that unfortunate incident at the party, about which they were disconcertingly well informed. But everyone's seen it now, haven't they? They know what she's capable of, and they are 100 per cent judging her for it. So why is she really here?

She gets why Amelia is here. Of all of them, she's the most obvious, now that they've been here for the best part of a day. It had seemed like a mistake. She didn't fit in with the others at all. Her personality, her skill set. None of it was right.

But, of course, it *was* right. She's the peacekeeper. She's the stable one. She's the confidante. And it had worked. She'd got Tiggy to admit to something she never thought she would voice. That thing with her not having the same tracker as everyone else had seemed suspicious, and it still does – but it means Amelia gets to probe in her own way. Even if their fancy tech can read their minds, having a real person teasing things out is much more effective. None of them trust the tech – but they all seem to trust Amelia.

But the tech simply can't do what they're claiming. Way too fantastically *Black Mirror*. Though how else to explain it? Where could the footage have come from? That was a very exclusive party. No cameras. Definitely no filming. And it had been shot from *her* point of view. She'd have had to be fitted with a helmet-cam or something.

From the Timeo presentation, it seems that the whole story had unfurled from inside herself . . . that this was Tiggy's own memory, released via the tracker that is still pinned above her left ear. It seems too impossibly far-fetched, and yet – she knows it's accurate. She was there. It happened exactly as it was projected.

She touches the earpiece, wiggles it slightly, trying to see if she can pull it out. But they'd shown that particular option pretty clearly in the presentation – the design of the prototype. The single metal prong is in fact two prongs that spring open once they penetrate the skin, like those special fittings for hanging heavy pictures on thin internal walls. She'd watched a handyman hanging pictures at her parents' Chelsea penthouse. He'd showed her the spring action of the wall fitting and explained it to her like she was stupid. She'd had an urge to ram it into his forehead, but had to content herself with imagining it instead of doing it.

Most of the time, she only imagined her violent episodes. The champagne flute had been the first one that she'd followed through on, which might explain why it was so vivid in her mind. If the technology *does* work as they claim, then it makes sense that that's the memory it was going to project.

Damn them. She should never have come. Her curiosity and her urge to get one up on her fellow influencers had been too strong to ignore – and getting to come along with Giles had sealed it. A fancy trip to a secluded island. What could possibly go wrong?

Everything, it seems.

She's blocked out the sounds of the others now. Hasn't even looked back to see if they're following. She's made her way over the rocks and is almost at the next section of the cliff path. She doesn't know if this is the official route, but from her memory of where the big house is located, it seems right. She pauses for a moment to catch her breath, realising that she's been half hiking, half climbing for quite some time. There's an inlet behind the rocks, another small bay, with a narrow shingled beach in contrast to the sandy bay she's left behind. Waves are already beginning to lap past the wrack line, seaweed and other debris swirling in the clear water as the retreat of the waves becomes ever smaller.

The tide is coming in.

She turns to look for the others and sees that although they're still quite far behind, they are following her path. Brenda and Scott are both limping, and the other three are trying to help them along.

The sea is much closer to the tiki hut now.

Amelia will no doubt be trying to keep everyone calm, but she can't have failed to notice that the sea is much closer to them than it was before.

She thinks about waiting, or going back and offering to help. But, no. She doesn't know them. She doesn't owe them anything.

Lucy is clearly wary of her now, after seeing the screening of the party. The others are a little less hostile, but they have definitely seen her in a different light. Even Brenda, who she was sure she'd won over with her inane chatter.

She doesn't even care about Giles anymore. She thought she would. She truly did think she loved him, for a while at least. But seeing him in full action with those two girls has brought her to her senses.

Enough.

No doubt the others think she's done him in . . . and right now, she wishes she had.

She scrambles up a jutting section of rocks onto the cliff path, heading towards the shingled inlet. She hauls herself up the final few steps, away from the cliff edge. Loose stones skitter across the narrow path, and she slides in closer still, hugging the bank. There are boulders up ahead, and as she heads towards them something moves in the corner of her eye, her peripheral vision just picking it up. Something in the shingled inlet below, washing in with the incoming tide. She stops walking and peers down. It's either a plastic bag wrapped around seaweed or a dead fish. A big dead fish. A flash of turquoise and a flash of red under the clear water at the shore.

She keeps staring at it, even after she's realised what it is. She can't peel her eyes away from it. There's a heavy feeling deep in her stomach, and her heart starts to beat a little too fast, bringing a wave of nausea as she catches a strong briny smell from the seaweed below, and that strange off scent that comes from slimy algae around rocks. And something else, although it could be her imagination. A coppery tang, with a sour, rotten undertone. Slithering its way in and out of the inlet, until an incoming wave forces it further. And further. And then it is there, washed up on the rocks.

His face swims into her vision. Beautiful eyes, sensual mouth. Desperate for her, ready to drink her up. Strong arms, pinning her down – now slapping weakly at the shoreline.

'Giles,' she says. To herself, because the others are still too far behind, and there's no way Giles can hear her from down there.

'Giles.' She says it again. Then she starts to scream.

Summer 2000

George sits in the den alone, sad that Anne has gone. Hopefully she went straight back to her grandparents' cottage, and she won't tell – but you never know what someone is going to do. George always tries to be good. To be friendly and kind and do all the chores as requested. But still Father isn't happy.

Father wasn't always so bad.

But as he's got older, and many of his loyal flock have deserted him – too tired of his old ways – he's become angry.

Disappointed.

'Why do they choose the word of the Devil over mine?' he says. 'Why do they choose to live their unfulfilled, sinful lives?'

Sometimes he takes the bellows from the fire and beats Mother. Sometimes he goes off for days on end, to stay with another of the mothers. Sometimes he forbids the siblings from playing together, leaving them all alone in their own rooms.

Not that most of them are much use. Most of them are weak – it's too easy to just go along with the rules.

But George doesn't like the rules.

Sometimes Father tells George that if they aren't careful, he will row them all over to the island and lock them in the lighthouse with a madman, just like Grand-Father did to Father, all those years ago.

As Father gets older, he becomes more and more like Grand-Father, and everyone is scared now . . . and everyone wants to leave – even if they'll never admit it. And sometimes some of the mothers whisper together, while washing the clothes or beating the rugs, 'One of these days he's going to kill us, you know.'

And George sits quietly, helping with the chores, and thinks: *Not if I kill him first.*

Amelia

'Oh God, what now?' Amelia starts to run and James follows. 'Lucy, please can you stay with the others?' she calls over her shoulder.

She can see Tiggy beyond the rocks, but she has no idea why she is screaming. Her heart thumps as she clambers up the rocks, using her hands for balance, then feeling James's palms on her back, guiding her. She pulls away and climbs faster, her breath coming out in ragged gasps.

Tiggy is standing still, her hands clutching the sides of her head. She's screaming so loudly Amelia can almost feel the vibrations of the sound in her own chest. Something guttural and terrifying. Something that has made every nerve ending in her body start to tingle.

'What is it, Tiggy? What's happened?' She reaches the cliff path and bolts up the hill, hardly daring to look down at the harsh drop to the inlet. It's smaller than the bay they've just left, and with shingle instead of sand – and a dank smell that makes her want to turn back and get as far away from this place as she can. She keeps Tiggy in her sights, because Tiggy is standing too close to the edge. As she gets closer, a small flurry of stones tumbles off the side of the hill and down the deep drop below. She hears James close behind, the sound of his trainers hitting the loose dirt of the path.

As she reaches her, Tiggy stops screaming. Instead she starts to shake uncontrollably before collapsing to her knees, sending more stones skittering over the side.

James moves past Amelia and throws an arm around Tiggy, pulling her gently back from danger. 'Tiggy! What—'

Amelia sees it at the same time as James does. There's no mistaking it's a body, face down and trapped among the rocks in the inlet. Even from their vantage point high up on the hill, it's obvious that it's Giles, his T-shirt ripped across the back, a dark, open wound visible through the billowing fabric.

Is Giles . . . dead?

Tiggy starts to make a high-pitched keening sound as she rocks back and forth on her knees. 'Oh my God,' she wails. 'No! We need to get down there . . .'

James tries to pull her back to the side of the hill. She's still too close to the edge.

He turns to Amelia, his face ashen. 'We need to call someone.'

'I . . . I don't have my phone. It's in my bag. On the plane.' Amelia takes a few careful steps back in the direction she came from, checking on the others. They are halfway up the rocks. Lucy is guiding Brenda by the elbow. Scott is slightly in front, his face pink with exertion. He's practically on all fours, dragging his bad foot behind him.

She turns back to Tiggy and James. 'Tiggy, do you have your phone? You said you had Wi-Fi earlier. Can we—'

'Jesus, Amelia!' James's moment of calm has been replaced with panic. 'Who can we call? We don't have an emergency contact for this damn place.'

Amelia glances around. 'There are probably cameras here, right? They can see us. Surely they'll send help for us now. They can't leave us like this. They can't leave Giles—'

'Aww, hell.' Scott has made it over the last cluster of rocks and onto the cliff path, and he's seen it straight away. 'Is that . . . ?' He doesn't bother to finish. Just shakes his head. Then turns away, stretching out an arm and leaning towards the rocks, taking Brenda's hand to help her make the last push onto the path beside him.

Lucy is right behind her. 'What's all the commotion here then?' She makes the final scramble by herself. 'Has Tiggy broken a nail?'

Amelia tips her head towards the inlet. 'We, uh . . .' She pauses. 'We found Giles.'

Lucy casts her gaze down to where Amelia is gesturing, holding a hand up to her forehead to block the sun, which has sunk lower now. The day is running away from them faster than they can reach their destination.

'Oh, shit,' she says. 'Now what?'

While the others stand in shocked silence, listening to Tiggy's whimpering, Amelia is already thinking of the practicalities. This is not her first on-trip casualty. It's not that she is a cold person, but she's become slightly immune to death over the years. Working in places where death is as commonplace as running out of milk to make porridge for a hundred starving children, it becomes just another thing to deal with. To process and move on from.

She tried to explain this to her family once, and they said they understood – that her job must be so tough, and that she must need to deal with it this way – but her mum had come to her afterwards, as she was picking up her bag to leave for another trip, and told her that maybe she needed to talk to someone about all this. That it wasn't normal to be so indifferent to death. Amelia hadn't gone home much after that, instead choosing to spend time at friends' houses when she wasn't in some third-world country. Friends who'd seen the same as she had. Who understood.

Perhaps this is why she is here. To lead the group onwards to safety, in the face of a tragedy. A tragic accident, that's all. He'd been drinking. He'd fallen out with Tiggy and he'd disappeared on his own.

Poor Giles. No matter what he'd done, he didn't deserve to be washed up on a beach like this with only a bunch of strangers, miles from home.

Another wave moves him again, his face tips to the side, and she feels a smattering of something that might be hope. She stares at his arms again. The hands are curled . . . as if he might be trying to claw himself to safety.

Lucy sees it too. 'Guys . . . I think we need to get down there. Fast.'

'Tiggy?' Amelia crouches beside her and takes her hand. 'Can I borrow your phone?'

Tiggy, clearly in shock, takes her phone out of her pocket and wordlessly hands it over, pressing on the thumb-pad first to wake up the screen. Amelia is in the process of dialling 999 when Scott speaks.

'Help us!' He shouts it into the air above the inlet, then turns round and repeats it. 'Help us. Please.'

They stand there, not making a sound. Listening to the waves crash onto the rocks below, coming in closer. Amelia stands, scrambles up the hill. The sandy bay they've just come from is partially submerged. The water is three quarters of the way up the legs of the stools around the bar. She slips the phone into her pocket. 'Help us!' she calls. 'We need help.'

'Help!' Brenda shouts. 'There's been an accident.'

Soon everyone is shouting, and there are beeps and screeches as each person's tracker emits a distress signal. Amelia feels her watch vibrate and looks down at the screen. 'Keep them calm,' scrolls across the face.

'Ow.' Scott smacks at his ear. 'It's doing something. Is anyone else getting a little stabbing pain right about now?'

The rest of them murmur and nod. Amelia feels nothing, of course. She has no mental sensor penetrating her scalp. 'Let's just sit here for a moment,' she says. 'Let's all take a few deep breaths.'

They sit down, one after another, but they are all simply staring vacantly ahead.

'Guys?' she says. 'What . . . ?' She feels a flutter of fear slide across her chest, squeezing her tight. She's about to say something else. About to lean over and give James a shake. It's like they've all fallen into a trance. Shock, probably. It's good that she's here. She's about to speak when she hears a sound in the distance, getting closer. The mechanical hum of an engine. Lapping sounds of the waves. A buzzing whine. Then she sees it. A small motor boat, making its way into the inlet. The captain is dressed in dark clothes, wearing a cap. Behind him, a familiar figure dressed in white.

Harvey.

Behind him, someone else dressed in white – another man, dark-haired and slimmer than Harvey, but evidently another employee of Timeo, in the same clean uniform. Not the right clothes to pull a body out of the sea. They should have thought about that.

The engine noise dwindles to an idle, then stops. The men on the boat are saying something, but it's too far away to make it out.

'What's going on?' James says, his voice groggy. 'I don't know what happened there. One minute I was trying to help Tiggy, then . . . it's like I dozed off. But one of those sleeps when you're aware of everything going on.'

'I think they've sedated us again,' Lucy says blearily. 'This is *seriously* fucked up.' She points to the rocks in the inlet. 'Look . . . the cavalry has arrived. I guess they didn't want us down there . . . or, you know – maybe this is all part of the game?'

'Pretty sick game.' Scott rubs the skin behind his ear. 'What would be the point?'

'To freak us out?' Lucy shrugs. 'I don't know.'

The men are already off the boat, walking around what's left of the narrow beach, heading towards a rough overgrown path that snakes up towards where they are sitting. One of the men has something on his back.

Amelia thinks they're coming up to meet them, to take them down to the boat – which doesn't look big enough to hold all of them, but she knows that you can always squeeze more people into any sort of transport if you're desperate enough. She's been driven across unmarked roads in ancient vans, folded into the footwell of the passenger seat, feeling every bump, every pothole and rock as if she were being dragged along the ground.

But then they turn off the path and towards the edge of the rocks, leaning over to where Giles lies sprawled. She turns to Tiggy, but the girl is still crouching on the path, hands clamped around her knees. She's no longer crying, or making any noise at all. She's staring down at the inlet, frozen.

Harvey steps into the water, placing a hand on a large rock for balance. He doesn't seem bothered that he's getting wet. He leans forward and grabs Giles under the armpits. Then the other man steps in to join him, and the two of them pull Giles away from the stony beach. They drag him up onto the path and lay him there, and while Harvey checks his pulse and leans his ear down to his mouth, the other man unfolds what Amelia can now see is a compact stretcher. He sets it out on the path and they roll Giles onto it. Then they lift it and begin to carefully walk towards the boat, where the captain is waiting – one foot on the gunwale of the boat as it bobs with the current.

'Giles.' Tiggy speaks at last, her voice a strangled croak. Her head whips round to Amelia. 'I want to go with him.'

'Give them a minute,' James says, putting a hand on her shoulder. 'We'll all be going down there and—'

The familiar screech of the tannoy cuts him off. Amelia circles around slowly, trying to see where it is, but it's hidden somewhere – just like the cameras.

'Please remain where you are,' the disembodied voice booms out. 'We will remove the casualty, and one of you to accompany him to the medical centre, but the rest of you must carry on and complete the journey as planned. As you are aware, we are now at T minus 8 and there is still much to be done and much to be arranged for the party. Please rest assured that the casualty will be taken care of. Can the one accompanying member please make their way down towards the boat immediately.'

The tannoy screeches again, and then stops.

'What's this bullshit?' Lucy stomps towards Amelia and James. She rubs at her eyes, shakes her head. 'Why only one of us? They can't expect us to carry on as normal after this, surely? I mean, I hope Giles is OK, obviously . . . and it's right that Tiggy goes with him. But Scott needs help too. And Brenda. How much further do we have to walk anyway?'

'It's not much further,' James says. 'We can make it.'

'How the hell do you know?' Lucy points at his chest. 'How could *you* possibly know how much further it is?'

'Guys, please,' Amelia says. 'We need to stick together right now.'

Lucy looks like she wants to say more, but instead she sighs and her shoulders sag, deflated. 'Sorry,' she mutters. 'This is just kind of messed up, you know?'

Tiggy stands up and starts to walk slowly down the hill, her leg movements jagged and irregular – maybe from crouching, or from the shock. Whatever the cause, she's lurching like a zombie.

'Wait. Let me help you.' Amelia jogs after her, takes her arm. 'Are you sure you want to go? Maybe you should stay with us.'

Something about this feels wrong. Isolating Tiggy from the rest of the group.

Everyone else is in shock, and Lucy's suggestion that they've been given something through the trackers to keep them calm seems to make sense. Amelia is the only one with a clear head now, and she has to remember that to help them all get through this.

They're almost at the bottom of the hill, and Harvey is walking up towards them. 'I'm very sorry about your friend,' he says to Tiggy. 'We must get him to the medical centre straight away.'

'Is . . . he . . . alive?' Her words are slow and drawn out.

Harvey takes her by the arm and leads her towards the boat. 'Barely,' he says. 'Come on. Time is of the essence.'

'Wait,' Amelia says, suddenly realising that Lucy's outburst earlier was completely justified. 'You can't just leave us all here.'

Harvey looks back and shakes his head. 'I'm sorry. Just following orders. You'll be at the house soon, and all will be fine, OK? Just keep heading up the cliff path, then keep to the left. You're close. You're all doing great. I know this has been a bit of a shock, but trust me – it's better if you carry on and let us deal with this. I'm sure Giles wouldn't want you to miss out due to his misfortune.'

'Tiggy?'

The girl ignores her as she lets Harvey help her onto the boat, and all Amelia can do is stand and watch helplessly.

She bites her lip as the boat reverses, then turns and pulls away. Tiggy is sitting at the back, a blanket wrapped around her, facing out to sea. But just as the boat turns, Tiggy swivels round to face her – and Amelia sees her blank expression sliding away. There's something else there, just under the surface. Fear, maybe – or could it be guilt?

After all, Tiggy has already shown herself to be an adept chameleon . . . and she was the last one to see Giles alive.

Lucy

Lucy is sitting pressed tight against a smooth rock, arms wrapped around her knees, unconsciously mirroring Tiggy's habitual protective stance. 'I hate this place,' she says, kicking a stone and watching it fly over the edge and bounce down towards the inlet. 'I wish I'd never come.' And she really means it. It had been fun for about five minutes, but now it's just weird and wrong, and she can't actually believe she signed up for it. She stands, kicks another stone, then slips on the loose gravel path. James grabs her and pulls her back from the edge.

'You need to calm down. There's no point in us all getting freaked out here. The boat is gone. They're not coming back for us. We need to work out what to do.'

'We could try getting someone else to come and goddamn help us.' Scott yanks a small branch off one of the overhanging trees and snaps it into pieces. He throws the pieces into a bush, then roots around in the leg pocket of his shorts and pulls out his phone. 'Right, so I can't make any proper calls, but I can sure as hell send someone a message. WhatsApp works on Wi-Fi, right? Messaging at least, if not audio?' He starts tapping away at the screen, angry stabs of his finger peppered with an array of curses muttered under his breath.

'Maybe we should just keep going,' Brenda says quietly. She's sitting on a rock, absentmindedly rubbing her leg. She looks pale and her face is a little clammy – but then they have just scrambled up a steep incline over awkward, misshapen rocks, and the sun, although low in the sky, is still pumping out heat.

Amelia has made it back up from the bay, rosy-cheeked but otherwise unscathed. 'I think Brenda's right,' she says. 'There's no point in us sitting around here, is there? Harvey told me we're nearly there.' She taps her watch. 'Can we have some directions, please?'

'Oh, please,' Lucy says. 'This is ridiculous. We can't just keep going. I don't understand what the hell is going on here.'

The beep that always comes before a hologram cuts her off.

'Oh, great,' Scott says, snapping another branch. 'Which one of us is getting humiliated next? Maybe I should just jump off this cliff and be done with it.'

Lucy feels a wave of nausea. She'd forgotten about the memory projections. None of them are immune from the reveals, are they? She tries to make light of what Scott has said. 'Got something juicy to share, have you?'

'I doubt it's as juicy as yours, lady. The more I look at you, the more I see some sort of heartless deviant just itching to burst out.'

Lucy is trying her best to laugh as the holographic letters appear in front of her. Her own secret, the one she desperately hopes is never revealed, is momentarily pushed out of her mind. She turns away, looking at the sky to get the clearest view.

THINGS HAVE NOT GONE TO PLAN, BUT PLEASE DO NOT PANIC. YOUR FRIENDS ARE SAFE, AND YOU WILL BE TOO. IT'S NOT MUCH FURTHER, AND WE HAVE SOME SURPRISES IN STORE THAT WILL MAKE ALL OF THIS WORTH IT.

PLEASE SEPARATE INTO GROUPS AS DETAILED BELOW, AND THEN FOLLOW THE MAP ALLOCATED TO YOU. YOU CAN ACCESS IT AGAIN ANYTIME – YOU JUST NEED TO ASK. REMEMBER, THIS IS A TAILORED EXPERIENCE – DON'T BE AFRAID TO ASK FOR WHATEVER YOU WANT . . . OR NEED. WE WANT YOU TO BE HAPPY.

AGAIN, DO NOT WORRY ABOUT YOUR FRIENDS. THEY ARE SAFE.

TRUST US.

. . .

. . .

THE GROUPS ARE AS FOLLOWS:

. . .

. . .

SCOTT AND BRENDA

. . .

. . .

LUCY AND AMELIA

. . .

. . .

JAMES – PLEASE SPEND SOME TIME ON YOUR OWN.

. . .

. . .

THE MAPS ARE AS FOLLOWS . . .

A series of maps appears on the screen, each one showing the sandy bay and the stony inlet where they are now, and on the other side of the island, somewhere that seems still so far away, something labelled as 'the big house'. Although it doesn't look particularly big, but perhaps the map isn't really to scale.

Lucy blinks as the holographic image fades. 'Interesting selection of groups.'

James has been isolated, which is a bit worrying as there's something about him that seems too good to be true, and Lucy's spidey-senses have been tingling for some time now. They've put her with Amelia, the person she's spent the least time talking to so far, probably to see what happens when there's no one else there to distract them. She looks across at Amelia, with her khaki shorts and her neat, shiny hair. She reminds her of one of those hardcore Girl Guides – the ones who knew how to read maps and could find their way back to the tent when orienteering.

Amelia shakes her head. 'This is wrong. Scott and Brenda are the weakest.'

'Excuse me,' Brenda says, standing up straight. 'There is nothing weak about me, young lady. If I'm not very light on my feet today, it's because of this damn heat, and the shock of everything that's gone on – but I am certainly not *weak*, and I am more than capable of dealing with this oaf.' She nods her head towards Scott, who is staring at her open-mouthed.

Lucy can't control her laughter. 'Glad to have you back, Brenda. Thought we'd lost you.' She gives Brenda a double thumbs up, then turns to Amelia. 'Come on then, let's go.'

'Wait,' James says. He puts a hand on her shoulder, and she automatically shrugs him off. She's not OK with people touching her without permission. Not much *with* permission either, come to think of it. 'I don't really need to spend time on my own,' he says. 'I could just tag along with either of the groups—'

'Big Brother is watching, Jamesy. He's got some sort of plan.' Scott stands up, testing his bad ankle. 'Personally, I would also not describe myself as weak. So why don't you girls run along, and we'll see you later on when we get the next set of instructions . . . mmmm-k?'

Amelia's face has turned bright red, and it's not from sunburn. 'I'm sorry, I—'

'Save it, lady.' He turns to Brenda. 'What say you and me show these kids how it's done, huh? I'm already thinking of a few things I'm going to ask for. The first being a top-up of this water bottle. Those cocktails were nice and all, but this water is something else. Don'cha think?'

Brenda shakes her head, but she's smiling. Scott offers her his arm and she takes it, and the two of them shuffle off up the hill, in the direction their map had pointed them in.

'Piss off then, James,' Lucy says. 'I'm starting to think this might be a race, and I'm not losing out to you or those two crazies.' She tips her head towards Scott and Brenda, still close enough to have heard her, and Scott curls his spare arm around his back and gives her the finger.

James opens his mouth to speak, then closes it again. He's pale too, like Brenda, and he's shaking ever so slightly.

Amelia is looking at him too. 'James, are you—'

'I'm fine.' He cuts her off and turns away from them. They watch as he heads off up the path behind Scott and Brenda. He quickly gains on them, but before he reaches them, he turns left and starts to hike up an unmarked trail.

'Right then,' Lucy says. 'Where're we headed?'

Amelia says nothing. She shoulders her backpack and heads up the hill, following the same path as Brenda and Scott. Before long, the others are out of sight, and the two of them are at the brow of the hill. There's a cluster of worn rectangular stones arranged in a square, piled up at different heights on each side. Bright green succulents poke out of the gaps, and a fluorescent moss covers most of the flat surfaces. They stop walking and glance around at this place they've stumbled across. There are more rows, more walls.

'I think these are ruins,' Amelia says, running a hand across one of the stones. 'Small cottages, maybe. Or some kind of shelter, anyway. Looks like they've been abandoned for a very long time though.'

'I did one of those haunted house things once, for a piece,' Lucy says. 'I had to accompany a B-lister from *The Only Way Is Essex* – who couldn't stop screaming every time someone moved – and that couple who're always on morning TV talking about their psychic experiences. Best five hundred quid I've ever made. In fact, I'd do it again for free, just to watch that reality TV dork shit his pants again.' She laughs. 'I'm sure this spooky wee place is fine though. But I'd rather not stick around. How far to the next stage, do you think?'

'Hmm?' Amelia hasn't been paying attention. She taps her watch. 'You know,' she says, 'I just remembered . . . Scott mentioned he was going to message someone. Do you think he got through?'

'Does it matter?' Lucy shrugs, feeling a bit dejected that her funny anecdote has fallen on deaf ears. 'We're not with him, are we? They could be getting airlifted to safety as we speak . . . and we don't have a phone.'

'I think we'd notice if there was a helicopter coming in to land.'

'S'pose so.' She walks around the walls of the small building, peering over into the middle. Inside, the light is different. Darker, even though there's no roof to block the sun. The walls on the inside are blackened, as though charred. She reaches a gap that was obviously once a door, but she doesn't want to go in there. She's not sure why, but there is something wrong with these buildings. These cottages or shelters or whatever they are. The energy is off-kilter. There's a strange old-smoke smell that makes her feel sick. Or maybe she's just tired and hungry, and fed up with this 'adventure'. Whether the ruins are haunted or not, Amelia is not nearly as much fun as those TV people she'd hung out with.

'Jeez,' she says, breaking the silence. 'Remind me never to accept another weird invitation again, will you? If something sounds too good to be true, then it probably is. Look at Tiggy' – she pauses, walking around to the next building – 'she was definitely too good to be true.'

'We don't really know that. We don't know if these projections are real – I mean, Tiggy told me about it all, because I couldn't see them for myself, but I don't know . . . she might've been lying. We don't even know if that was really Giles down there in the water, do we? He was too far away to be sure.'

'Lying about glassing a girl at a party, or lying about not doing it? Plus, you went down there to the boat with her. Didn't you get a better look at him? Didn't she?'

Amelia shakes her head. 'They'd already moved him by the time we got to the bottom. And I don't know about Tiggy. I can't work her out. She looked back at me from the boat, but I don't know if she was trying to communicate something or if she was still in shock . . .'

'Right. Anyway, forget that. What does your watch say? Where are we going? I want to get away from these . . . things.' She scowls at the blackened buildings. 'They're seriously giving me the creeps.'

Amelia taps her watch again. 'Bad news.' She looks Lucy in the eye. 'It's telling me we need to go inside this cottage.'

'What?' She feels her chest tighten. 'Go inside? It's barely got four walls. I just told you: I'm not going in there. I don't like it. It feels weird. We don't know what these things are, or what happened here.'

'They're just old cottages. What's the big deal?'

'What's the big deal? You do it, then. I'm not doing it.'

'Lucy . . .' Amelia's voice trails off as the familiar beep sounds, signalling that a projection is about to start.

Lucy's tracker vibrates hard, as if someone is trying to drill into her skull. She screams in pain.

'Go into the cottage, Lucy,' the voice says in her ear. 'It's the only way.'

'No. I'm not doing it.'

'My God, Lucy, are you OK?' Amelia takes a few steps towards her. 'What's happening? Tell me . . .'

The vibration increases until Lucy feels her whole body shake. The noise is too loud. She grabs hold of the tracker.

'Don't!' Amelia cries. 'You'll make it worse.'

'Go inside the house, Lucy.' The voice is more insistent now.

She tries to ignore it, but she can't. Her teeth rattle. She lurches forward through the doorway and falls to her knees – and with that, the vibration stops.

'Well done, Lucy,' the voice says. 'Now enjoy the show.'

Amelia is in the doorway, staring at her in horror. But she's not staring quite at her; she's staring above her, at the projection, which has soundlessly started to play, projected from Amelia's wrist-tracker for them both to see.

'Why . . .' Lucy says. 'Why is it only coming out via *your* tracker?'

'I guess they want us to watch it together,' Amelia says. 'Maybe it's something about me . . .'

But, of course, it isn't about Amelia.

It was only a matter of time before this happened. Lucy watches as the camera view shows things through her eyes. She knows this because she recognises the glass door that she's opening, which leads into a large modern house. Her hand on the door handle is encased in a black glove, and she can hear breathing – her own breathing – as it comes out in icy puffs in the darkness.

She remembers how cold it was that night. Remembers how she hesitated, giving herself one last chance to stop.

The camera view rotates as Lucy turns round, checking behind her, taking in the thick copse of trees and the heavy clouds hanging low in the darkening sky. As she turns back, her face, her whole body – and what she is carrying in one hand – are briefly reflected in the glass of the door.

Amelia gasps.

'No,' Lucy says weakly. 'This isn't real. It's not me.'

The projection carries on. She walks slowly through the house, looking at the floor as she pours out the contents of the petrol can, making a long, thin snake. She stops at the foot of the stairs and the view tilts upwards, then back down as her foot is carefully placed on the first stair. A pause. Silence, but for the light sound of her breathing. The view tilts upwards again. Up, up to the top. Then another pause as the view rotates slowly to the left, before pausing again. More breathing. Then the carpeted floor of the landing, the petrol still flowing in a steady stream from the can. The view tilts up again. Straight ahead, there's a partially open door and, visible through the doorway, the corner of a white blanket hanging off the end of a bed.

Her gloved hand comes into shot as she pushes the door open wider. The sound of breathing is louder, more ragged. Then it stops, and the faint sound of snoring comes from inside the room.

'No,' Lucy whimpers now, shaking her head as she sits curled up on the floor of the ruined cottage. 'No.'

Amelia stands motionless, watching. 'It's only another trick,' she says quietly. 'Just like Tiggy and Giles.'

Lucy jumps to her feet as Lucy on-screen moves away from the door, the camera swivelling round as she makes her way back down the landing, past another door – with a pink teddy bear engraved on it, along with the words *Milly's Room*. She hesitates. Her breathing stops for a moment. Then the camera shows the staircase, the image moving quickly as she hurries back down the stairs.

Lucy in the ruin turns away from the screen, but another screen appears, then another and another, whichever way she turns. 'I can't watch this,' she says, just as Lucy on-screen steps outside the front door, the camera turning for a final glance up the stairs. Her breath coming out in a gentle wheeze. The view tilts down again, to her gloved hand rummaging in a pocket. She pulls out a box of matches.

Amelia staggers backwards, out through the ruin's doorway.

There's a *whoomph*, followed by the sound of crackling as Lucy runs out of the ruined cottage, while Lucy on-screen stares at the house, her vision fixed on the roaring flames.

Brenda

T - 6

Brenda and Scott make it up the hill and onto a flat plain. Scott lets go of her and limps across to the edge, but there is no barrier of any kind so he leans over for a quick careful look down, then steps back. Brenda follows close behind. They're on top of steep cliffs. It looks like they've made it to the other end of the island, but it's a long way down to the sea. She hopes they don't have to go down there. The pain in her thigh is extreme now. It feels stiff and difficult to move. She daren't touch it – the last time her hand brushed against her shorts the pain was excruciating, radiating all the way through her leg. She takes another small step closer to the edge and stands awkwardly beside Scott, trying to peer down at the sea without risking being blown off the edge by one of the frequent squalls. The waves crash into the rocks, and the movement is mesmerising. Hypnotic. She steps back before she loses her balance.

'I feel like we're at the end of the world,' she says. 'There's nothing ahead. I've no idea where we are.'

Scott points to the left, the opposite side from the cliff path they've just climbed. 'There's land over there, in the distance. Another island, maybe.'

'Or the mainland?' Brenda feels a prickle of hope, but when she turns to look at where he's pointing it slides away into nothing. She nods. 'No, you're right. Another island. A bit bigger than this one, do you think? Maybe we should start a fire or something.'

'Smoke signals?' Scott laughs. 'Oh, hang on.' He takes his phone out of his pocket and holds it up towards her. 'Got a message. Remember I sent that WhatsApp earlier? Didn't really think it would go through. I must've picked up that Wi-Fi Tiggy mentioned.'

'Who did you send a message to? Are they coming to help us?'

He grins, rocks back on his heels. 'You betcha. I messaged my mate Mark. He's one of those people who always knows a way to get out of a bind, if you catch my drift.'

She doesn't really, but she doesn't care either. Scott's mate could be a Russian spy for all she cares. Her own phone is in her handbag on the plane, and she's no idea of anyone's number – so if Scott has some sort of 'fixer' in his contacts, then good. She hopes he can come soon though, because the pain in her leg is starting to make her feel sick.

'I'm hoping he can somehow find us with GPS, you know, with us having no idea where we are . . .' His voice trails off, as if he's just realised this.

What's the point in asking for help if no one knows where to find you?

Brenda swallows. 'Listen, I don't normally take anything myself – I mean, I never get sick. But I don't suppose you have any painkillers on you? I thought I saw you taking something when we first started out.'

'They aren't painkillers,' he snaps. 'What I mean is . . . they aren't your usual over-the-counter type of things. I, um . . .'

'I thought you were a health guru. I assumed you'd have some sort of herbal remedy.'

He laughs, then raises both his palms in a 'you got me' gesture. 'Well, they do come from some sort of natural resource. You're welcome to one, but, well . . . they're not like M&M's, you know. I'm not sure of your tolerance.'

She blows out a breath, readying herself, then slowly lifts the left leg of her shorts. She tries to roll it up, but her leg has swollen so much she can barely move the fabric.

'Holy shit!' Scott recoils from her as he takes it in.

Her skin is roasting hot, sticky with sweat and something else that she doesn't even want to think about. A pale, gummy trail oozes from the wound towards her knee. The site of the snakebite is even redder, almost purple, a thick welt with a yellowing crust around the two puncture marks that seem to have swollen wide open.

Scott's voice comes out in a choked whisper. 'I thought you said it didn't bite you?'

'I lied. I think I was in some sort of denial. Besides, I didn't want to make a fuss.'

'Make a fuss? For Pete's sake, Brenda. They would've sent help for you, like they did for Giles. You need medical attention. You might need an antivenin – do you even know what kind of snake it was?'

She shakes her head slowly. Having the breeze on her leg feels good, and she doesn't want to roll her shorts back down. 'I thought it was just an adder, maybe, or a grass snake – not that I really know anything about them. Snakes in general, I mean. I hate them. I can't even look at a picture of one without feeling like I'm going to have a panic attack. But it had this weird white mouth – I couldn't stop staring at it. It was sort of mesmerising.'

'That doesn't sound much like a harmless grass snake,' Scott says. 'Jeez, if you'd gotten help sooner, it'd be nothing but a memory by now. But that' – he points at her leg – 'that does not look good.' He turns round, looking here and there, as if trying to find somewhere for them to sit. There's a raised, flat rock. Behind it, a couple of crates that look like they've been abandoned for some time. They're peppered with bits of moss and spatterings of bird droppings. He shifts one of them and the lid slides off. 'Well, what d'ya know?' He takes out a bottle of water, offers it to Brenda, then takes out another for himself. He flips off the cap and drinks greedily. 'This stuff is gooooood. I can't work out what's in it, but did you notice that James never drank any of his? No alcohol either. No prizes for guessing what his big dark secret might involve.'

Brenda takes a sip. 'You think this water is drugged? And that James is a recovering addict?'

'No such thing, in my book. You're either addicted or you ain't. I'm the latter of the two. I know what I like, but I know I don't need it. I just like it. All that vitamin stuff I sell to those yoga-hippies and alpha-moms? Total B-S.' He takes another swig, then reaches into the deep pocket in his shorts – this time pulling out a small plastic bag. He holds it up, shakes it. It's full of different-coloured, different-shaped pills. 'So . . . I got uppers, downers, sleepers, jiggers and holee shit that's good'ers. Looking at you though, I think you might need some combination therapy.'

'Anything. Please. I just need to get rid of this pain.'

'Okey-dokey,' Scott says, digging around in the bag. He hands her a pink capsule and a small round yellow pill. 'Knock yourself out. Literally.'

'Don't we need to keep going . . . and get to the house?'

He shakes his head. Pops a red capsule in his mouth and washes it down with the rest of his water. 'Don't worry about that. My mate Mark will find us. I promise.'

Brenda sucks in a breath, lets it out slowly. If the snakebite is going to kill her, she might as well float off on a high.

Amelia

Amelia is glad to have some time alone. She's not a person who gets stressed very often, but the collective tension of the group is starting to get to her, and those last few, horrific minutes there with Lucy in that hellish burned-out cottage had been too intense. She taps her tracker, willing it to tell her where to go next, and hoping that wherever it leads will give her a chance to pull herself together. What happened with Lucy had pushed her to the brink, and she's glad that Lucy has run off on her own. It was all from Lucy's own memory, but the shock had been clear on her face. Amelia would need time to come to terms with what had just been shared, and Lucy would need to do the same. Just like Tiggy, Amelia can't quite believe that Lucy is a monster. There had to be a reason why she set fire to someone's house – a house where there was at least one person inside. She doesn't even want to think about the kid's bedroom. But something drove Lucy to do what she did, and until she knows what it is, she will reserve judgement.

She heads down into a dip along the coastal path, a narrow, winding track lined with parched bracken and occasional thorny fronds of wild brambles. It doesn't appear that any of the others have gone this way. The sandy path is damp in parts, but there are no footprints.

She pauses for a moment to take in the view. To her right, the vast ocean is dark and impenetrable, nothing visible for miles. The water is calm for now, the waves undulating gently. The path becomes steeper again as she climbs out from the dip, and she feels the burn in her calves as she presses on. There's barely a sound, except for the high-pitched screech of a kittiwake nearby, circling and swooping – letting her know that there's a nest and to keep her distance.

Just as she's feeling she must be getting close to the headland, she rounds a sharp bend and the remains of a lighthouse come into view. Previously hidden from her due to the angle of the path and the undulating terrain, she stops to take it in. The walls are still painted white in places, but most of it has flaked off. They're broken and crumbled, but there is still a light on top – presumably it doesn't work. She walks closer and then the path disappears completely and she's walking over dense brush that has not seen other footsteps in a long while.

The sea breeze makes her shiver, and she hugs her arms around herself. *Am I supposed to be here?*

It's not safe, that's for sure. But nothing has been cordoned off. There's nothing to stop her exploring.

She's glad to have found her own place of quiet.

She skirts around the lighthouse and takes a few steps closer to the edge, keeping her weight on her heels, leaning back towards the safety and shelter of the building as she peers down at the sharp drop below. She'd thought it strange at first that the lighthouse would be hidden from view from the rest of the island, not perched on the highest point but in the dip behind. But seeing these rocks, it makes sense. Huge Jurassic boulders are piled precariously together, the erosion of the sea creating sharp, rugged lines further below. A boat hitting these rocks would stand no chance at all.

As she steps even closer to the edge, a strange feeling flits over her. Déjà vu – although she knows she hasn't been here before. She would remember it, she's sure. And yet there is something familiar about it.

She hunkers down to peer at the rocks, and through the gaps she can see the waves crashing, their white foam spraying high. And further out, past this cacophony and the quieter sea beyond, she can see something else.

Another headland, off in the distance. A mirror of this – the hill, and the drop down onto the rocks, huge breakers smashing against them.

Another island.

A chill runs through her, despite the ever-present heat of the sun. Something about the island in the distance. The hill, the rocks, but in between the two, a rocky ledge jutting out.

The kittiwake shrieks and swoops towards her, and she stumbles back.

She knows this place. Not where she is now, but the tip of the island across the water.

She was there. A long time ago.

She turns towards the lighthouse. Touches the cold, wet stone. Remembers a voice, cross and childlike: 'Of course we can't go over there. That island is private. No one lives there now. No one has even been there for years and years.'

'Why? What's wrong with it?'

'It's a bad place. An evil place . . . Father says no one should go back there. Not *ever*.'

Amelia

She runs until her lungs start to ache and she has to stop to catch her breath, to cough, to suck in great mouthfuls of air. She slumps forward, hands on her knees, waiting for her heart rate to slow and her breathing to ease, then she unhooks the straps of her backpack and throws it onto the ground. She grapples with the zip, eventually pulls out her water bottle and takes a long, slow gulp. She drops to the ground, cross-legged, and frowns.

This so-called game. It had to be about her, didn't it?

Why couldn't it have been about one of the others – Lucy or Tiggy, or even Brenda. They've all done shitty, horrible things in their time – and what has *she* done? Other than devote her whole life to helping others.

It's all she's ever wanted to do. Ever since she read that news story about the refugee who had died trying to climb onto an island in the South of England. He'd managed to get all the way across the Channel on a small boat that was meant for picnicking on ponds, not escaping across the sea, risking life and limb. Losing life, in the end. How awful must your existence be if you think that's a good idea? Obviously it's worth the risk, because so many try it – and many succeed.

But many don't.

She read about that man one summer, after she'd spent a week on an island with her grandparents, bored to tears with none of her friends around her – not that she'd ever had many. That was another reason she got into humanitarian aid – because she'd never be short of people who wanted to spend time with her.

She's tried to block out what happened that summer on the island, but she knows it's close to the surface now. Ending up at that lighthouse was no coincidence.

She drinks a bit more of the water and feels a little calmer. Scott is convinced that the water is drugged, and she's not entirely sure he's wrong – and right now, she's not entirely sure that she minds if it is. She's never taken drugs, other than paracetamol for a headache, and maybe some antacids now and again. She's not even much of a drinker, although she enjoyed the cocktails at the tiki hut. Brought back some happy memories of someone she met while working on a project in Ghana. Someone she'll probably never see again, and that's fine too. She's used to being on her own. The more her parents had pushed her to 'be like the other girls', the more she had pulled away from them. But it's not been in vain. She's been responsible for a lot of good things, and earned recognition for them – magazine profiles, interviews on the major news channels – sufficient to raise awareness that has in turn led to more funding for bigger projects. Tiggy might be a celebrity within her own circle, but Amelia is well known by much higher profile people, for much bigger things. All those celebrities who make tearful vlogs of their time spent helping starving children and digging wells need to have someone in the background to talk them through it all, don't they? She might not be famous in the traditional sense, but she has made a name for herself in a way that truly matters. That hasn't been the point, certainly, but it's something she reminds herself of when she's on her own – as she nearly always seems to be – in some dire, bleak situation or another, and finds herself questioning just what kind of life she's chosen to lead.

Not that this qualifies as one of those times. True, it's been a little dire – certainly has been for Giles – but it's far too scenic to be bleak. Though now that the sun has dipped, it's starting to get a bit chilly, and they haven't made it to the house yet. The thought of a party makes her stomach flip, but then again, she would like some food. When did she – or any of the others – last eat? Although, she's not actually hungry. Maybe the drugged water is an appetite suppressant too?

She heads down the hill, through an overgrown trail that may or may not be the right way to go. No one else seems to have arrived at the lighthouse, so it's clearly not meant to be found – and yet, she found it. Knowing that she's come around the headland, with the sea to her right again, and the other island just across the stretch of water in the near distance, she figures that the house can't be far, based on the map. Of course, she could ask her tracker again, but she's sick of being told what to do.

Surprisingly, she hasn't come across Lucy. Not that she's been looking for her. She'd expected her to come back to the ruins, but when she didn't appear after a few minutes, Amelia had set off on her own. Did Lucy go back the way they came? That would make no sense, but then Lucy was in shock and who knows what she might have done. Hopefully the others have made it further. Maybe they're already at the house.

The path dips steeply into a marshy area that seems too overgrown to pass through, but she knows if she just keeps going she'll get out. Unless there's some hidden danger to deal with in the undergrowth. Landmines or snakes, or quicksand, even. One of those phenomena that used to scare kids but rarely exist in any real place.

'Don't worry, it's safe to cross.'

James's voice comes from her right and she whirls round, but she can't see him.

'In here,' he says, his smile evident in his voice.

She walks in the direction of his voice and sees his hand waving from under a green tarpaulin. He's in some sort of makeshift shelter propped up with poles, leaving a space just high enough to stand.

'Am I glad to find you!' She pushes through the marsh grass, ignoring the scratches on her bare legs. As she gets closer, a distinct, comforting aroma hits her nostrils and her mouth waters. 'Oh my God – are you brewing coffee?'

'Ethiopian Arabica,' he says. 'I'm assuming you'd like a cup?'

He lifts the edge of the tarpaulin and she bends her head slightly as she walks into the shelter. In the middle, James is on one knee, tending to a small stove with a metal coffee pot on top, and the whole floor area is covered in blankets and cushions. 'Wow. What is this place?'

He pours coffee into a tin mug and hands it to her. 'It's my comfort den. I asked for it. Said if I had to be on my own, I wanted to be somewhere I felt safe.' He takes a sip from his mug and looks away from her.

'You didn't feel safe earlier?' She lifts her mug to her lips and inhales the scent. 'With us?'

He shakes his head. 'I wear a good game face. How else do you think I can do my job?' He sits down on the floor, wraps a blanket around his shoulders. 'But no. I don't feel safe. I never feel safe. I knew what they were trying to do when they told me to go and spend time on my own. They were trying to freak me out. To see how I would react. You all thought I was fine, didn't you? Being part of the team, getting on with the task in hand.' He pauses, takes another sip. 'But I'm very much not OK. I thought . . . well, if I just stayed in here, I'd be fine. I knew I'd have to come out eventually and start looking for the others, or finding my way to this house, but I couldn't do it. I thought if I stayed here then someone would find me. I wanted someone to find me.'

His eyes are wild when he looks back at her, and she realises he's quite agitated. Something about this situation has triggered something in him, but she doesn't want to pry.

'I was a bit of a loner when I was young,' she says. 'I probably still am – although with my job, I have to push myself into the crowd. I'm always out of my comfort zone, and it never gets any easier. I've tried to have friends, but it's never really worked out. I've always found it hard to go along with what other people wanted. I had one of those holiday friends once. You know the ones. They've been there before so they think they know it all. Try to convince you to do things you know you shouldn't do.'

James smiles sadly, then looks away. 'I never went on holiday as a kid. My dad . . . well, let's just say he was tricky. My mum couldn't cope. She . . . she drank. Tried to blot it all out.' He stares at his coffee cup. 'One day she went out for a pint of milk and never came back. I was six . . .' He turns back to face her, tears in the corners of his eyes.

'Oh, James . . .' She leans over and puts a hand on his knee.

'A neighbour found me. One of my mum's friends. They took me in. But she had her own kid and it was hard. For a long time, I barely spoke. Barely interacted. I just kept saying, "I thought she was coming back."'

Amelia wipes a tear away. 'Well, you're not alone now. You've got me, OK? Now, let's leave this den – as snug as it is – and go and find the others.'

He smiles and gets to his feet. He takes her cup and lays it down next to his on the floor. 'Thanks for listening to me. I try not to let my past get to me, but . . . well. It does. Often. People think that the paparazzi must be ruthless, amoral gold-diggers – but to be honest, the only reason I started doing it was because I thought it was a job where I was always going to be in a crowd, so I'd always be safe. Watching celebrities and taking their photos – it's such a break from reality that sometimes it makes me forget that I exist.'

Amelia walks out of the shelter and back into the long grass. James follows. What is it about this place, she thinks, that's making everyone bring their long-suppressed memories to the surface?

Lucy

T - 3

Lucy knows there's no point in running. It's an island. They're not just going to let her leave. Not now.

She can't work out how they got hold of this *video*. Where was the camera? Even if there was CCTV at that big fancy house, it couldn't have tracked her like that, from the door to upstairs, back down and out. She's replayed the whole scene inside her head, many, many times. And now Amelia has seen it too – conveniently projected out of her tracker so that they could watch the horror unfold together.

But who is she kidding? There was no camera. It came from her own head.

She's willing to accept now – as bonkers as it seems – that Timeo has mined her memories. But how did they know where to look? How did they know she had such a secret to hide?

The worst part is, it's not even finished. At some point, the rest of it is going to unfold – what she did, who she did it to – and how it ended.

It was never meant to end the way it did.

She rubs at her face, angrily wiping away tears as she meanders back down the path, heading past the ruins, taking a quick look to see if Amelia is still there but not wanting to go anywhere near them. Amelia isn't there, of course. Why would she be? She's probably back on the other side of the island now, trying to escape the psychopath.

Lucy isn't a psychopath though. She's sure of it. She's just damaged and torn and broken into bits. She's a cracked mirror, bringing her own seven years of bad luck. It's been six and a half, actually. She'd thought she was close to getting through it.

'How far is the big house?' she says out loud.

A holographic map pops up in front of her. A big arrow showing where she is now, and another pointing to the big house.

'Thanks,' she mutters. She's apparently accepted the technology, but she doesn't want to.

She blinks as the map pixelates then disintegrates, and she picks up the pace. It's not far now, and she'd like to get there before sundown.

'It's T minus 3 hours,' the disembodied voice tells her, even though she didn't ask.

She doesn't care about this party that's meant to be happening. Doesn't want to do anything now, except go home. The last message to the group told them they were to ask for anything they wanted, but there's nothing. Not now. That memory being unleashed has crushed what spirit she had. It had been fine to mock Tiggy, but only because she knew she had something much worse festering away inside her.

The house was supposed to be empty. *Her* house.

Her ex and his new wife were meant to be in New York.

The child – she can barely bring herself to recall her name, Milly, was supposed to be at her grandparents'.

How was Lucy to know they'd cancelled the trip because the baby was ill? That woman had taken her husband and given him the child she could never produce. She wasn't going to have her beloved home as well.

That had been the plan.

But when she'd seen the rumpled blanket hanging off the end of the bed, heard the heavy breathing in the bedroom, even though she knew rationally that it was a second chance – an opportunity to stop and think about what she was doing – she'd gone ahead with it anyway. In too deep, the adrenaline surging through her – the buzz of it blocked her from stopping and led her to make the biggest mistake of her life.

She *is* a monster.

A sharp pain shoots through her stomach, spasms doubling her over as she falls to her knees and vomits. There's nothing in there but clear liquid, but it burns as it empties out and the spasms finally subside. Brushing her hand across her mouth, she gets to her feet again. Clenches her hands into fists, bites hard on her bottom lip to stop herself from screaming.

She takes a few slow, calming breaths. Then carries on. She'd been questioned, of course, but there had been nothing to link her to the event, and somehow she'd got away with it. Except she hadn't, of course. Because she still has to live with it. Every minute. Every day.

She forces herself out of her head, scans her surroundings. Off to her right she can see the blinking lights of another island. She can't work out how far away it is, but it definitely looks too far to make a swim for it. She's already getting cold as the sun has dipped, and she's not that strong a swimmer.

She climbs a small hill, barely noticing the surroundings now. The exotic plants and varied landscape were interesting before, but now it's all just something that's there, a reminder that she's somewhere she doesn't want to be.

As she descends the hill, she sees a copse of tall trees ahead. And nearby, two figures, walking away from her. She sighs. Might as well join them.

'Hey, Amelia? James!' She shouts it across the marshy plain, and her voice seems to be dulled somehow. Grabbed by the breeze and shaken away. 'Hey, you two,' she cries again.

This time, James turns round, sees her. Waves. Amelia stands beside him. Perhaps she hasn't told him yet. Perhaps Lucy has a few more moments before James finds out what a monster she is. She waves back, starts jogging towards them. The ground is a bit spongy underfoot and it slows her down. But they wait. James is smiling. Amelia's expression is wary.

She definitely hasn't told him.

'Hi.' James walks towards her. 'I was wondering where you'd got to. Amelia and I were chatting about . . . things. I forgot myself for a while.'

Lucy frowns. James seems different to when she last saw him. He'd seemed confident, ready for action. Now he seems smaller, deflated. Like he's ready to give up. She'd started to get suspicious of him before, thinking he knew more about the 'game' than he was letting on, but now he looks just as fed up as she feels. Not that surprising, really. They're all tired. They're all in the same boat. She smiles inwardly. If only they had an actual boat. They could row to that island and get help. Get away. Go back home and pretend none of this ever happened. They all signed a non-disclosure agreement and she's more than happy to stick to it.

She doesn't want anyone to know anything about this place. She definitely doesn't want anyone to know anything about the technology they've been testing.

'I was just about to tell James what happened in the ruins,' Amelia says carefully. 'Thought he might need to know . . .'

Lucy bristles. Clenches and unclenches her fists. Why? It's not going to make any difference to him, is it? She says nothing.

Amelia presses: 'Best that we get everything out in the open, don't you think? I have a feeling that's why we're all here. It's an experiment. They've selected us because of our repressed memories, and they want us to release them.'

It makes sense, but Lucy's still not sure why. Why her? There must be millions of people on the planet who are suppressing terrible memories. Why has she been chosen? No doubt they'll all find out soon enough.

'Do you mind if I tell the full story, though?' Lucy says. She sucks in a fast breath, lets it out slowly. 'It'd be better in context. For you too.'

'Fine. Let's walk and talk. It'll be dark soon.' Amelia turns and starts walking.

'Go on,' James says, his voice gentle.

She walks in step with him, but she can't look at him. 'I think Amelia might be right with the memories thing.' She taps the tracker. 'I thought these things were nonsense at first, but after the presentation . . . and what happened in the ruins.' She pauses, blows out a long breath. 'I think maybe they are tapped into our neurons. Or something, at least. There was an . . . an incident projected. Amelia saw it. It was a video, like Tiggy's. But the thing is, I know there was no way a camera could've filmed it. The only footage of that night is inside my own head—'

'Hang on.' James stops walking. 'You're saying that film we watched earlier, of Tiggy, came from her own memory? And that the same thing just happened to you?'

Amelia realises they've stopped walking. She sighs and turns round, heads back towards them. 'There's another possibility,' she says. 'Maybe the memories are false. There's a psychological condition – false memory syndrome. It's been well documented.

Remember that "satanic panic" stuff? It was all disproved, and it turns out the kids had been almost hypnotised to believe that this stuff happened to them when it didn't. I'm wondering if maybe they've inserted something into your bloodstreams with that tracker probe. Maybe it's not pulling out repressed memories – maybe it's putting some garbled garbage in there instead.'

Lucy shakes her head sadly. 'I'd like to believe that, but I'm afraid I know for sure that what you saw really did happen.' She rolls up her sleeve, revealing pink, puckered skin. 'I spilled petrol on my arm.'

'I didn't see that happen . . .' Amelia says.

'I know you didn't. Because I didn't look at my arm when it happened. So you didn't see that part. It's evidence, isn't it? It's my constant reminder. I can cover my arm up with long sleeves, but I can't cover up the fact that it itches every night, and sometimes it still bleeds.'

'Are you going to tell us what happened that night?'

Lucy nods. 'I think I have to. I think that's the only way for us to end the game.' She's about to say more when a loud crack of thunder sounds overhead. They all look up at the sky as the sun fades out as though someone has turned a dimmer switch.

'I agree,' James says. 'But first, I think we need to find Scott and Brenda . . . then we need to get to the big house before we're caught in the storm.'

Brenda

Brenda's head is pounding, but the pain in her leg has gone. She daren't look at it again, knowing it can only be getting worse – but at least for now, she can't feel it. She sits up, rubs her eyes. 'How long were we asleep?' The light has faded, the sky a dark purple. She's propped up against the plastic crate that Scott found. It's still only the two of them. At the top of the hill near the tip of the island. 'Scott? Wake up. I think it's going to rain.' She pokes him with a finger in the ribs and he groans. 'Scott?'

'All right, all right.' He pulls himself up into a sitting position, glances around. 'Where are we? Where is everyone?'

Brenda is beginning to feel more awake, and as well as her head, her body has started to tingle with pins and needles, her muscles straining to get back into position after she's been slumped for however long. 'What time is it?' she says, louder.

The holographic text starts to scroll. 'It is T minus 3. Thank you for using this service.'

'Three hours to go,' she mutters. 'Three hours until what, though?'

'Huh?' Scott looks confused.

'I think we need to get going. Can you give me something for my head?'

He drags the bag out of his pocket, his movements seemingly in slow motion. He digs about and finds a red-and-white capsule. 'Pain at the base of your skull, as if someone has whacked you with an axe?'

She nods.

'This'll sort it. Might make you drowsy again though.'

Brenda laughs, but the sound seems alien to her. 'Drowsy? We've been asleep for two hours.'

'That's one way to avoid this crap. Right?'

She pops the pill with a long swig of water, then shoves her backpack behind her as a cushion and lies back against the plastic crate. 'Maybe we could just stay here a bit longer.'

'Mmm-hmm.' Scott is looking at his phone. 'Well, I had a reply from Mark. Only, I don't know if it's actually from him.' He runs a hand through his hair, tugging at it. His earlier neat styling is long gone.

'Oh?' Brenda tries to be interested but she feels herself drifting off again. 'What makes you say that?' She's trying to remember who Mark is, and wonders if it's relevant. If she gets out of this alive, she's definitely going to be making more use of pharmaceuticals in the future. She's always been put off, seeing the obvious effects of coke on the workaholic players that do her bidding, and she'd assumed that anything else was for neurotics and fools. But what Scott has given her has been a revelation. Numb the pain, doze off, treat the side effects with something else. It's easy to see how addiction can creep in.

Scott pauses. 'Might be a stupid thing, but it's the fact that he's replied to me using my name. He never calls me Scott, or Scottie or anything like that. He calls me "Doodle", as in "Yankee Doodle". He thinks it's hilarious.'

Brenda sits up straighter. 'Well, that's interesting. What did he say though – in response to your call for help?'

'"Don't worry, Scott. Everything is under control."'

'That doesn't sound like the sort of response you were looking for, does it?'

He shakes his head. 'He's a man of few words at times, but this . . . well, this doesn't help us. I thought he'd have mentioned our location – if he'd been able to track it via my message. I think it's safe to say that my communication attempt has been intercepted.'

'Maybe there's a firewall of some sort?' Her leg is starting to itch again now, but it feels different from before. It's more of a crawling, squirming feeling than an itch. She can't tell if it's getting better or worse.

A patter of rain starts to fall. Light at first, but by the colour of the sky it's going to get worse soon.

'We need to find shelter,' Scott says, sounding distracted. He's still tapping at his phone.

Brenda drags herself up but feels unsteady on her feet. Scott drops his phone in his pocket and gets up from the ground, then walks over and takes Brenda's arm. 'Come on.'

As they start walking, jets of pain begin to shoot through her leg. This is definitely not good. 'Do you . . . do you think he even got your message?'

Scott is walking too fast, limping with his bad ankle, trying to support her too. 'Well, someone got it. Someone replied. Harvey, probably. Or one of the other Timeo minions.'

She glances at him, but he's still looking straight ahead. There's a small pulsing in his cheek. She's seen it before, in some of her consultants. When everything's about to hit the fan. When they're trying to avoid the inevitable. 'Scott?'

He keeps walking, practically dragging her along beside him. She'd always thought she was in decent shape for her age, but now she feels every one of her sixty-two years. Like one of those awful women she refuses to look at in the high street, gossipy and doddery and buying the latest cardigan from Per Una and thinking it makes them look young. Yes, she lied on her information form – but what difference was it going to make? Do they think for a minute that she's too old to do something like this? She's still running her business like a woman half her age, while most people she's encountered along the way have burned out, or lost it all and thrown themselves off a tall building.

She sucks in a breath and tries to remember the mantra her long-term counsellor told her: *Mind over matter, take the first choice – not the latter, too much sleep makes you fatter*. She smiles to herself. It's a stupid mantra. A parody of a mantra. But it still holds true. She can do this. She can take control. And that enforced sleep she had can only stand her in good stead to get through the rest of this horrendous day.

The rain comes then, the real rain. Not that pathetic hair-frizzing pretence at rain. This is hard rain, coming at them from all angles in their exposed position on the cliff. They're drenched within seconds. There's no point hurrying now. A bright flash of lightning shatters the sky, followed a few seconds later by a loud crack of thunder. It's this they need to take shelter from. She's always hated electrical storms. Always been secretly terrified of being burned from the inside out.

Scott speaks at last. 'There,' he says, pointing ahead. A cluster of rocks juts out from the side of the central hill of the island. She'd realised earlier, after the quick look at the map, that the whole thing is shaped like a figure eight. The airport at the bottom, the lighthouse at the top. The tiki hut bay at one side, the big house on the other. It would have been helpful if they'd been shown this map right at the start – but thinking back, none of them asked for a map; they just followed that first arrow, then things took their own course: stage-managed, no doubt, by their elusive 'host'.

However, she knows the layout now, and she knows they are close.

They just need to get out of this storm.

'There,' he says again. 'Do you see it?'

She's struggling to see anything, now that the rain is hitting them in sheets. She puts a hand to her forehead, trying to shelter her eyes enough to see what he's pointing at. Other than the rocks, there's . . . then she sees it.

The overhanging rock is the entrance to a cave.

Scott takes a firmer grip on her arm and starts to run as best he can. She tries to follow, slipping and sliding on the wet path. Stumbling more than once as her leg gives way. But then somehow they're there. He drags her under the overhanging rock and into the mouth of the cave, then he switches on the torch on his phone, directing it inside.

Sitting inside, wrapped in blankets, faces frozen in surprise, are Lucy, Amelia and James.

Amelia

Amelia jumps to her feet. 'Oh, thank God! Are you OK? Where have you been? You're drenched!' She grabs her blanket from where it has dropped to the ground and rushes towards Brenda, draping it around her shoulders and ushering her into the dry warmth. Brenda is pale and shaking quite violently. Scott, apart from being soaked to the skin, seems to be OK. He lays his phone on the ground, leaving the torch on to give them some light.

James gets up and hands a blanket to Scott. 'Jeez, you two don't look like you're having much fun.' He gestures to a wooden crate just inside the mouth of the cave. 'We haven't got a lot to offer, but we seem to have unlimited blankets.'

Scott starts laughing. He can't stop. James joins in, but Amelia can't bring herself to, not with Brenda looking like this. She picks up another blanket and uses it to try and get the worst of the rain off, drying her hair, dabbing her face. Brenda lets her, almost child-like in her demeanour now. She looks older too – with the rain having washed off her make-up, it's clear to Amelia that she is a lot older than they thought.

It's also clear that there is something very wrong with her.

'Brenda? Are you OK? Talk to me. Are you in pain?' She turns round to the others. Lucy is still sitting on the floor, red-faced from crying and apparently in a bit of a trance. She hasn't reacted at all to

Brenda and Scott's arrival. Amelia has seen this before, when people have fallen into a semi-catatonic state from shock. Clearly Lucy's video-memory and her subsequent recall of the story to her and James has pushed her somewhere deep inside herself. She'd blurted the story out in a wash of tears the minute they'd entered the cave. All she and James could do was sit there in shock, while trying to comfort her – and she still needs comforting. But for now, Amelia knows she has to focus on Brenda, whose needs are more physical.

'Can't really feel it now,' Brenda says. 'Red and white and yellow and pink.' She giggles. Then her legs seem to collapse from under her. Amelia makes a grab for her, but she's a dead weight. 'James—'

James is there in a flash, grabbing Brenda under the armpits, half dragging, half walking her over towards Lucy, to the area where they've kept themselves warm wrapped in the blankets. As he lays her on the floor, her shorts ride up her legs and she starts to scream.

'Shit.' James steps away, points at her leg. 'That does *not* look good. Jeez, Brenda, I thought you said it didn't bite you?'

'She lied, didn't she?' Scott says. 'She told me, then we partied for a while. She's pretty good fun for an old lady.'

Amelia ignores him. 'This is bad.' She crouches down and inspects Brenda's leg. It's swollen up like a balloon, the shorts sticking to her clammy skin. The bite area is leaking yellow pus. 'It looks like an infection.' She leans forward and puts a hand to Brenda's forehead. She's burning up. Amelia frowns. 'We need to lower her temperature. Has anyone got any paracetamol?' She stares out of the mouth of the cave, then turns to James. 'Soak one of the blankets in the rain, then wring it out. I need a cold compress.'

Scott limps towards her, holding out his plastic bag. 'That's Tylenol, right? The red gel ones are the rapid release. Maybe you could burst it and squeeze it into her mouth.'

Amelia raises her eyebrows at his sensible suggestion. Not shocked that he has a bag of random mixed drugs and knows what they all are by sight, but that he's realised they might struggle to get Brenda to swallow a pill right now. There's just one problem. 'What did you give her before, Scott? I want to reduce her fever, but I don't want to kill her with a drug reaction.'

Scott snorts. 'Funny you should say that. Most of the lunatics who come in for vitamin infusions have ended up in the emergency room after doing something like that. People pop these like they're candy, but you gotta know what you're doing.'

'Scott, I'm not looking for a lesson in illegal pharmaceutical combination therapy and its consequences. I just need to know if she's already had any paracetamol, because I think the state her body is in right now, her liver won't handle it.'

He shakes his head. 'She's had fentanyl and Demerol. I was going to give her a Percocet but she was already out of it.'

'Wow.' A drenched James has come back in from the rain. He stands at the entrance, wringing out the blanket and rolling it tight. 'Really going for it there, mate.' He hands the blanket to Amelia and raises an eyebrow.

'Whatever, *buddy*,' Scott shoots back. 'Don't make out like you're the innocent. I can see it in your eyes.'

Amelia lays the blanket over Brenda's leg, and she murmurs something incoherent. Amelia has managed to squeeze a couple of the capsules into Brenda's mouth, and now with that and the compress, all they can do is wait it out.

'They're not coming to help us, are they?' Lucy says. Her voice is flat. Emotionless. Amelia had almost forgotten she was there.

'Maybe we need to just ask,' James suggests. 'You know, like they keep telling us to?' He shrugs. 'I know it seems mad, but it does work. They're watching us. Listening to us. Whether it's via the trackers or more hidden cameras doesn't really matter.'

'They're not coming,' Lucy says again. 'If they can see us and hear us. If they can track us. If the tracker is measuring our bodily functions . . . they already know how sick Brenda is. They know we're all sitting here cold and tired. They know that whatever they're doing is triggering our worst ever memories, or biggest fears, the most awful things we've ever done. They know all this, and they don't care.' She pulls her blanket tighter. 'They want to destroy us.'

'Why, though?' James says. 'Why us?'

'It doesn't matter. People who do stuff like this? It doesn't matter.'

Scott slaps a palm on his forehead. 'I didn't tell you this yet, guys. The phones. Remember earlier, Tiggy said she used her phone to text Giles – that she was linked to their Wi-Fi? Well, I'm the only other one with a phone. I was linked too.' He runs a hand through his wet hair. 'After the boat came, I sent a message to a friend of mine. Someone I thought could get us out of this mess. He messaged me back when I was alone with Brenda. Only . . . only it wasn't him. It was a reply as if it came from his number. But it wasn't him.'

'How do you know? What did it say?'

Scott shakes his head. 'Doesn't matter. I just know it wasn't him. They're messing with us—'

'Wait, so when Tiggy got a message from Giles saying he was OK – that wasn't from Giles?' Lucy pulls her knees up to her chest. 'So we don't know when Giles was last OK. We don't know if he was OK when Tiggy left him.'

'And where *is* Tiggy?' Scott says.

'She went on the boat,' Amelia says. 'She's with Harvey – presumably others too – at the big house. With Giles.' She lifts the compress to check on Brenda's leg, and Brenda groans again. Her eyes are closed, sweat is dripping off her brow. Her fever is still raging, and there's nothing Amelia can do to fix it. 'Look, we need to get help. Can someone please tap their tracker and ask?' She looks back at Brenda. 'I really don't know how much longer she's going to last.'

Lucy

Scott limps towards the entrance and taps his tracker, shouts: 'We need help here, you bunch of sick fucks!' He stays there, staring out into the darkness.

'Giles, Tiggy and now Brenda. We're dropping like flies.' Lucy's voice is still wavering slightly. She's embarrassed about her breakdown, after she'd told her story to Amelia and James. Thankfully, they were sympathetic – as much as they could be, under the circumstances. She's been living with this for long enough. Having a couple of people know her secret doesn't change it. It's still a secret. It's still the thing that coats her heart, making it impossible for her to form any kind of bond with anyone, or anything, ever again. She'd bought a dog – a small terrier cross-breed – thinking that having something in her house that relied on her might help her come to some sort of peace within herself. But the dog had seen right through her. Shied away from her touch. It was back in the dog's home before the week was out, and she hadn't even given it a name, other than 'Dog' – which to someone with a functioning heart might have come across as cute and ironic. But it just reminded her that she was too hardened to even find affection for an animal, much less earn any in return.

She looks around the cave at the sorry bunch she's been lumbered with, and wonders what the point is anymore. She should walk out of here right now. Walk to the end of the island, where that crumbling lighthouse stands, and throw herself into the sea.

No one is going to mourn the death of a cynical, washed-up gossip columnist.

Amelia clears her throat. 'Brenda is going to be fine.'

It's obviously a lie. Brenda's leg is festering before their eyes, and her temperature is so high Lucy can feel the heat radiating from four feet away.

She wants to say that she doesn't think Brenda is going to be fine, and that neither are the rest of them, but she decides to change tack. 'You know, I'm thinking we all need to sue the organisers of this thing. Once we get out of here. The invite said "luxury", and here we all are, huddled together in a cave. Sheltering from the rain while one of us battles a serious infection. Two of our party are gone and we don't know where . . .'

'I think Giles and Tiggy are being looked after,' James says. 'I want to believe that, at least.'

'It didn't work out so well for anyone who went to Fyre Festival though, did it? Thousands of dollars for supposed luxury, but they ended up with collapsing tents, their belongings looted, barely anything to eat . . .'

'We didn't pay for this though, did we?' Amelia says. 'We were all willing to come here and be pampered for free. We've all got our reasons for being here. We all hoped to get something out of it.'

'Sure,' Lucy says. 'I tried to check them out, remember? I told you all this. There was nothing on their website. Nothing at all in any search engines. It's like Timeo doesn't even exist, or if it does, they're keeping themselves way below the radar—'

'You saw the presentation.' James raises his palms. 'That's the whole point of them. They make stuff and sell the copyright. They don't want people to know who they are. These tech companies with all their innovations need to sell the dream that they've invented their own products. They assign credit to the people they want to assign it to – the people that are the best "fronts" for the company. In fact' – he pauses, takes a breath – 'I'm pretty impressed. All the things that Timeo has come up with—'

'But how do we even know it's true?' Lucy says. 'How do we know anything is true? You know . . . Giles looked pretty dead to me, lying face down in that inlet.' She nods at Amelia. 'But you say they told you on the beach that he was going to be looked after?' She shakes her head. 'I don't trust a word they say. They've forbidden us from sharing things with each other, unless on *their* say so, and now they're picking us off, one by one . . .'

Brenda's eyes fly open and she cries out in pain. Then she murmurs something, too quiet and garbled for them to make sense of. Her eyes close again.

'Brenda?' Amelia crouches again and wipes the woman's brow. 'Stay with us. We'll be home soon.' She turns round to the others. 'Did anyone ask for help yet?'

'For Christ's sake, Amelia,' Lucy spits. 'No one is going to help us.'

'OK, OK, let's calm down,' Scott says, limping back to the group and lowering himself to the ground. 'I asked already. Didn't you hear me over by the entrance?' He taps his tracker and yells at the roof of the cave. 'OK, guys, the fun's over. Maybe you didn't much like me cursing at you before, and I am *real* sorry about that, OK? But Brenda really needs your help. In fact, I think we all do. Can someone come and get us now? Please?'

Another scream of pain from Brenda, and she sits bolt upright. 'The island! I remember, I remember. No, no, no, no, no! Cornwall – I was there . . . so long ago. On the news . . . a man died . . . a child gone. All the stories . . . scared. Everyone scared . . .' Then she closes her eyes and collapses back onto the floor.

Amelia leans down and grabs her by the shoulders. 'Brenda? What are you talking about? Are you OK? Answer me! I want to help you—'

'Of course she's not OK,' Lucy says. 'She's got a fever that will probably kill her, if the infection doesn't shut down her organs first. She's out of her mind. She doesn't know who *she* is, never mind who you are. Or where we are. Cornwall? We're not in bloody Cornwall.'

Amelia pulls away and sits down hard on the cave floor. She looks scared, and Lucy is intrigued. Something Brenda said has triggered something. She wonders what Amelia's secret is, but without the embedded tracker there's a good chance they're not going to find out.

'Wait a minute,' Lucy says, 'aren't the Scilly Isles near Cornwall?'

'Yes,' James says. 'Of course. Some of them are uninhabited too, I think. I mean, I don't know, but I'm guessing this could be one of them. But I haven't seen any boats nearby, and that island you can see from the lighthouse doesn't look that far away . . . but' – his face pulls into a frown – 'wasn't there something weird about one of the islands? One where they did some sort of chemical testing, or where they put people who had an infectious disease—'

'You mean like a leper colony? Or one of those anthrax island places?' Lucy remembers something about these from school, but she can't remember where they were. But anyway, it was so long ago there wouldn't be any risk of infection now. Would there? 'Scott – be useful for once and help us out here? You know about medical stuff . . .'

'Listen, lady – I don't do historical disease outbreaks. As I already told you, I help stressed moms and hipster types with a bunch of vitamins they don't really need. You know that no one with a balanced diet actually needs vitamin supplementation? For the majority of the world's population, it's an expensive racket.

Those companies that send out brochures advertising all these wonder cures? Most of it is bullshit. Most of those supplements do nothing at all.' He pauses, shakes his head. 'You know, most of the people who think they benefit from my concoctions are really just benefitting from having some fluid pumped into them. Most people are chronically dehydrated . . . that's the real problem we have. Fast food, unhealthy lifestyles—'

'Yeah, OK, thanks, Scott,' Lucy says. 'We're a bit more concerned about right here, right now, and what might be in the soil on this island. Or the air—'

'Or this cave,' James says, running a finger down the damp wall. 'I think we should get out of here.'

'But look at the rain.' Amelia gestures to the opening, where the rain is still battering the earth, bouncing up off the hard-packed soil, spraying droplets towards them. It's pitch-dark out there now.

Lucy is about to say something else when there's a beep and the green holographic text that they haven't seen for a while starts to scroll.

IT'S NOT SAFE OUTSIDE RIGHT NOW. PLEASE STAY WHERE YOU ARE.

ASSISTANCE WILL BE WITH YOU SHORTLY.

APOLOGIES FOR THE INCONVENIENCE.

'What? Are they crazy?' Lucy says. 'We can't stay here.'

'I think we're going to have to.' James sits down beside Brenda and Amelia. 'How is she?' he says, picking up one of Brenda's hands. Lucy can see Brenda's chest rising and falling, and occasionally she lets out a random stream of words.

'What's she saying?' Amelia looks distracted. 'Can you make it out?'

James shakes his head. 'Just nonsense, I think. Nothing to worry about.'

Lucy sees Amelia's mouth draw into a tight line. She's bothering at the skin around her thumbnail, ripping it off, then balling her hands into fists.

Well, well, well, Lucy thinks. *I wonder what's got Little Miss Perfect so worried?*

Amelia

Amelia knows that Lucy is watching her, and she tries not to catch her eye. She looks down at her hands and realises she has ripped the skin off around both thumbnails and they're now ragged and bleeding. *Idiot!* Especially after what Lucy and James have just been saying about infectious diseases and quarantined islands. Is that really what's going on here? Of course not.

She knows exactly where they are now. And although it might seem like rambling nonsense, Brenda knows something too. Not about her – there's no way she could know that – but about what happened on the island. It was all over the news. Amelia recalled it herself earlier. But there's one piece of the puzzle she can't get hold of. Or that she's blocking, not willing to deal with it just yet.

Is this why Brenda was brought here? Another person with a link – a memory – to force Amelia to remember?

She looks down at the older woman, at her pale, clammy skin, and she can tell that without intervention she's not going to survive. There's nothing Amelia can do about it. She's tried her best to make her comfortable and reduce the fever. She's not a medic. Brenda's condition isn't something that can be fixed with makeshift splints and boiling water.

What she can't understand is why she didn't tell them she'd been bitten. If they'd known, she could have taken her down to the boat when they came for Giles, and now she'd be off somewhere warm and safe, getting the help she needs. There *must* be medical help available at the big house. This is what she chooses to believe . . . because the alternative is far worse.

She hopes she's wrong about where they are. Despite recognising the lighthouse, and the island in the distance – and the memories that tried to push themselves to the surface – she's still hoping she's got it all wrong.

That maybe none of this has anything to do with her at all.

Apart from her recent suspicions about Brenda, she hasn't worked out any possible link between her and the others yet, and she has a horrible feeling that perhaps there isn't one. That they've been chosen on the strength of their own secrets, to help illustrate a point.

Or maybe it's nothing. Maybe she's just paranoid. It's been a long day.

'Hey,' Lucy says, 'you doing OK there, Amelia? You look like you're miles away.'

'Just getting a bit fed up of all this.' She doesn't want Lucy to sense any weakness in her. Lucy is on edge after her big reveal, and she's desperate for something to take the heat off her. Amelia is about to say something else when there's another beep, and her tracker projects a pixelated screen in front of the entrance to the cave.

'Oh, *great*,' Lucy says. 'I wonder which poor sod is next for mental destruction, eh?'

Amelia closes her eyes. *It's fine. It won't be mine.* She opens them again. Her heart is pounding. *Just start. Just get it over with.*

She can tell by the others' stillness and the odd, glazed looks on their faces that they're seeing something she's not. She taps her tracker in frustration, but it stays as it is; nothing but the undulating green line of her heart rate, spiking high.

'Guys, can one of you—'

'I'm on a canal towpath,' Lucy says. 'I can see a small arched bridge up ahead. It's dimly lit. Only one dull street lamp. There's a pile of junk or something on one side, shoved up against the wall. It looks like a ton of black bin liners. Loads of crap spilling out. There's breathing. But that's me, I think. Well, not me. Whoever's vision this is. I can't work out who it is yet.'

A canal towpath? Amelia relaxes. None of it has anything to do with her. She glances around. Brenda is lying with her eyes closed, not part of this. Scott is staring at one of the cave walls, transfixed. But James is looking down at the floor, his shoulders shaking slightly. He's gently sobbing.

'James,' she says, walking over to him. She lays a hand on his shoulder, but he shrugs her off.

His head snaps up. 'It's fine.' He wipes the back of his hand across his face. 'I'm going to close my eyes now. I don't need to see this.'

'OK,' Lucy says. 'It's James, then? We're still walking along the towpath. Had to swerve to avoid the first pile of rubbish. Christ, what a mess this place is. Need to get the council in to clean up.' She shakes her head. 'Someone's talking to me. I can't really make it out. I think I'm wearing headphones.' Lucy takes a breath. 'Not very safety conscious, in an area like this . . .'

'Come on,' Amelia says. What they're seeing has nothing to do with her, but the green line on her tracker is a steady repeating line of bumps now, much higher than they should be. 'What's happening now?'

'Oh, shit!' Lucy reels backwards as if she's been grabbed from behind. She twists round quickly, ducking low. 'There's a man . . . It wasn't a pile of rubbish, it was a den. Ooof. I'm on the ground. I almost felt that. The man . . . the man is after me!'

'My camera . . .' James's voice is flat.

Amelia spins to look at him. 'Where *is* your camera, James? I don't think I've seen it since we left the visitor centre.'

'It's here, in my bag. I dropped it earlier, cracked the lens. So I put it in my bag.' He takes his backpack off, opens the top and rifles around inside. Pulls out his camera and hangs it around his neck.

Amelia is puzzled for a moment, remembering the visitor centre – James's mission was to take promotional shots, but she can't remember him using the camera at all – but she pushes this aside, turns back to Lucy.

'What now, Lucy?'

Something flutters in Amelia's chest as she waits for Lucy to respond. She turns to James, who has his eyes open, glazed like the others', staring at whatever's unfolding in his mind.

'Lucy?'

Tears spring to her eyes as she imagines the next scene. She's already worked it out. The tramp has attacked James, and James is going to retaliate. An accident. He would never mean to hurt him. He was only defending himself . . .

But that is not what happens.

'Hang on,' Lucy says at last. 'This is weird. The view has shifted. I'm not on the ground. I'm looking *down* at the man on the ground. He has a camera on a strap around his neck.' She turns to James. 'I don't get it. I thought I was inside *your* head.'

James is frowning. 'They're clever, those Timeo bastards. I'll give them that. Up to now, we've been seeing it unfold from the perspective of the CCTV camera on the other bridge – the one behind you.'

'Huh?' Scott says.

'Keep watching. You're getting to the good part.' James closes his eyes again.

'There's more light here,' Lucy says. 'Closer to that street lamp. There's blood on the ground, a big pool of it.' She closes her eyes. 'Oh God. No. This is horrible . . . I don't want to watch.'

Scott continues for her. 'I'm . . . I'm kicking the man on the ground. I'm wearing black boots. I'm pushing him with my foot. Jeez. He's trying to get up. The side of his face is covered in blood. His camera – damn, James, is that you? Oh Christ. Your camera's on the ground next to you. It's smashed. You're . . . or he, I don't know who this guy is . . . whoever it is, he's groaning. He's trying to get his hands onto the ground, trying to lever himself up. But I'm pushing him with my boot again.' Scott clutches his head. 'Holy shit, this is . . . this is like the worst virtual reality game I've ever played. I can't . . . Lucy, take over again? Saying it out loud makes it even worse.'

Lucy is pale with shock, but she takes over, her voice little more than a whisper. 'I'm, um . . . he's bending down to the man on the ground. Jesus, James, is that you? You're just lying there. I don't know if you can't move, or if you're pretending so that . . . so that you won't get another kicking. But I'm . . . he's kicking you. Or whoever that is. Fuck. This is brutal.' She pauses, takes a breath. 'OK. I've stopped. Thank God. I'm leaning down, rummaging through his pockets. Grabbing what I can. I've picked up his camera, I'm turning it over in my hands. The lens has a crack running down it, but other than that it's still intact. It's just light enough that I can see my face reflected back in the cracked lens. I, um . . . I'm *so* thin, my face is all angles and dark circles. Dark shadows around my mouth, like sores, maybe. I . . . he . . . I just look broken, and . . . sad. I look like someone who's lost even the memory of hope. I look like—'

Scott sees it first. 'Ho-lee-crap.' He spins round to face James, eyes wide in shock. 'Gotta tell you, buddy, I did *not* expect that.'

'What do you mean?' Amelia says. Her voice is high-pitched, frantic. 'Who is it?'

Scott is still staring at James. 'I was right about you being an addict, huh?' Scott cocks his head, looking partly pleased with himself, but partly disturbed at what he's just seen.

Amelia can't take it in. James has been her strongest ally from the moment they arrived. They'd been drawn to one another from the moment he'd walked up the steps just as she'd woken on the plane, confused and alone. He'd been the first one to help anyone who'd needed it.

But who *is* James?

Giles's secret was almost predictable, but just like Tiggy's and Lucy's, James's big reveal has come completely from left field. It makes her feel better about her own. Although the memory is still hazy and not yet fully formed, there is a familiarity about James in the video that resonates.

James's voice comes out in a croak. 'I was a different person back then.'

'No shit,' Lucy mutters. No doubt turning her own memory over and over in her head.

James clears his throat. 'Why are they doing this to us?' He looks around at them all. None of them are looking at him now, except for Amelia, who wants to simultaneously hug him and shake him. She's the only one who's heard his story. His mum, his abandonment at a precious age. Is it any wonder that he turned to drugs? Scott *was* right about him being an addict, but so what? James is different now. He's no longer the skinny, disease-addled junkie from that horrible projection. But what if the story he told her earlier was a lie?

She doesn't know what to think anymore.

'Look, I'll just say it because no one else is going to.' Scott crosses his arms. 'Did you kick him into the canal? Because that seemed to be where that little performance was heading. Am I right?'

James shakes his head. 'No. Jesus. I didn't kill him. I'm not a monster.'

Lucy raises her head, catches Amelia's eye. Neither of them speaks, but there is plenty conveyed in that look. Just as Scott has seen James, Lucy has seen her. She can feel it. A kindred link that she wants to sever straight away. *You're wrong about me*, she thinks. *I'm good. I've always been good.*

'That was a turning point for me,' James says quietly. 'I took a picture of myself with that camera. Looked at it on the screen. I saw what I'd become, and I knew I had to stop. I was heading in one direction, and I didn't want to be that man. That damaged kid living a ruined life. I kept the camera. I used it to turn my life around.' He lifts the camera hanging from his neck. The lens cracked, in a horrible symmetry with the memory that's just been shared. 'That's why I couldn't ditch it. Even though it's useless to me right now. I fixed it before, and I can fix it again. I keep it, because of what it means . . .' His voice trails off and he lets the camera go. It swings back into his chest with a thump. He raises his head and stares into Amelia's eyes. 'That was me then. It's not me now.'

Amelia nods. 'I know.' It's the same thing she's been telling herself.

Tiggy

They won't let her see Giles. On the boat she'd been in shock and let them tell her what to do – to stay back from him as he was receiving treatment, to keep herself warm. They gave her hot, sugary tea, which she hated but drank anyway.

But they've been in the house now for four hours, and she has no idea where Giles is. She taps the tracker and asks again: 'Hey. When am I getting out of here?' But it's as if since she's been indoors, the tracker no longer does anything – like they've turned it off – which makes no sense whatsoever. She'd thought maybe they'd come and take it. Odd, but they haven't done that either. In fact, since she was brought here on the boat, and Harvey led her into this bedroom to rest, she hasn't seen anyone at all.

The house is pretty much what she expected. When they'd bundled her in, wrapped in blankets – head fuzzy from the tea, which must have had something other than sugar dissolved in it – she'd seen the white walls, ornate pillars and the huge wooden door. But even from her rushed transit from outdoors to in, she could tell that this wasn't a genuine old mansion.

She sits up against the pile of white cotton pillows, rubs her eyes and has a good look around the room. Fancy cornices, dado rails, long navy velvet curtains hung on brass poles. The furniture looks expensive, but probably isn't. Like the facade and the fittings, this fancy house is nothing more than a replica.

She should know.

Growing up in one of the most prestigious white houses in Chelsea, one of those built in the 1840s by a famous London architect, she can spot a fake a mile off. She runs a hand across the bedside table, with its pretty brass lamp and its velvet shade to match the curtains. Someone has spent a lot of time making this place *look* expensive. But all this smacks of to her is the classless nouveau riche. The hideous sorts that have begun to infiltrate SW3, despite the best efforts of the long-term residents to keep them out. The Russians are the worst. Their money comes from unspecified means and their women, although immaculate, ooze venom. The Arabs, at least, have slightly more class, due to them having actual assets to brag about, and their women are dripping in gold yet oddly demure – in public, at least. The changing face of Kensington and Chelsea is a source of constant fascination, and if she's honest she actually quite likes it – although her braying Sloaney Pony friends all disagree. But if that memory replay did anything, it was to serve a timely reminder that most of those people are *not* her friends.

Come to think of it, she doesn't know if she has any true friends.

When she'd first met Giles – at a party in Kensington Roof Gardens, where he'd looked bored and she'd been sitting alone, waiting for her so-called friend Veronique to return with another bottle of Bolly – she'd thought that maybe he was different from the others. He'd seemed genuinely interested in what she had to say – and that was before she even told him that she was an influencer with 1.5 million followers, and before he'd told her that he was the biggest name in gaming. Hmph. She'd felt like an idiot then. In *her* business, with all the endorsements and freebies and specialised subliminal advertising she was involved in, it was prudent to understand every aspect of life. Or 'modern life', as Mummy always said, laughing about Tiggy to her old-money Chelsea friends that she still called on her Bakelite landline. Tiggy had never used the old phone to make a call – how would she, when all her contacts were stored in her iPhone? But she had used it in a photograph when she'd been asked to advertise some retro furniture store on the Kings Road. That post had got a hideous number of hits, and loads of comments about Mummy's old phone. Mummy had been quite pleased about that, although she'd never tell Tiggy so. All Mummy wanted her to do was find a man with a big bank balance to settle down with and have babies. She'd been interested in Giles when Tiggy had told her his net worth, but quickly lost interest when informed that he didn't own any property, or even a car – as he believed these to be old-fashioned entrapments.

Monogamy, it seems, was another one of those things.

She'd cried into a large tub of Häagen-Dazs Coconut Caramel Chocolate in Mummy's sun lounge the first time she'd found out about Giles's cheating, and Mummy had shaken her head and said, 'Don't you understand, Tiggy-wigs? This is what men *do*.' She'd raised her hands towards her Baccarat crystal chandelier and said, 'That's the sacrifice that must be made if a lady wants to have nice things.'

Tiggy thought that maybe she could get used to it, but the more she let him get away with it, the more he carried on. Becoming more blatant, less discreet every time. To give him credit, he always apologised when she found out, always said he didn't love the other woman – or women – and always bought her a beautiful gift to make it up to her. After Cressida and Lorena, he'd bought her two of her favourite Baobab Powdered Rose candles and taken her for drinks at Gong – the highest cocktail bar in Western Europe, he'd proudly told her.

She sighs. Maybe it wasn't worth kicking off at him earlier on. It's not like she didn't know about his threesome at the W Hotel last summer – but there was no need for her to be *shown* it like that. She'd thought she was done with him, but when he'd floated into the inlet like that, her heart had sunk to her feet. Of course she loves him. He makes her laugh, he tells her she's pretty – even when she knows she's not as pretty as those bitches who call her names. He takes her to nice places, buys her appropriate gifts. She'd quite liked Albert, a young French sommelier she'd met when dining at Nobu one evening. She went out with him because he was cute and charming and had given her and the rest of her party several extra wines with their tasting menu – but he'd turned up for their second date with a taster-sized box of Ladurée macarons. She couldn't even be bothered to explain why this was not appropriate, and had been sad for a moment that he was never going to be 'the one'.

She swings her legs off the bed and walks to the door. She'd tried the handle earlier and it wouldn't budge. But this time it turns effortlessly. The door opens with a soft click. Her heart thumps a bit faster than before. Is it really this simple? Why have they unlocked the door? When she arrived, Harvey told her they were locking her in for her own safety, and given her more hot tea. She'd been exhausted then and glad of the rest. And she'd enjoyed the sinking feeling of collapsing into the cushions as the tea kicked in, sending her into a deep, dreamless sleep.

But she's awake now. Maybe everything that happened before was just the way it had to be so they could appreciate real luxury. A proper rest, and now hopefully a good meal and some perfectly matched wines. That's one thing Albert would've been good for.

She opens the door and tiptoes down the hallway. There's no sound, due to the thick pile of the carpet and the fact that she isn't wearing shoes. She should go back for her shoes, she supposes, but she doesn't think she's going outside again tonight. The storm had been coming in by the time they'd arrived here on the boat. Hopefully the others are all downstairs, and Giles has recovered enough to join them for dinner.

One foot is raised mid-air, ready to take the first step down the lavish staircase, when a gloved hand forces something rough and foul-smelling over her mouth and nose, and she feels her legs disappear and her head start to fizz; and then she feels nothing.

Brenda

The pain has gone now. All that's left is a dull ache. She feels as if she's floating. Drifting towards the ceiling with nothing to hold her back. Their voices come in and out of range, sharp, soft, echoing as if she's sinking underwater then being forced back to the surface again. She can't seem to open her eyes. It's as if something has taken away that ability, and when she tries to force it, they snap shut, keeping her locked away from whatever it is out there.

She heard the beep announcing a new message earlier. Were there just words or pictures? It doesn't matter. The group had fallen silent, and then Scott had spoken, and James . . . and now James sounds sad.

What did you do, James? It's probably best she doesn't know. She doesn't need to know. It's not going to help her now.

The pain comes back – short, sharp bursts – then it goes away again and she's drifting once more. Hot in here, then cold. Dark behind her eyelids, then light.

She opens her mouth, says, 'I'm scared.' But it comes out as a groan, not words. Someone lays a hand on her arm. Squeezes her hand. 'You're OK,' the voice says. Amelia? From so far away now.

Fragments of memories swirl around her head, and she tries to screw her eyes tight, push them away. *I don't want to remember.*

They are trying to force her.

Voices inside her head – goading her, cajoling her. *Tell them what you did, Brenda . . . show them what you did . . . show them who you are . . .*

'No!'

The voice again, close to her ear. 'Brenda? What did you say? Can you hear me? Help is coming.' Far away: 'I think she's trying to speak.' Close again: 'Help is on its way, Brenda.'

No it isn't.

'Brenda?' The voice swims away again. Another beep . . . loud and piercing, this time inside her head. They're trying to show her memory. They're trying to show them all who she is.

No!

'What's happening to her? Is she having a fit?' The voice is close.

She feels her body writhe and buck, but she can't control it. Pain comes, different now. In her arm, fast and sharp. Across her chest. She bucks again. She opens her mouth but it's another groan.

The beep sounds again.

'It's another projection.' Far away. 'I don't even know if I want to watch it.'

Her body bucks again, as if it's being electrocuted.

The voice is closer now. 'What's happening to her? Do something!'

'The memory feed . . .' The voice is far away. 'It's Brenda.'

Her body stops twitching, and for a moment everything feels OK. She opens her eyes, squints across the room. Amelia is holding her wrist-device, aiming it at the far wall of the cave.

'This one is projecting from mine,' she says. 'This happened earlier, with Lucy. We're all linked together, somehow . . . Can you guys see it here with me, or is it coming through all the trackers?'

Brenda can see herself via her own private screening, but she doesn't bother to respond. She's sitting at her dressing table, gazing into a vanity mirror. A younger version of herself, with bouncy, glossy blonde hair. Bright red lips, cold hard eyes.

Behind her, reflected in the mirror, there's another woman on-screen, dark-haired, worry etched on her face.

As Brenda stares at the screen she puts her fingers to her left ear, finding the tracker. Her hand shakes. In her periphery she sees Amelia glance at her, her mouth falling open at Brenda's sudden moment of lucidity. But Brenda ignores her, pulls gently on her tracker, testing to see how firmly fixed it really is.

The dark-haired woman on-screen is holding hands with a young girl. Her blonde hair is tied in bunches, and she's holding a small stuffed monkey under one arm. The dark-haired woman is trying to coax her away from the younger Brenda, but the girl cottons on and her mouth opens wide in a scream. 'No.' She throws the monkey on the ground. 'No! I want to stay here! I want to stay here with Mummy!'

'Take her,' the younger Brenda says. 'We all know she'll be better off with you.'

Brenda yanks the tracker out. The pain is excruciating. A jet of blood arcs up and over, travelling far enough to spatter across Amelia's arm. Brenda howls, and the projection stops.

The tracker has landed in Amelia's lap, she picks it up and turns to Brenda, who only manages to blink then open her mouth to speak before pains shoot through her body once more and she collapses back onto the ground.

'Brenda? Oh God.' Amelia grips her shoulders. 'Brenda?' Her voice shrinks away. 'Can I get some help here?'

There's the sound of footsteps, muffled voices. She feels other hands on her, touching her face, her shoulders. She just wants them to stop now, but she can't seem to find the words, and she can't move her arms to bat them all away from her. She can't move anything now. She tries to speak but it comes out as a groan.

‘They’ve said they’ll send help,’ someone says, ‘but it’s difficult with the buggies when there’s an electrical storm.’

Her body judders once more and the voices slip away. Pain shoots across her body – as if she’s been struck hard in the chest – and then the dull light that she can still make out through her closed eyelids fades slowly to black.

Amelia

It's fully dark now. Amelia watches James run after the buggy as it pulls away at speed, carrying Brenda. After a moment he gives up, walks back to the cave. He's shaking his head, sending droplets of rain spraying around him.

'I just can't believe this. That they'd leave us here.'

Amelia hands him one of the blankets they've been using as a towel. He's drenched again from being out in that crazy rain.

'This is insane,' Scott says. 'I say we brave the weather and get out of here.'

'And go where, genius?' Lucy says. 'It's pitch-dark.' She gets up from where she's been sitting since she arrived at the cave. She seems to have recovered from her earlier distress after her projection – but then, is it really so surprising? If you keep a secret like that locked away for years, you have to find coping mechanisms. Amelia knows that from personal experience. The deeper you bury something, the harder it is to find.

'The rain has to stop at some point,' Amelia says. 'We're warm and dry. We just need to wait it out for a bit.'

Lucy turns to her. 'How come you're so calm all the time, Amelia? Everyone else has had something horrible happen to them today, except you. What's that all about?'

Amelia tries to keep her voice neutral. 'I told you at the start. I'm used to extreme situations.'

Lucy puffs out air. 'Right. But this one is not entirely normal, is it?' She cocks her head. 'It's almost as if you know exactly how to deal with it all. As if you're expecting it, even. That whole thing with your tracker . . .' She lurches forward and grabs Amelia by the wrist. 'How come you got this one? How come you aren't asking it to help us out of here?' She grips harder.

Amelia yanks her arm away, catching Lucy on the shoulder and sending her spinning backwards. 'Hey—' she starts, but Amelia is having none of it.

She surges forward, thrusts her face close to Lucy, who backs off further. 'We know what you did. And we know what you do now, destroying people's lives with your gossip and lies.'

'Hang on. Have a word with your boyfriend about that.' She nods at James. 'He takes the photos. That's just as bad, is it not?'

'Oh, come on,' James says, crossing his arms. 'It's not like that . . .'

'Thought you were a paparazzo?' Scott chimes in, amusement on his face. 'Long lens privacy destruction, right?'

James shakes his head. 'No. Not like that. I go to things that the press is invited to. I don't stalk people as they go about their lives.'

'You sell the photos though.' Scott raises an eyebrow.

'Of course I do – it's my job. But I mean, I go to a prearranged event and I hustle for the best position, and I try to get the best, most flattering shot. I'm not hiding in the bushes trying to take photos of royalty in their underwear.'

'So *you* say,' Lucy scoffs.

Amelia is still in her face. 'Shut up. Just shut up. You're the one writing the lies, bending the truth, putting stuff out there that can never disappear, even if they retract it all. It's even worse now with social media; people can screen-grab things before anyone else has even noticed – sell that to the highest bidder. You people make me sick.'

Lucy laughs. 'Oh, Saint Amelia! You do have a feisty belly on you after all. Glad to have awakened it.'

'Screw you,' Amelia says, then shoves Lucy in the chest. She doesn't think it was hard, and Lucy is no doubt milking it for all she's worth, but she slips back and crashes into the wall of the cave.

'You little—' She struggles to get to her feet, getting tangled in the blankets and sliding around on the floor. She falls back again and the wall judders. She stops moving, her mouth dropping wide open in shock as she slowly starts to fall backwards through the moving wall. 'What the . . .'

Amelia takes a step back. Scott and James appear on either side of her, all three of them watching now as Lucy falls back further until she's flat on the ground, and what they'd thought was the wall of the cave is now flipped up towards the roof, like a garage door.

'Are you *kidding* me?' Lucy sits up, grinning. 'An actual hidden door . . . like Aladdin's cave. This is absolutely mental.' She starts laughing, and she can't stop. She waves a hand in front of her face. 'Oh my God, seriously? I thought we'd had all the surprises today . . .'

Scott takes a few tentative steps until he is partially inside the concealed section. He scans the walls, the ceiling. Frowns. 'Well, it sure ain't lined with gold. You found a magic lamp yet, Lucy?'

Lucy starts laughing again, and Scott joins in. The sound of their manic laughter echoes around the small cave.

Amelia clamps her hands over her ears. 'Would you two shut up? I can't hear myself think.'

'Maybe you should come out of there,' James says from the mouth of the cave. He's the only calm one of them left now. 'It might not be safe.'

'It might not be *safe*?' Lucy cries. 'Oh, you are hilarious, Jamesy-boy.' Her laughter filters away. 'We haven't been safe *all day*.'

'I know, it's just . . .' He lets his sentence trail off. Lucy is right, obviously. But there's a reason they found this place. Isn't there?

Amelia take a few steps inside, looks around. It's not a lot different from the main part. They've just sectioned it off with that slide-up door – which was incredibly convincing in the murky muted light from Scott's phone. Lucy must have triggered it when she fell. She circuits the small space, tapping on the walls, pressing. But nothing else moves, and there are no hollow sounds when she taps.

'Are you thinking there might be more of these doors?' James takes her lead and starts tapping and pushing on the walls. 'Maybe it's a network . . . it might lead us to the big house.'

Amelia frowns. She hadn't really considered it, but it makes sense. 'I wouldn't be surprised. But it doesn't seem like there's anything else leading off here.'

'Maybe this is how they get around the island so fast,' Scott says. He starts tapping the walls too. 'Maybe there are underground tunnels and they just scoot around in those carts, keeping an eye on us.' He pauses. Stops tapping. 'Is this *instead* of the cameras that we already found and they confessed to, or *as well as*, do you think?'

'I think it's safe to assume they're watching us, listening to us and monitoring us in as many conceivable ways as possible,' Amelia says.

'And some inconceivable ways.' Lucy taps her tracker. 'Nice cave, guys,' she says. 'Now when are you coming back to get us?'

There's a beep, and then the holographic lettering starts to scroll.

YOU'LL BE REUNITED WITH YOUR FRIENDS
VERY SOON.

MEANWHILE, ENJOY THE REFRESHMENTS . . .
AND THE SHOW.

WELL DONE FOR GETTING THIS FAR.

YOU WILL BE REWARDED.

Lucy swears. 'Thanks, guys! You know what? This so-called game is doing my head in. Do you think we're being live-streamed? Are people at home on their sofas deciding which one of us gets obliterated next?' She glances around. 'Where are these *refreshments*, then?' She gets to her feet and wanders around the small section of cave, kicking at the base of the walls. A pile of different-sized rocks sits in a dark, recessed part of the space, with a couple of large boulders at the base and smaller ones scattered around. She picks up one of the smaller ones, examines it. 'Definitely a rock.' Then she tosses it to the back of the pile and pokes around a few of the others. When she gets to the larger ones, she kicks again . . . and one of them gives. 'Bingo!'

Amelia has watched this little performance with interest. She goes over to help, and the two of them remove all the smaller rocks. As they reach the final large rock, they look at each other and grin.

'What've you got there, ladies?' Scott says.

It's obvious, now that they've moved the real rocks out of the way, that these base-level boulders are not rocks at all – the tops are flat, and when Amelia runs a finger down the side, although well designed to look rock-like, it's clearly made of some sort of fibreglass. 'You do it.' She nods to Lucy, who looks pleased.

Lucy puts her hands around it and pulls. It slips off without much of an effort. She holds the rock-like facade aloft, like a silver cloche in a fancy French restaurant.

'Ta-da!'

Lucy

'Well, well, well,' Lucy says. Just when they think they've seen it all, they throw another curveball to knock them off balance. Whatever is in this box had better be worth it. She drops the fibreglass rock cover on the floor, then lifts the lid of the box underneath. Inside are two smaller boxes – one metal and fully sealed, the other plastic with a pop-off lid. She opens the plastic one first, handing the lid to Amelia, who is still hovering by her shoulder.

'What is it?'

'Hmm,' Lucy says. She pulls out the contents of the box in one big handful. 'Exciting, or not exciting?'

James picks up what she's dropped on the ground. Unrolls it, and something else drops out. 'Waterproof jackets . . . and a head torch. Intriguing.'

'Only intriguing if we're going caving, which, considering we can't find any other concealed entrances, I don't think we are?'

Scott disappears back into the main area. After a moment, the sounds of kicking and tapping echo through the space between the two sections of the cave.

'Good thinking, Scott,' Lucy calls through to him. Then to James and Amelia, she says, 'We should've checked the other walls through there. No rules to state that the connections have to come through here. Maybe this was just the easy one for us to find. So we'd work it all out.'

Amelia picks up a jacket and torch. 'Or maybe this is just so we can go outside in the rain . . . and dark.'

'Why go to all the effort of making concealed rooms and boxes disguised as rocks, though?' James pulls on a jacket and zips it up. 'Bit of a waste of effort.'

'All part of the amazing super-fun game though, Jamesy – eh?' Lucy rolls her eyes.

'Maybe. Just seems a bit elaborate.'

'Oh, come on,' Scott says. 'It's like Giles said right off the plane. It's. A. Game. They're tossing in as many ridiculous surprises as they can—'

'But what if we hadn't found the cave?' Lucy says, interested now. 'Then what?'

'Then it wouldn't matter,' Scott says. 'There'd be something else along the way.'

'Hmm. Maybe. Or maybe they have no fucking idea what they're doing yet, and we're the mugs who're testing out all the possibilities . . .'

'It could be one of those "choose your own adventure" type things,' Amelia suggests.

Lucy laughs. 'Well, whatever it is, I hope they're not expecting me to give them a favourable write-up.'

'We're not allowed to talk about it though, are we?' Amelia says.

Lucy clenches her hands into fists. Amelia is becoming more irritating as the day goes on. 'Seriously . . . what are they going to do to enforce us *not* talking about it? I'll be making sure I tell everyone I know not to sign up for this if they get asked – and I know a lot of people, remember?'

'Are you sure you want to do that?' James says. 'I imagine their enforcement will involve revealing your big secret more publicly.'

He's right, of course. But she's not going to tell him that. She's cold and tired. She's been subjected to a memory that she thought she'd done a good job of keeping locked up in a little box – and she's had to share it with these strangers, just to rub salt in the wound. They might be tolerating her now, but there's no doubt they think she's a monster. James's memory feed was pretty nasty, as was Tiggy's. From what little they saw of Brenda's, there was some serious heartache linked to that. But Lucy's wins in the evil-bitch stakes, hands down. Is it any wonder her moods flit back and forth like they do? Every single day, she has to find some way to live with herself.

'Whatever.' She turns back to the fake rock and starts to pull out the metal box. She tries, but it's too heavy and it slips out of her hands.

'Here, let me.' James leans in and grips the box with both hands, then slowly pulls it out. He lays it on the floor and looks over at Lucy, who's moved out of the way. His eyes are saying, 'Shall I open it?'

'Go ahead.'

He unclips the two metal clasps at each end, twisting them downwards. The lid pops up and he lifts it off. Lucy peers over his shoulder as he starts to unpack it, laying the contents on the floor. Four bottles of a pale yellow drink. Four shiny red apples. Four packets of crisps. Then something wrapped in waxed paper, which he unfolds to reveal a chocolate cake, pre-cut into four equal segments.

'Christ. This is like reality TV show bingo. We've gone from *Big Brother* to that celebrity jungle one, with our little "reward". Scott . . .' Lucy calls over her shoulder. 'Your dinner's here.' She lifts one of the bottles and inspects it. 'He's been moaning about being starving for hours. It's weird, though, because I'm not hungry at all.'

'Me neither,' Amelia says. 'James?'

He shakes his head. 'Well . . . it's not so much that I'm not hungry, it's just that I'm a bit wary of eating anything here. They put those cereal bars and things in our bags, and there were the nibbles at the tiki hut, but I just didn't want to risk it.'

'You're probably right.' Lucy places the bottle back in the box. 'They've drugged everything else they've given us. Maybe this will be all-out poison.' She takes an apple instead. 'This is so shiny it doesn't look real. This whole picnic thing reminds me of *The Famous Five* – I can't tell what's in the bottles yet, but it doesn't look like "lashings of ginger beer".'

'Who are the Famous Five?' Scott chips in. 'Were they the guys who blew up your Parliament with gunpowder?'

Lucy laughs. 'No, idiot. Think Nancy Drew, but with five annoying kids instead of one . . . or was one of them a dog?' She shakes her head. 'I can't remember.'

'If we're going for kids' stories, I'd say this apple is more like the one that poisoned Snow White,' Scott says, lifting out an apple, inspecting it, then putting it back. 'Do they really think we're going to eat fruit that we found in a box disguised as a rock? Who knows how long it's been here.'

James smiles. 'It's interesting you mention *The Famous Five*. I've been thinking the same all day. This whole island thing. What did they say the name of this place was?'

'Nirrik,' Scott says. 'Now, do *not* ask me how I remembered that. It just stuck in my head for some reason.'

'Did you say *Nirrik*?' Amelia says. She has gone very pale. She spells out the letters one by one. 'That's Kirrin, backwards—'

'Wait,' Lucy says. 'What? How did you happen to click to *that*?'

Amelia shrugs. 'My mind just works that way. Puzzles, word games.'

Lucy frowns, unsure where she's going with this. 'O . . . K . . .'

'Kirrin was the island the Famous Five went to.'

'Oh, of course,' says Lucy. 'Where they met George.'

Amelia looks away. 'Yes. It's where they met George.'

Amelia

Amelia needs to get away. Things are moving too close to the truth, but she doesn't want to reveal what she knows. Not yet. She steps outside and raises a palm upwards. 'I think the rain has finally stopped.' She walks further into the fresh air, takes a deep breath. 'It's called petrichor, that scent. Did you know that?' She turns to face James, who has followed her out. He shakes his head. 'The smell of the air after the rain – following a dry spell. You could tell it hadn't rained here for a while. The ground was so hard-packed.'

James just nods.

Lucy and Scott come out behind him.

'How come there were only four portions of food?' Lucy asks. 'If Brenda hadn't taken out her tracker—'

'They're manipulating us,' Scott says. 'They probably whispered something in her ear. Or maybe they just knew she wasn't going to last much longer, even if she hadn't tried to brain herself pulling out the tracker. They're watching us, remember?'

'Well, the four of us are OK now, aren't we?' Amelia says, forcing a smile. 'Even Scott's ankle seems to be holding up.'

'It's fine,' he mutters. 'Stopped hurting long ago.'

'Thanks to your little bag of tricks, eh?' James nods towards his pocket, where he's stashed his diminishing bag of mixed drugs.

Scott shrugs. 'I'm kinda thinking I might not take these anymore. I mean, I need to stay on them today, make sure I keep the pain in my ankle at bay until we get back home. But after that, I'm done. I'm gonna get help. Watching your memory feed made me feel sick. I thought . . . I guess I thought I could shift responsibility onto the user. That's what I've been telling myself for long enough. But seeing it like that? I took advantage. I'm responsible for that.'

James nods. 'Yeah. You are. But we're all taking responsibility now, aren't we? I mean, we didn't see much of Brenda's, and I don't even want to think what might've been going on there – I mean, it looked like she was giving her child away . . . And *you* didn't hear about Lucy's.'

'But what about Amelia?' Lucy butts in. 'She doesn't have this tracker. We saw what happened with Brenda – as soon as she pulled it off, the feed stopped. We're not going to see what Amelia's got to hide, are we?'

'It could still be projected out of my wrist-tracker,' Amelia says, hoping she's wrong.

Lucy taps the side of her head, just above her earpiece. 'Not attached to your *neurons*, is it?'

'Do we have to know?' James turns to Amelia. 'I think we get the picture.' He shrugs. 'We all did terrible things. We've all been brought here to be held accountable. I'm sure Amelia doesn't have to have hers projected for her to know she needs to deal with it?'

'Well, that's hardly fair,' Lucy snaps. 'Maybe Amelia should just tell us anyway.'

'Right,' Scott joins in. 'Come on, Amelia. It's not like you don't know what you did – give the rest of us a peek at your rotten core.'

'What about you, Scott?' James says. 'I don't recall seeing your memory yet.'

'Oh, don't worry,' Scott says, with a small laugh. 'I'm pretty sure they're saving the best for last.'

Amelia tightens her headlamp and switches it on. 'Guys, come on,' she says, trying to take control. 'I think we need to get going. It's not far now. Let's just get to the house and see what happens next.'

'Oh,' Lucy says, 'so that's a no then, Amelia? Not going to be sharing your little secret?'

'Let's just get to the house,' she repeats tightly, barely able to get the words past her constricting throat.

Lucy makes a disgusted sound, but drops it – at least for now.

'Maybe the cops'll be there.' Scott pulls on his waterproof jacket. It's too cold now to go outside with just shorts and a T-shirt; his sweater is long gone. 'They'll be there to check things out, after Harvey called an ambulance for Giles and Brenda, right?'

Lucy shakes her head. 'I doubt that. We're just guinea pigs, aren't we? They're going to give us a slap-up meal, say thanks for our time, then pay us off and tell us to keep our traps shut.' She flicks her headlamp on. 'That's what I think, anyway. I bet the others are all being pampered as we speak.'

'Even Brenda?' Amelia zips up her jacket.

'Especially Brenda. OK, so they left it a bit longer than they should've, but of course they were coming for her. Of course they have the medication she needs to get better. Right? I mean, what's the alternative? We've all said this: Giles called it right from the start. It's a game. They kicked it off with a fake plane crash, but none of us reacted. So they stepped it up—'

'Oh man, you're right!' Scott says, grinning. 'The clues were right there at the start. He's a goddamn games designer! That's why he disappeared early on. He's in on it all – I'd say Tiggy was part of it too. She was too calm when Giles's *body* washed up like that.'

'What do you mean, his *body*?' James says. 'Are you saying it wasn't his body at all? That this is all a big, stupid hoax?'

Lucy laughs. 'Have any of you seen that slasher flick called *April Fool's Day*? This bunch of teens head out to an island, and they start getting bumped off one by one, until there's one girl left – you know, that usual crap. Anyway, she's traumatised, crying her eyes out, she's just seen all her friends get horribly mutilated . . . then she goes into this room and they're all there going "Surprise!" because the whole thing was just some big elaborate stunt. Seriously? One of the sickest things I've ever seen. Can you *imagine*?'

'You think this is what's happening here?' Amelia crosses her arms, frowns. 'It's all just a joke?'

Lucy shrugs. 'Has to be. What did the invite say? "Luxury island adventure" or something like that? And it's been nothing of the sort. Top secret. Limited info. Then all this weird tech stuff . . . which, I have to say, I still can't explain. There's no doubt that my big secret is real. We've all confessed the same, right? Well, except *you*, Amelia. We're still waiting for that.'

'We're waiting for Scott's too,' Amelia snaps, turning away from the cave and letting her headlamp shine a path ahead. She starts walking and James catches her up, leaving Lucy to continue to wax lyrical with her theory, a few paces behind – with Scott avidly agreeing and adding his own thoughts on it all. They sound happy, now that they've convinced themselves it's a game. Scott is talking about the Michael Douglas movie now. *The Game* was a genius piece of cinema, to be fair. So realistic. So terrifying.

'You don't agree, do you?' James says quietly.

They are walking at a steady pace, being careful to follow the lamplight. On their right, the sea is barely visible, just a dark expanse with occasional breaking white waves, and that rhythmic lull as they crash into the rocks.

'I want to believe it,' she says. 'It's just that . . . well, I thought I had it worked out earlier. A very different scenario to the one that

Lucy and Scott are painting right now. One that involves *my* big secret. Someone I knew – a long time ago.'

He doesn't look at her. 'But why? Everyone's got a horrible secret. We're all the same . . . what makes you think otherwise?'

She frowns, unsure about whether to say more. She glances across at the blinking lights of the bigger island in the distance. She wants to be wrong, but the longer she's been here, the more her own long-buried memories have pushed their way to the surface. It sounds narcissistic, but it makes sense. She's the only one who has a real link to this place. All that Famous Five stuff had swung it for her in her mind. This is about *George*, trying to get a message to her. She knows it. But she also knows that if she says it out loud she'll sound crazy.

James lays a hand on her arm. 'You don't have to tell me. It's obviously not going to be forced out of you, like it has been for us.'

'That's the thing. That's why I'm sure I'm right and Lucy is wrong. You see . . . I don't think it's a coincidence that my tracker didn't work. I think our host wanted me to remember it all for myself.' She sighs. 'That's why I'm sure this is all about me. And the rest of you . . . the rest of you are just pawns.'

James looks back at the other two, and she does the same. They've got their arms linked and they're walking carefully, laughing at something. Both sure now that everything is going to be OK. 'Well, whatever you do,' James says, dropping his gaze, 'don't tell the others.'

'Oh?'

He looks like he wants to say more, then he stops, shakes his head. 'Forget I said anything.'

She frowns. She wants him to continue. Wouldn't it be better if she told the others now? At least then they could arrive at the house together, safe in the knowledge that everything will be fine, and that their secrets will be safe from the wider world. Because they might not know it yet, but Amelia does. This is all just a game. The host is showing off – toying with them all. Because the host doesn't care about them or what they've done.

The host only cares about Amelia.

She stares at James from the corner of her eye, taking in his expression. For a moment, she thinks he looks scared. 'James . . .'

His expression shifts again. Then he points at something up ahead. 'Look!'

She follows his line of sight and she can see what he's pointing at. Right there in front of them. Nestled into a dip in the wide expanse of dark, undulating grassland. Smoke from a chimney. Lights.

They've made it to the big house, at last.

Amelia

T - 1

The house looms bright before them. Hidden away from the rest of the island in this dip, with its own small bay. The lights around the building give it an eerie glow, and the water rolling up to the private beach twinkles in the moonlight. The big house is certainly that. Painted white, with ornate pillars on either side of the huge doorway. Two large windows split up by a grid of tiny frames. The interior light is muted, the view in obscured slightly by gauzy fabric hung at the windows. If it wasn't so dark outside, it's possible you wouldn't be able to see inside at all – but as they get closer, Amelia makes out shapes and shadows in the window to the left, the outline of various pieces of furniture and occasional movement inside. Behind the window to the right all is still.

'So much for our welcoming party,' James mutters.

They stop walking, waiting for Lucy and Scott to catch them up.

'Nice house,' Scott says when they arrive. 'Bit smaller than I expected.'

'You Yanks and your crazy McMansions.' Lucy punches him playfully on the shoulder.

They walk closer.

'Whatever. But the whole point of our big houses is we've got the space. Plenty of space here. Coulda made it twice this size.' He walks over to the window on the right and cups his hands around his face, pressing up close to the glass to peer inside. 'Nothing in there but a bookcase and a bunch of armchairs.' He takes a step back, turns to them, grinning. 'Maybe that's where we go for the after-dinner cigars.'

Amelia heads towards the window on the left. It's harder to see closer up, the curtain obscuring what's inside. But she can see a long dining table set with goblets and plates, candelabras in the centre, light flickering from the flames. The chairs are high-backed, and they are all unoccupied.

'Wonder where the others are?' James says, joining her.

'I don't care about that right now,' Amelia says. Her earlier vulnerability is gone. 'I just want to get in there and give the organisers of this whole stupid thing a piece of my mind. I'm not impressed. I want to go home. Right now. And when I get there, I'm going to be making some calls about this. Non-disclosure agreement or not.'

James raises his eyebrows at her, but says nothing.

She's done a good job of keeping herself in check, trying to do the best for the others, but the relief of finally making it here is tinged with anger over the ridiculous day they've had, and all that's happened along the way. It's hard to believe that they arrived here this morning, in glorious sunshine, all bursting with excitement for the day ahead – and now, several of them are injured, and all of them are mentally broken. All the arduous aid work she's done over the years, all the things she's seen – none of it has prepared her for this deliberate form of torture.

She's about to continue her internal tirade when there's a soft creak, and a shaft of light spills across them as the door swings open and someone appears in the porch.

'Well, hello!' Harvey says. 'What took you so long?' His voice is playful.

Amelia wants to punch him. 'Is this some sort of joke? What took us so long? Have you any idea—'

Harvey raises a hand. 'I'm sorry, that was insensitive of me. I know you've had a tough day. I understand it's probably not what you expected of your time here. Please, come inside. Everything is ready for you.'

Bone-tired, they trudge inside, removing their headlamps, which Harvey collects from them. They move through the porch into a wide hallway, unbuttoning their jackets as the warmth hits them.

'Well, this is nice.' Lucy looks around, taking it all in. Patterned tile flooring, grandfather clock, oil paintings and high ceilings.

There are several doors leading off the hallway, and a grand spiral staircase takes pride of place. Amelia's gaze follows the thick cream carpet upstairs to the landing, where she can just make out a series of doors separated by expanses of gold-papered walls adorned with more oil paintings. She brings her eyes back down, tries to find something aesthetically pleasing amid the gaudy decoration of the entrance hall, and fails. She stares at one of the paintings hanging on the wall next to her and takes in the scene: low, tumble-down cottages with high marsh grass all around. Just behind, in the distance, the murky grey of the sea – and in the foreground a stern-looking couple, both dressed in drab tweeds, she holding a bucket and he a long pitchfork. They don't look happy about being painted, and the scene is not uplifting in any way. It's executed well, but there is something horribly dark about it that gives her a small shiver down the back of her neck.

She looks away.

'Just one moment, please.' Harvey disappears through one of the doors, leaving them standing there.

James shrugs. 'So, what now? Dinner and bed?'

'Netflix and chill?' Lucy laughs.

Amelia shakes her head. 'I don't like this place. It's giving me bad vibes.'

'Whooo,' Scott says, wiggling his hands in front of her face. 'Heebie-jeebies.'

'Shut *up*!' She thrusts her hands into his chest and he flies back across the hallway, feet slipping on the tiles, and ends up crumpled on the floor at the foot of the stairs.

'Jesus, what is *wrong* with you?' Lucy barks at her, then rushes over to Scott and helps him to sit up. He's muttering that he's OK, rubbing the back of his head; he looks confused more than anything else. His eyes meet Amelia's.

'Scott, oh my God,' she says. 'I am so sorry. I don't know what happened. There's no excuse.'

He shrugs. 'No harm done, eh? We're all a bit wired.' He still looks wary.

James is looking at her oddly. 'Amelia? Are you OK?'

She turns away from them all and walks towards one of the closed doors. There's a narrow glass pane running down one side of it, giving her a perfect view of what's inside. It's another small reception room, like the one that Scott peered into from outside, with the bookcase and the armchairs. This one has a roaring fire and comfortable-looking couches. She can make out the faint sound of music playing. The couches are all facing inwards, towards the fire. Two people sit on one couch, and a third person on another, all facing away from her. The light in the room is dim, the candlelight flickering against the walls mixes with the flames of the fire, making shadows dance – making it look like the people are moving.

She gasps.

James comes up behind her and peers through the glass. 'It's the others,' he says, with a long sigh. 'Thank God . . .'

Amelia turns back towards Lucy and Scott. 'I think you two were right. 'They *are* fine.' Relief washes over her. She'd had a horrible feeling earlier, but seeing them here, alive and well, has pushed that feeling away. Maybe things are going to be OK after all? Well, they will be, once they talk to them. Make sure they're all right.

'Let's go in and join them then,' Scott says. 'What are we hanging around out here for?' He makes to stand up, but then falls back onto the bottom stair, gripping his ankle and swearing under his breath.

Lucy gently nudges Amelia out of the way and grabs the door handle. Turns it. Rattles it. But nothing happens. She tries again, but it's locked. She raises a fist and bangs on the glass. 'Guys, we're here – we made it!'

'Please step away from the door.'

They whirl round at the sound of the voice. Harvey is standing behind them, and his expression is stony. 'The others are waiting for you, but they won't hear you through that glass. The reason the music is so quiet out here is that the room is virtually soundproofed. Best way to have a music room, don't you think? Please, come with me. We need to get you warmed up and give you a change of clothes. And a little time to decompress. Then you can join the others and the party will begin. OK?' He's smiling again, but it doesn't quite reach his eyes.

Lucy and James shrug and step away from the door, following Harvey towards the staircase, where Scott is still sitting on the bottom stair.

'You all right there?' Lucy says. She holds out a hand towards him.

'I think my ankle's gone for good now.' He looks pained, but he takes Lucy's hand and gets to his feet.

Amelia turns back to peer through the glass once more. No one is moving. In fact, they are all sitting quite still. Too still. Only the shadows caused by the naked flames are creating any movement inside the room. The feeling of relief is replaced by something else. A nagging dread, slithering slowly down her spine.

Their silhouettes are in shadow, and she can't make out who is who. But as she continues to stare, she thinks she sees a movement on the back of one of their heads. A flickering that seems to bring the shape in and out of focus, a smattering of small coloured squares, just for a moment, before disappearing.

No . . . it can't be.

'Amelia, are you ready?' Harvey is next to her now. He places a hand on her elbow, urging her away from the door.

But it's too late. She's already seen it. She's seen it several times today. A glitch that they need to work on. Such a basic issue for a company so proud of its technology.

Pixelation.

Harvey looks at her as he leads her away, and she catches a hint of what might be fear in his eyes. He knows what she's seen. He knows what she knows. 'Please,' he whispers, close to her ear. 'Come with me now. Don't make things more difficult than they already are.'

The dread slides around her body, rooting itself in the pit of her stomach. She feels a sudden urge to throw up. Sucks in a deep breath, trying to keep it together. She should say something – call over to the others. But the fear roots her in place. Because it's clear now: those people on the couch are not their missing, injured friends.

Those figures on the couch are not real.

Summer 2000

She'd been a bit put off by the kid being so full-on friendly so soon, but she decided to throw caution to the wind. Islanders probably have to be pushy if they want to make friends with the holiday-makers, and it's not like she has anything else to do. The nickname thing seemed a bit silly, but she couldn't really find a good enough reason to go against it.

You be Anne . . . I'll be George.

Whatever.

She follows George away from the beach, around the back of the shop that sells everything from buckets and spades to small kitchen appliances, to an overgrown track with a broken wire fence. She stops, swinging her canvas satchel around her back and out of the way. It looks like a treacherous path – she imagines it will be lined with gorse, and she doesn't want the thorns catching on her bag. She looks down at her legs, pale and skinny in too-short shorts, and wishes she'd brought a pair of tracksuit bottoms with her.

'Is it very far?' she says.

'Not really,' George says. 'Why? Are you feeling particularly wimpish today?'

'No, of course not,' she snaps. She doesn't want this islander kid to think she's some spoiled city brat who doesn't know how to look after herself in the wild. She glances up the path as it snakes its way up the hill. It's only a stupid hill. It's only a few thorns. It's not going to kill her. 'Let's go then.'

George reaches back to push some overhanging twigs and leaves out of the way, holds them up to let her through, then sets off at a pace. She takes a deep breath and follows.

The first bit of the ascent is tricky, the gradient and the pace causing her lungs to burn, and she soon gets a stitch and has to stop. 'Wait. Just a minute,' she says, panting. She swings her bag out of the way again. Takes a few deep breaths. 'OK, coming.'

George laughs. 'You mainlanders just don't have the stamina.'

'Well, you islanders have nothing better to do than climb up your one silly little hill all day long.'

'Aww . . . our silly little hill, eh? Just you wait until we get to the top.'

She starts walking again, leaning into the hill to try and make it easier. George is right though, about stamina. She'd thought she was fairly fit with her four-times-a-week swimming, but hiking at a steep incline is something else altogether. Her legs will be aching tomorrow, but it might give her more strength to the back of her thighs if she keeps it up. Imagine how strong her freestyle would be if she could power it even more with her legs? The coach is always telling her she needs to do more land training.

She powers on, and before long she's caught up with George, who turns to her and grins. 'Nice work, city girl. Are you looking forward to the secret place?'

'Sure,' she says. 'Although I'm kind of surprised that anything is secret on this island. It's not exactly difficult to explore it.'

'Yeah, but no one comes up that path . . . couldn't you tell? An old woman slipped on loose stones there a few years ago and fell down it and died. The island council said it wasn't to be used anymore. Only they couldn't afford to block it off, so they just put up that wire fence and a "Keep Out" sign – but that's long gone, and so is most of the fence.'

'So who comes up here now?'

'Mostly just me . . . although Jago follows occasionally. He likes to take pictures,' George says with a shrug. 'The others obey the rules of the island council . . . and also, they're kind of scared of me, so they think if I'm up here, they're better to stay away.'

'Scared of you? Why?' She looks George up and down and doesn't find anything particularly scary. But then, they've only just met. For all she knows, anything George says could be a total fib.

George sighs. 'I'm not going to tell you, because it's nonsense, but you'd probably be scared too, and I'd quite like to have you as a friend . . . I think we were meant to meet, Anne. I think bumping into you was meant to be. Today is only the start.'

She thinks about this for a moment. She stops and turns. Looks back down the path, then takes in the view from being so high up. It's enough to snatch your breath away. The beaches, the beautiful blue sea. The seagulls swooping by, shrieking their cries – letting them know who's boss around here. It's all so far removed from her real life. Alone, she'd been bored, and despite the intensity and that wild gleam in George's eyes, the island has come alive for her since they met.

'OK,' she says, giving George a huge grin.

'Oh, fantastic. You won't regret it! I've got so many things to show you. They're all up here, in my den.' George points to a hollowed-out tree. The limbs have long fallen off, leaving an array of fat stumps. In front, there's a large round boulder. George rushes over and bends down, pushes it away, revealing an entrance to the tree.

'Wow,' she says, genuinely awed. 'This is so cool.'

'Told you!' George smiles shyly. 'We'll be safe in here.'

'Safe from what?'

'Never mind. I meant to ask . . . do you like sci-fi? You know, like *Star Trek* and stuff?'

She ducks down and follows George into the hollow. The place is lined with pillows and blankets, and boxes spilling over with comics.

'Oh, yes,' she says, grinning. 'I love science. It's my favourite subject at school. I keep wondering about all the inventions that we know about, and all the things that haven't even been invented yet. Do you think the stuff in *Star Trek* might happen one day? Like teleporting and holograms and finding life on other planets?'

George sits and gestures for her to follow, then flicks down a curtain from the top of the entrance and they are basked in muted darkness, until the light of George's torch brightens the space again.

'Definitely,' George says. 'Well – I'm not sure about the life on other planets part, or even the type of spaceships they have . . . but the rest of it is definitely going to happen. People are already working on it, you know – in America, and Russia, and Germany too. I can't wait to leave school and go to university. Because then I'm going to start up my own lab and I'm going to invent all of the things you could ever imagine.'

'Wow,' she says. 'That would be so cool. Maybe I could come and work for you?'

George frowns. 'Well, I reckon I'm going to have a *lot* of strong candidates. What makes you so special?'

She grins. She sits up straight and puts on her poshest, most formal voice. 'I'm loyal. I'm a quick learner . . . and we have the same shared vision.'

'How loyal?' George says. 'Because this is actually the key requirement. In fact, I need someone I know I can rely on.' George looks away. 'I don't just mean in the future. I mean now. I . . . need hope. I need to know that one day, I can get away from this place. Can you help me with that, Anne?'

George's gaze weighs heavy on her, and she feels butterflies fluttering in her tummy. It's as if there's a lot more at stake here than just a fantasy future job idea, and this strange island child is somehow making her feel significant. 'Of course . . .' She lets her sentence trail off when she sees what George is doing.

A drop of blood pops and glistens on George's thumb.

'Give me your hand.'

Mesmerised, she complies. The pain is quick and hot. Just a sting, then it's done. George takes hold of her thumb and presses it hard.

'We're blood now, Anne. You can't let me down. Promise?'

She nods. 'I promise.'

Tiggy

Tiggy feels sick. She opens her eyes, expecting to see the dressing table and stool in her room, and is surprised to find that they're not there. Also, the pink flocked wallpaper has been replaced with green and gold, with what looks like deer printed on it.

She pulls herself up to a sitting position, and the room spins and tilts for a moment before settling down. She's on a chaise longue that she doesn't remember seeing before, and she's wearing a long, floaty lemon dress that she definitely did not put on by herself. As her eyes swim back into focus, she takes in the rest of the room. Another similar chaise opposite, plus a selection of mismatched but all equally period armchairs, wing-backed chairs and a couple of footstools. Everything is upholstered in clashing, gaudy fabrics. The curtains are green, to match the wallpaper, and the carpet is a shimmering gold weave. The room is lit by orange glass wall lamps, and at the far end are folding partition doors.

Through the gap in the partition, she can make out the silhouettes of several people moving around.

They're here!

She blinks herself awake and jumps up. Then holds on to the end of the chaise to steady herself. She'll be OK in a minute. She must have slept too long. She has a vague recollection of leaving her bedroom to walk downstairs, but there's a black hole between then and getting changed and ending up asleep down here. There's an empty champagne flute on the small table next to where she was lying. That would explain it, if she'd had a few on an empty stomach. As if reading her mind, her stomach growls. She walks towards the partition and catches the scent of something delicious wafting through.

This might make the wasted day worth it then, she hopes. Especially once she's seen Giles.

But where *is* Giles?

Her head is fuzzy, and fragments of the last few hours are missing. She remembers that she and Giles had an argument. And she remembers being on the boat, and him not waking up. But he must be awake now, if the others are back and the food is being served?

The gap in the partition is narrow, but she's small, so she slips through without having to open it further. The first thing she notices when she enters the room is that everyone is on their own, doing their own thing. Have they fallen out with each other since she left them behind in the bay? Or are they just enjoying a bit of space?

She surveys the room, taking them all in. Lucy is wearing a navy velvet cocktail dress and very high heels. Her hair is pinned up, with small diamanté studs peppered throughout. When Tiggy's heels clip-clop on the tiled floor of the dining room, Lucy turns round. She's holding a champagne flute and her eyes are slightly glazed.

'Tiggy! Oh my God, I am so glad to see you!' She rushes forward, stumbling slightly in her shoes, and throws her arms around Tiggy. She smells of coconut and an expensive, heady perfume.

Tiggy pulls back, slightly bemused by her over-the-top display of affection, and Lucy senses it and laughs. 'Sorry. I've had a few of these. They brought a bottle up to my room, and two women with a load of fancy clothes to dress me. I felt like an eighteenth-century queen. Or a drag queen, more likely.' She laughs again.

The others hear the voices and laughter and come trickling over from their various positions.

Scott and James are both dressed in perfectly cut tuxedos, their hair neatly styled. They each lean in to kiss her; they smell of orange and sandalwood.

'Tiggy,' Scott says, touching her arm. 'You look sensational.'

'How are you?' James says. 'I bet you've been in the lap of luxury while we've been sheltering in a cave and staggering here in the pitch-dark.'

'A cave?' she says. 'Well, I'm glad I missed *that*. I'm not keen on small dark spaces.'

'Hello, Tiggy.' Amelia doesn't kiss her. It was obvious early on that she wasn't the kissing type. She looks lovely though, in a purple off-the-shoulder ball gown, her dark hair swept up to the side, adorned with a simple silver leaf-shaped clip. Her eyes scan the space around Tiggy. 'Where's Giles?' she says. 'Is he going to make it to dinner? Harvey told us it was going to be quite special, and that we'd be rewarded for our treacherous day.' She looks at the others. 'I don't know how you all feel, but I almost feel like today was just a bad dream . . . and that this' – she raises her palms, gesturing to the room – 'is what this trip was really about.'

'Totally agree,' James says. 'It might be the champagne they brought up to the room, but I can hardly even remember all the drama from earlier.'

'And my ankle doesn't hurt a bit, but I know I did something to it.' Scott holds out his foot, turns it from one side to the other. 'I couldn't have done this a few hours ago. I tried my best not to put weight on it, but it hurt like hell most of the day. Even more so when Amelia knocked me over in the hallway.'

'I *said* I was sorry,' Amelia says, her cheeks flushing.

Tiggy has no idea what's gone on since she left in the boat with Giles, but they are all acting very strangely. All day, they'd been questioning the 'game' and everything that was going on. Bickering with each other, trying to decide who to trust – and now they're all washed and changed and sipping champagne as if none of it even happened.

'Anyway,' Lucy says, her face still fixed in a grin. 'Giles? Where is he? The three of you were in the small sitting room by the fire when we arrived.'

Tiggy is even more confused now. 'The three of us?'

Lucy's smile slips, just a little. 'You, Giles and Brenda, of course. Who did you think I meant?'

Tiggy swallows hard. 'I . . . um . . . I don't remember seeing Brenda since I got here.' She looks at Amelia, pleading for help. 'I thought she was with you?'

'They brought her back here a bit before us,' Amelia says. 'She collapsed.' Her forehead pulls into a frown. 'You haven't seen her?'

'I haven't seen her *or* Giles!'

'What?' Lucy says. 'But—'

She doesn't get a chance to say any more. There's a double handclap, then Harvey appears through the partition. 'Ladies and gentlemen. Thank you for your patience.' Behind him, two men push the partition doors open wider, revealing the lounge room behind. Both men are youngish and awkward-looking in their white shirts and neat black trousers. Tiggy notices that her glass has been cleared away. 'It's time for our final presentations, before you meet our wonderful, yet elusive, host – the CEO and founder of the incredible Timeo Technologies, Merryn Hicks.'

Are they supposed to applaud? Scott catches her eye and shrugs, then starts a slow handclap. James joins in. Then Lucy.

The two young men stand watching, expressionless.

Behind her, Tiggy hears James whisper to Amelia. Something that sounds like, 'Is one of *them* your friend?' She whips her head round just in time to see Amelia give a small shake of her head and look away from Tiggy's gaze. James smiles, still clapping.

Her *friend*? What on earth is that all about?

She thinks back to the earlier presentations of the day. Giles's awful projection. Then hers. Then that really boring one on the beach afterwards, going through all the 'hashtag amazing' inventions that the company has come up with – that this host, this Merryn Hicks, has come up with, if they are supposed to believe all of that. Tiggy still can't understand why someone who's so bloody clever would want to keep it all a secret. Surely they'd want to be on TV and the front cover of *TIME*, telling the world what a genius they are – getting even more funding to invent even more things? Why would anyone want to share that across so many different companies and not take any of the credit? And why would they go to all this effort to test it in such secrecy?

'But first,' Harvey continues, 'please enjoy the feast . . . as you may have worked out by now, we've been suppressing your appetite all day to build you up for this.' He looks slightly sheepish.

'So you did drug us?' Tiggy folds her arms across her chest. 'How?'

'The water, dummy,' Scott mutters. 'Why do you think I drank so much of the stuff?' He turns to Harvey. 'Amphetamines, I assume?'

Harvey continues with his insipid smile. 'I expect so. Not really my department.'

'And the champagne?' Tiggy says. 'What was in that?'

'Just a little something to keep you calm. Help you get past the stresses of the day.' He pauses. 'Oh, come on. Don't tell me you don't like it?' He turns to Tiggy. 'You, of course, had a little something extra at the top of the stairs. But I don't suppose you remember that.'

A fragment of a scene flashes into her brain. Leaving the room. Heading for the stairs. Something holding her back.

'You grabbed me!' she says.

He shakes his head. 'Again – not my department.' He nods towards the two young men, who remain stony-faced. 'But we had to look after you, I'm afraid. You couldn't go wandering off on your own. Who knows what you might have found.' He laughs, but it sounds mirthless and forced, and after a moment he stops – his face falling serious once more.

'As I said, please enjoy your feast. You deserve a bit of luxury now – after all, isn't that what you signed up for?' He refuses to catch anyone's eye as he sweeps his arm towards the long dining table, laden with all sorts of fancy-looking treats.

'Well, I guess I am kinda hungry now.' Scott makes his way across to the table and picks up something small and round, topped with a pile of what looks like caviar. He pops it into his mouth, smacks his lips together. Lifts his flute. 'Any chance of a top-up here?'

Another staff member appears from a door to the side, a slight woman with her hair pulled back in a severe bun. She looks vaguely familiar, and Tiggy wonders if she might have been one of the women who dressed her earlier on. She rushes over clutching a bottle in a white linen napkin, and with one hand behind her back, expertly pours champagne into Scott's glass. She then walks over to James, who waves her away.

Tiggy picks up a glass and holds it out. But she doesn't look at the woman. She's back to looking at Harvey. Still waiting for him to say more. When he doesn't, she takes a sip of her champagne, then says, 'And what about the others? Aren't they getting to enjoy this treat?'

There's a murmuring from behind her: Lucy and Scott agreeing.

Harvey tips his head to the side and lifts a finger to his mouth, putting on an exaggerated look of confusion. 'The *others*?'

Tiggy puffs out a stream of angry air. She never thought she'd feel this again, but she has the urge to ram this champagne flute into his face. 'Yes,' she snaps. 'The *others*. Brenda and Giles, of course. Where are they?'

Harvey pales, his forced joviality gone. 'Oh, I see. My apologies. I thought you'd realised that all surviving players were present.'

Tiggy feels a burning in her gullet, as if the champagne is going to make a swift reappearance.

'*Surviving* players?' Scott holds another caviar blini, but he stares at Harvey now, leaving the canapé hovering close to his mouth. 'What in hell does that mean?'

'Where are Brenda and Giles?' Tiggy demands, clutching the flute tighter, her hand shaking. 'Tell us. Tell us right this second!'

Harvey taps his tracker. 'I'm sorry. I assumed you knew.' A holographic screen pops up. Two bodies, covered with white sheets. He taps the tracker again and it vanishes. He stares at them all, holds his palms up. 'I'm afraid Brenda and Giles are dead.'

Lucy

This is not happening, Lucy thinks. *We saw them . . . in the other room. Didn't we?* She feels sick. Walks over to a high-backed chair and leans her hands on it to steady herself.

Scott slams his glass down on the table and the stem snaps off. He flicks it angrily away. 'What the hell d'you mean, they're dead? Where are they? Did you take them to the hospital?'

Tiggy collapses onto the floor, sobbing. 'I can't believe it,' she manages, between wails. 'I know he was a . . . a . . .' She can't speak any more. James goes to her and crouches down, puts an arm around her shoulder, and she falls into him, broken.

The nice little drunken buzz that Lucy felt earlier is gone in an instant. Despite everything, she'd still thought it was all a game. Well, seems it *is* a game, but not one that has any winners. She looks over at Amelia, who is standing perfectly still, her face contorted in a mixture of shock and terror. She won't catch Lucy's eye.

None of this makes any sense. This is the kind of thing you see in a horror film. A group of strangers thrown together in an isolated place, forced to band together for certain challenges, but their bickering and in-fighting spilling over the more tired and hungry and scared they become. It's a classic set-up. But that's fiction. Fantasy.

This is supposed to be real life.

She'd just about bought the holographic projections and the trackers linking to their individual biometrics – but, if this latest holographic image is to be believed, two of them are dead, and the organisers don't seem to be the slightest bit concerned.

Scott is pacing up and down along the length of the dinner table, muttering to himself, occasionally taking a swipe at one of the platters, sending fancy canapés skittering across the floor.

James is comforting Tiggy.

Amelia still hasn't moved.

'Hey.' Lucy walks over to Harvey and stands right in front of him, putting her face close to his. 'I need to talk to you.'

He flinches slightly, taking a step back from her.

She pushes a finger into his chest. 'Now listen, pal. I've gone along with this charade. All. Fucking. Day.' She jabs his chest to punctuate each word. 'I've gone along with it, because I was promised something in return. I was promised—' Her sentence stops abruptly as she screams, grabbing her ear. 'Oww!' The tracker vibrates hard, giving her a sharp shock. 'What . . .'

'You were told not to talk about the conditions of your agreement,' Harvey says, smoothing a hand down the front of his shirt to remove the dents from Lucy's probing finger. 'You were warned.'

'This is insane!' Tiggy shouts, stepping away from James as she grabs hold of Lucy's arm and glares at Harvey. 'Stop this. Stop this now.'

'It's OK,' Lucy says, her voice faint. 'It's stopped.' The sharp pain has subsided, but there is still a dull ache, and she rubs the skin behind her ear as she addresses Harvey. 'I get it. No talking about our agreements . . .' She's fuming, but she tries to rein it in.

Finally, Amelia stirs – blinking, as if she's just zoned back in from a trance. 'I . . . I . . .' She shakes her head, trying to wake herself up. She turns to Harvey. 'Please. Can we talk to the host now?

Everything's got out of hand. We need to keep calm and work out how to deal with all this—'

'Keep calm?' Lucy is fizzing with rage now – Amelia's stoic attitude has lit her fuse. How is anyone supposed to be calm when they've just found out that two of their party are dead? She balls her hands into fists. '*You*, Amelia. This all seems a bit too easy for *you*. Remind us again why we haven't been privy to *your* big secret?'

'Something to do with my tracker . . . you already know this.' Her eyes flick away. 'There's no big conspiracy.'

Lucy pokes her in the chest and Amelia takes a step back. 'No big conspiracy? Why would you even say that? Are you in on this? Is this all your doing?'

Amelia locks her arms over her chest to shield herself from another jab. 'No. Of course not. Why are you saying that?'

'She does know something,' Tiggy sniffs, nodding towards James. 'I heard him asking her.'

Scott stops pacing. 'Asking her what?'

Now all of them are staring at Amelia.

'About her *friend*,' Tiggy says. 'Something to do with her friend.'

Amelia shakes her head, inching further away. 'No.' Her lower back hits the table and she stops.

Lucy advances on her. 'What *friend*, Amelia? Who is your *friend*? What's your *friend* done to Brenda and Giles?'

'No.' Amelia tries to take a step away from the table, but Lucy shoves her back. 'This has nothing to do with me.'

Lucy laughs. 'Nice try. Not buying it.' She shoves her again. 'Oh, you don't like the shoving? You seem to have no trouble shoving *us* when it suits you.'

Scott is beside her now, and he gives her a little shove too. 'Care to enlighten us, Amelia? Because I'd sure as hell like to know what in God's name is going on here. Right now, I would like to get on that plane, fly back to where we came from, then get home to my goddamn normal life.' He shoves her again, bouncing her against the table. 'But it seems like you're stopping that from happening.'

Though Lucy had been doing it herself, seeing Scott pushing Amelia snaps her awake. When did they become a pack of animals? She puts a hand on Scott's shoulder, gently tugging him back.

Silent tears are sliding down Amelia's cheeks. 'Please,' she begs.

'Leave her alone.' James has stepped to Amelia's side and put an arm around her. He's pulling her away from them. 'None of this is her fault. I promise you that. If you want someone to blame, I—'

The familiar beep sounds, signalling that something is going to be projected. They all turn around in the direction of the sound. They're not bothering to broadcast it through their trackers anymore. This house is clearly full of potential projection points. The image de-pixelates quickly, and a man's grinning face fills the space. 'Oh, but it really *is* Amelia's fault,' he says in a deep, accentless voice.

'Who are you?' Lucy demands. 'I assume this is live now. You can see us. You can hear us.'

The man chuckles, then the image pixelates again. When it comes back into focus, it's a different man – the first one had dark hair and glasses, but he's blond this time, no glasses. 'I've been watching and listening to you all day, my dear. My goodness, you *are* tedious.'

'Who the hell are you?' Scott walks closer to the image. 'Oh, hang on . . . I get it. There's no mysterious "host", is there? It's a conglomeration. Of course no one person could be responsible for all the things you've claimed. Am I right?'

The image scrambles and unscrambles again, and this time it's a young woman. Her hair is in a neat ponytail and she's grinning with huge, too-white teeth. She laughs. 'Nearly, Scott. *You're* not as dumb as you look.' Higher pitched, but the same accentless voice.

The image flickers, and then another face appears. A younger man, bald, with thick-framed glasses. 'I'm going to stick with this one for the rest of the presentation,' he says. 'I don't want to confuse you all any further.' He grins, and his teeth glow bright – same teeth as the girl, Lucy realises. She looks closely at his eyes. Yes. Those too.

'You're just superimposing faces,' she says, trying to sound unimpressed when actually she is.

'Oh, just superimposing faces? Come on, now. Credit where credit's due: this is some impressively deep faking.' The teeth glow. 'I ought to know,' he says. 'I pioneered the technology.'

'Oh, whatever,' Lucy says. 'I'm getting bored now. Get to the point and then we can all go home.'

The man on-screen laughs. The sound of his laughter is still going when his face vanishes. Then a new visual appears in front of them.

It's someone leaning over a toilet, emptying things from his pockets into the bowl, yanking on the flush over and over, but the tank isn't refilling as quickly as he needs it to. There's a banging on the cubicle door.

'Come out of there please, sir. We need to have a word.'

Whoever it is swears under his breath. More emptying. More flushing – the water pours in this time, and whatever it is swirls away. 'One minute . . . please. I've got a bad stomach. Something I ate, I think.' His voice is ragged, frantic. He tosses in some paper, tries to flush again. Nothing.

'Sir, we're going to have to insist that you come out of there now, or we may have to use force. The club is being evacuated. There are health and safety concerns.'

'One minute, please.' The man turns from the toilet to the mirror over the sink. It's Scott, looking a little younger but completely wasted.

Lucy looks over at him now. His expression is stony.

'It's OK,' she says, her voice soothing. 'We've all had to face it.'

He gives her a small smile, then turns his eyes back to the screen. She does the same, just in time to see Scott being escorted from the bathroom of what looks like a nightclub – he's flanked by two police officers. The walls are bright pink, the strobe lights flickering. They walk into the body of the club, which is mainly deserted. The music is still playing, some *thump thump* dance music, while paramedics in yellow jackets help people outside.

'This bit looks like it's coming from CCTV,' Lucy says. 'It's not a memory feed, like the rest of it.'

Scott shrugs. 'Yeah. I guess it was pretty simple to get hold of this footage. Maybe this is how they picked me for this "adventure" in the first place.'

'There's sound, though,' Amelia says. 'I didn't think CCTV had sound.'

'They had it on my canal CCTV too,' James says. 'I'm guessing this is some kind of enhancement to the normal set-up.'

Lucy turns back to the screen. Two paramedics appear from somewhere near the stage, carrying a stretcher. A young woman is lying on it, hooked up to an IV bag. Her arms twitch spasmodically. As Scott on-screen watches, her head falls to the side and her eyes seem to bore into him. But they are deep pools of blankness. Wherever she is, she is not currently in there.

'Is she going to be OK?' Scott asks one of the paramedics.

The woman shrugs. 'We don't know yet. Be helpful to know what she's taken. This is the fourth one we've stretchered out. There are several others still upright but mainly incoherent. Are you OK, sir? Do you need assistance?' Her eyes flit from Scott to the two police officers.

'We've got him,' the officer on the left says. A young woman, probably not much older than the one on the stretcher.

Scott on-screen looks like a rabbit trapped in the headlights. While Scott at the dinner party is no longer watching the events unfold.

The screen pixelates, then goes dark.

'Scott . . .' Lucy starts, but he waves a hand, dismissing her.

The screen glows white again and the bald man reappears. His face is solemn. 'That girl on the stretcher died, you know. As did three others. They never did find out what concoction of drugs they'd taken. Toxicology came back inconclusive. It got put down to a bad batch, misadventure. No one was ever caught for supplying them.' He shakes his head. 'Sickening, isn't it? People really should take responsibility for their actions.'

The screen pixelates and disappears once more.

Tiggy

'OK, that's enough now.' Tiggy sits down at the dining table. She's deflated. No fight left in her at all. Her gaze rests on the flickering candles of the centrepiece, and for a moment she feels calmer. 'This has to be enough,' she says quietly. 'Let's just have a few drinks, go to bed, and tomorrow they can fly us out of here. We'll go to the police when we get home, and send them here to deal with everything. There's nothing else for it. I'll call Daddy as soon as we land. He'll help sort this out.' She picks up a fresh glass and holds it aloft. 'I'd like a drink, please.'

One of the waitresses from earlier scurries over and fills her glass with champagne. One by one, the others come and sit at the table. They're all weary now, the spirit knocked out of them. Everyone is drinking champagne, except for James, who refuses. Scott starts picking at the nibbles again. The stuff he'd knocked onto the floor has been tidied away and replaced.

None of them speaks. What is there to say?

Tiggy nibbles absentmindedly on a cheese stick and wipes away an angry tear. Just wait until she gets home. People will be so distraught about Giles. His profile will go through the roof, as will hers. People are always more interesting when there's a tragedy attached to them.

After a time, James speaks up. 'Where's Harvey?'

'Forget him. He's not going to help us.' Tiggy picks up another cheese stick. They're pretty good, and now that she's started it's going to be hard to stop. This is why she tries not to eat much. Eating only makes you eat more. You only have to look at a fat person to see that. She's been watching what she eats since she was a child, when Mummy explained how important it was. 'No one wants a fat wife,' she always told her. 'See how pretty and slim Mummy always stays for Daddy? You have to be careful, darling. There are plenty of eager replacements waiting in the wings, and your husband should never have to be forced into looking elsewhere due to your slovenly ways. Always remember that.' Mummy wasn't right about everything, but she was right about that. Besides, hunger isn't something to be scared of. OK, sometimes it's made her feel a little lightheaded – led to her making some wrong decisions, especially after a couple of glasses of fizz. But overall, it's healthy to feel in control. Isn't it? She picks up her glass and is surprised to find it empty . . . and another cheese stick gone.

'I don't know what's in these,' she says, 'but they are very moreish.' She picks up the tub and shakes it at the others. 'Go on, have some. Before I eat them all.'

Scott takes one, and then Lucy. Scott shoves half of it in his mouth at once, makes a mmm-mmm noise, and takes another. Lucy starts nibbling, but soon she's nearly done with hers too. 'You're not wrong, Tigs. These are insanely good.' Lucy takes the tub and holds it towards Amelia and James, who both shake their heads.

'I don't eat cheese,' Amelia says. 'Makes me feel queasy.'

Lucy sighs. 'Don't give me any of your lactose intolerance nonsense.'

'It's not that.'

Lucy shakes the tub at James. 'And, of course, you barely eat at all.'

He frowns. 'I do eat. Of course I eat. I just . . . I'm just not really comfortable eating this food.'

'What? You reckon they're going to poison us now?' Lucy puts the tub back on the table. She touches another, but then seemingly changes her mind. Reaches for a handful of nuts instead. Tiggy pulls the tub closer and takes another cheese stick – she's past caring about the consequences. Meanwhile, the waitress has been over and silently filled up all their glasses.

'Could I have a bottle of Coke?' James says. A few moments later, a waiter returns with a bottle and an opener. He opens it in front of James, then disappears without a word.

'I suppose it's your feed next, Amelia?' Tiggy says. 'They must have something on you, mustn't they?' Her head is a little fuzzy again; she's lost count of how many top-ups she's had.

'I suppose so. I—'

Whatever she was going to say is cut off when Lucy starts coughing. It starts with a small, throat-clearing cough, before getting harsher. Louder. She thumps herself on the chest. Her face is bright red and she's almost barking now, trying to dislodge something from her throat. Tiggy tries to stand up to help but falls back to her seat, too dizzy to manage it.

'Jesus Christ,' James says, jumping out of his seat and rushing around to Lucy. He pulls her up and bends her over, then knocks her hard on the back.

Nothing happens.

She keeps coughing, even harder. A high-pitched whine is coming from her lungs. Her eyes are wide with fear. Tiggy wants to help, but as she makes to stand up again she falls back once more. And then she starts to cough. Just a little at first. She grabs her glass, but it's empty.

'Here, take this.' Amelia grabs James's bottle of Coke and slides it down the table to her.

Tiggy seizes it and tries to drink, but as soon as it hits the back of her throat she gags, chokes – sprays the drink all over herself.

Lucy is still coughing hard, her face red, her eyes bulging. James looks around with terrified eyes. 'Amelia? I don't know what to do. I don't know what's happening!'

'Tiggy.' Amelia turns to her and sees that she is struggling too. 'Oh God, I—'

Tiggy is still coughing, but it's not as bad as Lucy – more like a coughing fit when you have a cold, whereas Lucy seems to be actually choking. 'Help us,' she manages, although it comes out as a squeak.

There's a beep and the screen appears. Blank. Just laughing.

'Scott?' James whirls round, leaving Lucy bent over the chair, trying to grip on to the sides. 'Oh no . . . oh no . . .'

Tiggy manages to stand, holding on to the chair. She sees Scott, his head slumped onto the table. His body is convulsing, and a pool of lumpy white vomit is growing out from his mouth like a mushroom cloud.

Lucy stops coughing at last. Tiggy's cough is still ongoing, but it's merely irritating now, like hiccups. Lucy is still bent over the chair. Tiggy puts a hand on her back, rubbing it gently. 'It's OK,' she says. 'You're OK.'

But she knows that's not true.

It's clear that Lucy is dead, as is Scott. They'd both eaten several things from the table. Amelia and James have had none.

Tiggy has eaten plenty. It's only a matter of time before her body gives in and she chokes to death too.

Across the table, close to Scott's outstretched hand, is the stem of the champagne flute he smashed earlier. It doesn't take her long to decide. Mummy's voice is inside her head: 'Take control, darling. Never forget that.'

She turns to Amelia and James. 'You two need to get the hell out of here.' She picks up the broken stem.

'No!' James shouts, launching himself at her. She's looking him in the eye, defiant as she thrusts the weapon into her own neck.

She barely feels it. Her head swims further away, and in the background there's a beep, followed by laughter.

Amelia

'No!' Amelia lunges at Tiggy an instant behind James, but they're too late.

Tiggy's head falls back, blood spurting from the sides of the wound. Her eyes bulge with shock for a moment, and there's a horrible gurgling sound as her blood pumps out profusely.

'We need to do something,' James says. He reaches for the stem. 'We can stop the blood.'

Amelia grabs his wrist. 'No . . . don't pull it out. You'll only make it worse.' She falls to her knees. Takes hold of Tiggy's limp hand, squeezes it, feels Tiggy's fingers gently squeezing back. There's another choking gurgle, and she looks up at Tiggy's face as it falls slack. The light in her eyes dulls, and her grip falls away.

'Oh no. Oh no.' Amelia drops her head into her hands. She feels a palm on her shoulder and looks up to see James. He takes her elbow and helps support her as she stands, then he leads her away from the table. She glances back, watching the staff who have already come over to tend to the wounded.

Wounded? That's a joke.

She turns away, lets James lead her into the other room, with the sofas and the clashing furnishings. 'They're all dead, aren't they?' she says quietly. She starts to shake. Despite the horror of it all, she feels distant – as if it's happening to someone else. Her mind taking her away from it, trying to protect her.

Just like her mind tried to protect her all those years ago: that summer.

Because she remembers it now. All of it.

James nods. He leads her over to one of the chaises longues and sits her down, then sits beside her. He takes her hand.

'OK,' he says. 'So I get that we are both in shock right now. In fact, it hasn't fully kicked in yet. What just happened through there is the most horrific thing I've ever witnessed, and as I told you earlier, I've been through a lot. That video of me on the canal was only one incident.'

Amelia sighs, drops her gaze. 'I know. I get it . . . Me too.' Still determined to distance herself from the reality of what's happening right now, she reflects on the other nightmares she's had to deal with in her past. 'Not things I've caused, so not exactly the same, but I've seen people die in agony from Ebola – me, fully protected from head-to-toe in a hazmat suit, unable to do a thing for them as they writhe in pain. I've seen horrific things in the jungle. I've seen—'

James squeezes her hand and she looks up.

The projection has started silently this time.

The virtual screen is above the fireplace now. A larger image than usual, showing a lush, green island.

This is it then, she thinks. *My turn.*

The view pans over a headland, showing a rocky outcrop, huge waves lashing against the secluded shoreline. The camera starts a 360, panning to another island across a stretch of water – a lighthouse on top; a small, sandy bay. The camera slides across and a cluster of ruins appears, then a wide stretch of marshland, and finally a house – but in a bad state of repair. The camera darts away, as if it has been shot via drone and speeded up, back to the first island, where two small figures are crawling out of a hollow tree. The projection pauses.

James squeezes Amelia's hand. 'Do you recognise this?'

She doesn't answer. It doesn't really matter what's on this video. There's only her and James left now, and it's unlikely they're going to get out of this alive.

'The smaller island looks like here, doesn't it?' he says softly. He's trying to coax it out of her – why? – but she's not ready. She's scared to speak. Terrified to see what's coming next. Her body starts to shake suddenly, and she feels cold. So, so cold. Perhaps sensing the change in her, he doesn't push further. Instead, he lets go of her hand and gets up. Folded blankets are draped over the backs of the other chairs across the room.

He comes back, wraps a blanket around her shoulders. 'It's OK,' he says. 'It doesn't matter now.' He pauses. 'I'm sorry, Amelia. I didn't know it was going to end like this.'

Amelia is puzzled. How would James have any idea how it was meant to end?

The two small figures on the screen walk up the hill to the headland. The one with the long hair walks over to a small copse of drooping trees and starts gathering sticks. The one with the short hair stands watching, hands on hips. The sounds are muffled, their voices carried away by the wind. She can't work out whose memory feed this is. It was only the two of them there that day, wasn't it?

Amelia in the blanket watches as the feed switches to another perspective, and she sees now what George saw, all those years ago. The man appearing from over the side of the cliff behind the small long-haired figure. An old man with wild hair, his clothes tattered. His arms are raised out in front of him, zombielike, and he opens his mouth to speak.

But before he can, a voice cries out to the long-haired figure: 'Behind you!'

The figure turns to face the man, whose arms drop to his sides as they regard each other for a silent moment. Then the long-haired figure rushes towards him with arms thrust forward and pushes the man's chest, toppling him over the edge.

Then the perspective changes again, taking in the two figures as the long-haired one spins round from the cliff edge. It's a much younger Amelia – frozen in shock – looking back at the shorter-haired girl who had called out to warn her of the man's approach . . .

Of course, Amelia knew all of this was coming. Her younger self was right there, after all. She's the girl standing on the cliff edge. But whose memory is this? Who saw the two of them?

James stands up. 'Enough of this now,' he says to the room, to whoever is showing them this scene. 'We don't need to see any more. You've tortured us enough.'

Amelia is crying now, her shoulders shaking under the blanket. 'I'm sorry.' Her words are punctuated by sobs. 'I thought it was a . . . a game. And then I wanted to help him.' She shakes her head angrily, pointing at the place where the screen was, where it's now just air. 'It was her,' she says, her finger trembling as she points at the empty space where the short-haired girl had been. The holographic screen might be blank, but she still has the image etched in her mind. 'She told me we couldn't save him . . .'

'You ran away, remember?'

They both turn at the sound of the voice. Behind them, from a door they hadn't paid any attention to before, stands a woman with short, dark hair. She's dressed in neatly cut black trousers and a black, fitted polo-neck sweater. She smiles.

'I've been looking forward to this—'

'You!' James leaps from his seat and lunges towards her. 'Who the hell are you?' His voice shakes as he shouts. He has the woman pinned up against the wall, his hands on her shoulders. 'Is this all your doing? Are you the other girl in that projection?'

But the woman doesn't struggle. She just smirks.

'Are you quite finished, Jago? Your acting has been tolerable up until now, but you seem to have lapsed into melodrama. Maybe seeing your own dark secret wasn't such a good plan after all . . .'

James keeps her pinned to the wall, but his shoulders sag. After a long, silent moment, he says in a hollow voice, 'You bitch, Merryn.'

He turns his head towards Amelia. 'I'm sorry. I really am.' He draws in a long breath, releases it in a sigh. 'I should never have gone along with this. I just thought she wanted to ruffle a few feathers. Make some sort of point. She promised to help get me back on my feet.'

'What?' Amelia says. 'Help you . . . ?'

'I've been struggling, ever since I moved to the mainland. That terrible scene you watched on the canal was only part of it.'

'You were always weak, Jago,' the woman he called Merryn says. 'Did you really think I was going to give you a new chance at life? It's not as if you helped me out when I needed you.'

Who *is* this man? Amelia wonders. And why did the woman call him Jago?

He turns back to the woman, who is still pinned up against the wall and not attempting to struggle at all. She clearly feels no threat from this man. 'We were kids, Merryn,' he continues. 'We both suffered at Father's hands. I thought you just wanted to bring Amelia back into your life. But people are dead . . . and Amelia still wants nothing to do with you.'

'We'll see about—'

In one swift move, James's hands have shifted to the woman's throat. Her face starts to turn red and her eyes bulge. Her arms go to his, grabbing him at the elbows, trying to push him off. But Amelia can see she has no real strength.

Amelia's mind whirrs as she watches this man she knows as James continue to throttle her. Obviously the woman is behind all this, and getting rid of her means they might be able to get away. But if he kills her, there's no chance of justice for any of the others, not to mention any insight into everything that's gone on. Who the hell does she think she is, brandishing her moral compass . . . punishing them like this? Killing her isn't the answer – she owes them an explanation at the very least.

Amelia throws off her blanket and rushes over to stop him from choking her to death, but before she can get to him he flinches and releases the woman's neck, then he starts to buck and writhe, as though he's being electrocuted. He falls to the floor, still shuddering, until a rush of bloody foam pours out of his mouth and his whole body goes slack.

'James!' Amelia cries out. But it's too late.

The woman steps over him and walks over to the dining table in the main room, pulls out two chairs. 'Come on then,' she says.

'What . . . what did you do to him?'

The woman shrugs. 'The trackers' tasering function is new. I hadn't actually trialled it before. Might need to dial down the voltage a little. I got a slight shock myself with the first burst.'

Amelia grabs the back of the chair, feels her legs ready to buckle. 'You killed him. Killed them all.'

The woman sighs. 'Yes,' she says. 'Yes, I did. But it's *your* fault.'

Amelia

Amelia sits down hard on the dining chair, her body heavy and numb. Her head falls forward, the weight of it too much now on her shoulders.

What have I just witnessed?

She can't take it in. These people have died because of her. Six innocent people. OK, maybe not so innocent. Maybe they have done some terrible things – but hasn't everyone?

The woman in black turns the other chair around, then sits on it, legs astride, leaning on the back. 'Let he who is without sin cast the first stone.'

Amelia's head snaps up at the sound of the familiar voice.

'Hello, Anne. It's been a long time.'

She looks away. 'Don't call me that. My name is Amelia.'

'And mine is Merryn, but I never really liked it. I always saw myself as George. Just like the one in the stories. Living on that island, desperate for friends. When you came along that summer, I thought I'd made a friend at last. We're *blood*, Anne. Don't you remember?'

Amelia turns back to face the woman sitting before her. *This* is . . . George?

This woman who, according to Harvey and the various presentations, is the most gifted technological scientist in the world.

This woman's inventions have made the impossible possible. The implausible come to life.

Amelia remembers that day on the island with that strange, bright-eyed, watchful girl. The comic books, the talk of *Star Trek* and all the futuristic powers that *George* was going to harness. And then the old man. The wild-haired, desperate old man on the cliff.

She looks away, her eyes moving slowly around the room, watching the staff carry out their duties. Clearing up.

Not the food and drinks. Not the upturned chairs and the smashed glasses.

Bodies.

James's head is still turned towards her at an unnatural angle, his eyes wide open. His mouth set forever in a silent scream. She'd thought he was a friend. An ally. He'd been part of this? But then he'd tried to help her? She still doesn't understand.

Did all these people really die because of her? All because of one stupid mistake she'd made such a long time ago? *An accident.*

'Tell me, Anne,' this madwoman says. 'Did you think about me much over the years? Because I thought about you. I thought about you all the time. On the days when I had to kneel for hours at a time, with bare knees on rough hessian sacks, repeating the prayers. Begging Father . . . atoning for my sins – I thought about you.'

'My name is Amelia!' She shakes her head. 'But . . . but what are you *talking* about? What have I got to do with your praying, or your weird bloody father? It was me who pushed that old man . . .' She pauses, wipes away a tear. 'But we could have saved him. There was time.'

'There was no time.'

'Of course there was! You brought me up that winding path to see your den and to show me the lighthouse over here, but the main path was quicker – I got to the bottom and I ran to the shop, but . . . I was too scared to tell anyone.'

'It doesn't matter now anyway,' Merryn says. 'I told you about this island, and the lighthouse – and how Father said we shouldn't come here. The island is cursed, he said. Father was damaged . . . tainted . . . but he wasn't wrong. If it hadn't been that man with his broken boat, and if it hadn't been you – something would've happened eventually.' Her face falls, and she looks almost genuinely sad. 'I could've coped with it all, if you'd stayed my friend. But you ran . . . just like all the other children did. No one wanted to be around me. Not with me living there with Father. Even Jago was bloody useless.'

'I don't know what you're talking about. Who *is* Jago?'

Merryn nods towards James's body. 'Your best friend there. Bloody useless. When he came to us after his mother died, I thought – at last, company! A little brother. Well, *half*-brother. But a companion, at least. A *partner*, maybe. Or at least someone other than just me and Father. But no, none of that. All I got was Jago skulking around, snapping his infernal pictures.'

'Jago?'

A flash of annoyance at her obtuseness. More than that – rage. But Amelia watches her rein it in. 'He was there that day, you know,' Merryn says. 'Hiding in the bushes. He saw everything – as you've just seen, from his memory feed that I spliced with my own. He ran off down the hill back to the village shortly after you did. I'm surprised you didn't see him. Maybe you did and just didn't know it.'

'I still don't get it,' Amelia says. 'Who is Jago?'

Merryn flaps a hand in front of her face. 'Jago . . . James . . . whatever. He took on the anglicised version of his name when he moved to the mainland. Disappeared down to London. He was no use to me, but then he got himself into a mess and he needed my help. So I helped him . . . and then he was meant to help me today. Help facilitate this little "adventure". I was hoping he might've helped *you* . . . to stop hiding from everything. Face up to it. Face up to what you've done.' She pauses. 'If you'd admitted to it all earlier on in the day, I might've spared the others, you know.' She's grinning now. 'But it turned out to be quite fun, setting everyone against each other. Pawns. That's all they were. You're the queen, Amelia. *My* queen. You always were.'

Amelia wants to ignore all this. Wants to beg to be taken home. But is there any point? This woman – Merryn or George or The Host, as she likes to call herself – is completely mad. Aren't all geniuses mad in some way? But *this* level of mad . . . She sighs. 'Tell me then. About *Father*. What did he do to you?'

Merryn shakes her head. 'I told you the stories. That day. I'm not sure I can tell you them again.'

'Why not? Because you made them up and you're not sure you'll stay consistent?'

Merryn laughs, but there's no humour in it. 'I only wish I *could* forget. Everything he did to me – to us all – it's imprinted in my brain. Why do you think I'm so fascinated by memory? It's the most powerful thing. It can be manipulated so easily. To help draw you here, I picked those people based on their profiles, which I had my staff dredge through. They searched keywords, millions of names in thousands of databases. I have access to them all. I watched hours upon endless hours of CCTV feeds, looking for things to use. Why do you think I create things for others? Because then *I* have them all. I have everything, and I can do what the hell I want with it. You think each social media platform controls its own algorithms? Each search engine? Cookies? All of that is mine. Those paranoids who think that Big Brother is watching them through their machines and their feeds – they're not wrong. I *am* watching. I see everything. And believe me, there's no glory in it. People are disgusting. I make people's choices for them, since none of them deserve to make their own.'

Amelia says nothing. The woman is a megalomaniac as well as a psychopath. From what she remembers, 'Father' was deeply religious and deeply controlling. What Merryn is suffering from is PTSD.

'All I want to do is stop the memories,' she says. 'I thought I'd have to implant false ones via the trackers, but those people you spent the day with – they had plenty of big secrets. Huge suppressed memories. As do you . . .'

'So why not give me the tracker? You could've made this a whole lot simpler for yourself.'

She shakes her head. 'What would have been the point in that? You'd obviously suppressed your memories of that summer so deeply there was a chance they might never resurface. I needed you to remember it for yourself. I needed you to remember *me*.'

Amelia swallows and a lump sticks in her throat. This is exactly what she'd thought earlier, in the cave. This is what she'd told James as they'd walked together to the big house. But he'd told her not to tell the others, so she hadn't – and now they're dead and it's all her fault. Everything is her fault.

'What happened that day . . . it was an accident.'

Merryn slams her hand down on the table and the plates and glasses jump. A couple of them fall over, rolling across the table. 'It doesn't matter. That's not the point! It was something we shared. Something we should've dealt with together. I never got over what happened – and you were long gone. I *needed* you, Anne.'

'I keep telling you . . . I'm not Anne.' A glass rolls off the table, smashing on the floor. 'You've got some twisted idea that we were friends. But we were never friends—'

'We could've been,' Merryn says, pulling her chair closer. 'We should've been.' She shakes her head. 'You didn't give me a chance. But we shared blood! Does that mean nothing to you?'

Amelia is struggling to find the words. The woman in front of her is clearly very ill. Delusional, among other things, and for all these years harbouring this strange, twisted obsession with a young girl she spent time with for one day – many years before. Yes, they shared a traumatic event together. But that can't be what defines them both forever.

Merryn changes tack. 'I know what you're thinking. It was one day . . . how could we be friends? But it was a *special* day, Anne. We formed a bond. What happened that day set the course for both our lives, did it not?'

She can't deny that. The number of times she'd wanted to tell her parents what had happened, and decided not to. She'd been petrified. Her parents weren't harsh people, but they were law-abiding and they would have wanted to do the right thing – go to the police, tell the truth. But what might have happened to her? She'd read things, seen things on the news about children who do terrible things being taken away – put in care – and what might have been done to her there? Being away from her parents and friends? Being known as 'the bad girl' . . . 'the evil girl'. The man from the boat was dead. Nothing was going to bring him back. She'd spent over twenty years trying to make up for it, and although she'd had to push her family away – to protect them from what she'd done – she'd managed to get on with her life. Somehow.

Stupidly, she'd assumed George – or Merryn, as she was calling herself – had done the same.

'You don't even know what happened to me,' Merryn said. 'Do you even care? It was fine for you. You just ran away, went home and pretended it didn't happen—'

'But I—'

'Don't interrupt me!' Merryn jumps up from her chair and sweeps a hand across the table, knocking plates and glasses flying. 'Look at all this. Look at all the lovely food I had made for you . . .

and you didn't eat a thing. Why? Why, Anne? I did this for you. I wanted you to enjoy the party.'

Amelia feels sick. She's struggling to cope with Merryn's flashing mood changes. 'You killed all those people, Merryn. Those people had nothing to do with this . . . with us.' She sighs. 'With anything that happened.'

'Do you know what Father did to me when he found out, Anne?'

Amelia says nothing. She doesn't want to know, but she's trapped her now, and she knows she's not getting out of this place. She glances around at the staff still carrying out their duties. What stories do these people have? Because surely only people with everything to lose would be willing to knowingly participate in this whole sick charade.

Amelia

Merryn sits down again, her expression calm. 'One of the fishermen found the boat, Anne. They told Father. They had to tell Father. He was in charge of everything, back then. He was born in this house, you know. Although it was very different at that time. A proper working house. His father was the Father, then. His mother lived with the other mothers, and they all shared the care of the children. They were self-sufficient, in every way. No one came onto the island. No one went away. But then the authorities on the mainland decided to send someone over. Said it was to check on the children.' She picks up a strawberry and rolls it around in her hand, before popping it into her mouth. She chews with her mouth open, strawberry juice running down her chin.

Amelia looks away. She tries to catch the eye of one of the staff, but they keep their eyes fixed ahead. They won't get involved with this.

'Some of the children were quite . . . ill,' Merryn continues. 'I suppose you'd call them deformities, or disabilities. Some of the illnesses had been passed down over many generations of Fathers. And my Father's Father . . . well, he was quite mad. Mine, despite his strict adherence to the rules, was mostly kind. To me, certainly. To some of the others, not so much. But when they found the boat man, they traced a path back until they found my den.'

'How? He was lying at the bottom of the cliffs, next to his smashed boat . . . you didn't even go near him. How could they have thought it was anything to do with you? Why didn't you tell them about me?'

She waves a hand, dismissing Amelia's questions. 'No one knew anything about you. You were long gone.'

Amelia still doesn't understand. But there's something more pressing that she wants answered. 'What did your father do to you?'

Merryn laughs, a sad, broken laugh. 'He punished me, of course. Kept me locked up. Said he wanted to help me atone for my sin. For the only true sin that Father believed in was the taking of another's life, and that, of course, is what I did. He'd decided that it was true, and there was no point in me denying it.'

'But . . . no,' Amelia says. 'I pushed him. *I* left him.'

Merryn smiles. 'Maybe it'd be easier if you just watch.' She taps the side of her head and a screen appears behind her. She doesn't turn round, but moves a little to the left, making sure that Amelia has a clear view.

The memory picks up where it left off in the other room. The last part that Amelia watched with James. Amelia as a girl, running down the hill back to the village, stumbling, half blinded by tears. Arriving at the shop, and hesitating . . . before she turns away, shoulders shaking with all the crying, and heads back to the beach.

'I don't understand,' Amelia says. 'How can you have my memory in here? I don't have the tracker—'

Merryn shakes her head. 'It's not your perspective though, is it? You were being watched. I've already told you . . . Jago saw the whole thing, didn't he?'

James. She still can't take it in.

Then the view cuts back to the cliff. Strands of short, straggly hair flip against her face as the view pans around quickly. A hand pushes a couple of overgrown branches out of the way, before the view tilts down the cliff, right over the edge – showing now the thing that Amelia couldn't have seen from her own vantage point back at the top. A steep, snaking path, overrun with grasses, all the way down to the rocks. A gull circles ahead, swoops down and opens its beak wide with that whooping warning cry.

This is George's memory.

Amelia feels as if she's experiencing this through a virtual reality simulator. She's in George's head, seeing through her eyes as she walks down the path, slowly, carefully, holding herself low, keeping close to the inside of the cliff face to keep out of the whirling wind.

She rounds the bend in the path and finds herself on the rocks, where she scrambles hand over foot, to reach the boat man, who is still half on, half off the flat rock. His hair moves gently with the waves, his hand draped over the rock, flipping upwards as the water clutches it, slapping back down as the waves diminish and retreat into the sea.

She makes it across the rocks to the man's body. She bends over, the wind grabbing her hair again, whipping it across her face. She takes his hand and pulls, with some difficulty, flipping the man onto his back. She bends closer, puts an ear close to his face. And then the man's hand moves. It reaches for her and she pulls away as his mouth opens in a cry. She falls back onto the flat rock, arms smacking down, breaking her fall as the man grabs at air, tries to turn himself over. Tries to grip onto the rock. The back of his head is dark and wet, with water and blood and matted hair. She crawls away, running her hands across the smaller rocks wedged into the shale at the foot of the cliff.

'Oh God . . .' Amelia says, tears springing into her eyes. 'He was still alive.'

She blinks, before fixing her gaze back to the projection of George's memory. The man is almost on his knees when she finds the rock, grips it tight.

She gets to her feet as the man tries to get to his, but he's injured from his fall. His leg buckles under him, probably broken . . . and he lets out a cry of frustration, which turns into a scream as she lurches forward and brings the rock down on the back of his head.

Again.

Again.

Amelia flinches, almost feeling the force of the blows juddering up her arm as they rain down – the tightness in her fists as she grips the rock.

Then the man slumps into the water again and she scrambles away, tossing the rock into the roaring sea. She turns, stumbles. The bottom of her T-shirt gets trapped and she yanks it hard, ripping it as she manages to pull it away. Then she looks up, finding the cliff path once more, takes a deep breath, and runs as best she can against the steep incline without a backwards glance.

The scrap of T-shirt. So that's how the fisherman knew that George had been there?

Amelia hadn't even realised she was crying, but now she wipes away tears with the backs of her hands. The screen is frozen in place, showing the broken man lying on the rock.

'You're a monster.' She says it under her breath, her eyes still fixed on the screen.

Merryn taps the side of her head again and the screen vanishes. 'Maybe.' She shrugs. 'I guess I was born that way. You can't have generations of inbreeding and fail to display some undesirable traits. At least I was physically normal – that's how I've always consoled myself.'

'You could've left . . . run away . . .'

'I did, eventually. Although I had to wait until I was sixteen, and they had to send me to school on the mainland. I taught myself all I could from books, while I was locked away – and I got myself into college and then university using a fake name.'

'But I assume Merryn Hicks *is* your name? Why did you change it back?'

'I had to. So I could apply for ownership of the island. They took all the other descendants away, and Jago was already gone – so when Father died, it was only me who could lay claim. Only me who wanted to. You'd been fascinated by the island and the lighthouse, and I wanted to turn it into something nice for you.'

Amelia feels sick. 'Wait, what? You did this for me? But you didn't even know me. You don't know me—'

'You were a friend to me that day, Anne. I told you this. I didn't want you to go through life feeling guilty for something you didn't actually do . . . but I couldn't find you. Not at first.'

'Not at first?' Amelia feels goosebumps sliding all over her arms. 'When did you find me?'

'I found you via your university applications. That was one of the first systems I accessed—'

'Accessed? You mean hacked . . .'

'Yes, but I wasn't doing it to cause trouble for anyone. Not like those idiot boys in their bedrooms bringing down banking systems and blackmailing people when they find their profiles on extramarital dating sites. I mean, I *could* do all that, but it's pretty pathetic, is it not?'

'So what *did* you do?'

Merryn grins. 'Once I saw where you'd been accepted, I made sure you were given the full maintenance grant. Plus a few extras that I was able to swing here and there. Nothing too ostentatious. I didn't want you to get suspicious and question it with anyone.'

Amelia closes her eyes. 'I did notice the extra payments. And I couldn't understand how I got the full grant, when I hadn't even applied because I didn't think I was eligible. I said something about money to my grandmother, and she answered quite cryptically – so

I just assumed it was her. I knew she'd set up a trust fund for me when I was little . . .'

'Your grandmother's payments were about fifty quid a month,' Merryn says. 'Nice for a few drinks in the union bar and the occasional fancy burger at the weekend, but nothing more than that. But *I* made sure you'd never get into debt.' She lays a hand on Amelia's arm. 'I was pleased that you never went to the bank and asked them about it. I understood that in some way you probably knew.'

'What?' Amelia's eyes fly open. 'How could I have known that you were . . .' She bats Merryn's hand away. 'Don't touch me. Stay away from me. I can't . . . have you been monitoring me all this time?'

'Of course I have. I've been looking out for you. Things have been hard, despite all the honourable work you've done, haven't they?'

Amelia sighs. She has nothing else to say to this woman. She's completely insane, and she's been spying on her, manipulating her life since she was eighteen years old – after one chance meeting one summer when they were children. There is no way to rationalise it. All she can do now is try to get out of here alive. But she can't tell what Merryn's endgame might be. Does she want her to stay on the island with her? She looks away. She doesn't want to engage with this lunatic any further.

'Did you know you'd found Father?' Merryn says.

Amelia shakes her head. 'What are you talking about?' A horrible sick feeling starts to roll over her stomach. 'Found him where?'

'He wasn't old when he died. He was strong. He might've lived another twenty, thirty years. He might have become Father to others. I couldn't have that. Like I said, the other families had been taken away to the mainland to start new lives. Safe lives. It was only me and my mother left, but there was always the possibility that

Father could lie his way into starting a new family. I couldn't let him hurt anyone else.'

'What did you do?'

'I told him I wanted to meet him, here. In this house.' She raises her hands, gestures around the room. 'I told him I wanted to know all about the old ways, about where he'd come from, about how life was before the authorities moved everyone across to the other island and burned this place down.' She laughs sadly. 'He agreed. I think he was still convinced that the old ways were the right ways. That his "family" had been wronged.

'I brought him here, and I killed him. It was simple, actually. I knew after the boat man that I could do it. That I could switch my brain to a different place and kill without remorse. Besides, I did them both a favour. The boat man *and* my father. I left his body out on the hillside, let the birds do their work. I knew no one would come here and find him. I came back a couple of years later to start work on the house, and I had one of the staff scatter the bones around the island. It gave me a little thrill when you held a piece of him in your hand. Powerless. Nothing left of him but bones.'

'You need help, Merryn. You've suffered terrible trauma.' Amelia shakes her head. 'What's happened today is terrible, of course it is. But I don't think you know what you're doing . . . or what you've done. Your family history, everything that happened to you . . .'

Merryn stands up, shaking her head in exasperation. 'I thought you would get it. I thought if I could just get you here, then . . .'

'Then what? That I'd understand? You killed six people today. People who had no reason to die.'

'They did terrible things, Anne. If you do terrible things, then you must be punished. You know that. You've punished yourself enough over the years, and for what?' She laughs, but it sounds hollow. 'You didn't even kill the boat man.'

Amelia stares at her. 'I was there. I pushed him . . .'

'It doesn't matter now.' Merryn pulls the tub of cheese straws across the table. Offers it to Amelia.

She shakes her head. 'Jesus. No. I'm not touching anything that's been on this table. I saw what happened to the others.'

Merryn nods. 'I knew you'd be safe, if it came down to this. I read your dietary preferences questionnaire that I sent out with the invitation. No dairy.' She takes a bite of a cheese stick. 'These really are good, you know. You don't know what you're missing.' She shoves the rest in her mouth, then starts on another. 'Jago's pathetic "I don't eat" thing presented a problem, but it gave me a chance to try out my new toy. The tasering was quite a thrill. I'm on Prototype III, by the way. I have a chip embedded in my skull. I've been monitoring my own brainwaves and I'm close to achieving what I wanted. To remove chunks of memory without affecting the flow of everything else. So close. Such a pity. All the data are safely stored though.' She grins, taps the side of her head again. 'All linked to your own biometrics, of course.' She takes another bite of the cheese stick, then looks down at the remaining piece, turning it over between her fingers. 'I modified a cyanide analogue. Normally it's instant death with that stuff, but I was able to tweak it. Lost a few rodents along the way, but I don't think anyone is crying over a few dead rats . . .' She coughs.

Amelia looks on, horrified. 'Merryn, no . . . don't do this . . .'

Merryn coughs again, and a spray of spittle shoots out of her mouth. Her face is already turning pink. 'Too late.' She continues to cough. 'There was always a Plan A and a Plan B.' She falls forward, grips the table. Manages to twist her head to the side. Her eyes are bulging now. 'Plan A was the one where you thanked me for being a friend . . . where you told me you wanted to stay here with me.' White foam spurts out of her mouth. 'Plan B is the one where you need to deal with it all alone.'

Amelia throws herself forward, grabs Merryn by the chin. 'Merryn, no,' she says again. 'Please, you must have an antidote for this. I don't know what you mean. Deal with what? I don't know what you want me to do.'

Merryn smiles one last time as her head falls backwards, her eyes rolling up into white. 'Goodbye, Anne.'

Amelia

Emily, one of the waitresses from earlier, appears, carrying a tray with a bottle of brandy and several glasses. Following close behind is Harvey. He gives Amelia a brief smile, then picks up the bottle and twists the cap, breaking the seal. He pours a large measure into each glass, then sets the bottle down. He slides a glass towards her, but she ignores it. Does he think she's stupid enough to drink anything else these people are offering?

Harvey picks up a glass and drains it, then refills it. The other staff members, who have been slowly filing into the room, follow his lead. Amelia looks at them all – at the relief on their faces, at their shaking hands – and decides that maybe, just maybe, they are not all the same as their boss.

She picks up a glass and takes a tentative sip. The liquid burns her throat, seems to do something to her head immediately. It's harsh, but then it calms down. And she calms down along with it. 'I suppose you're in charge now?'

Harvey offers a small laugh. 'Nope.'

She glances around at the other staff. They look exhausted, and Amelia wonders how long they've all been here, carrying out Merryn's deranged plans.

She turns back to Harvey. 'Who is in charge, then? Is there someone else I haven't met yet? Someone else who's been hiding behind a screen?'

He shakes his head. 'Haven't you worked it out yet?'

She takes another sip of her drink, then another. Harvey leans forward and refills her glass. When she doesn't respond, he lays a hand on her arm.

'It's you, Amelia. It was always going to be you.'

She shakes her head. 'What? No. God, I don't want anything to do with it. I don't want to know anything more about it. I want to go home and forget all of this ever happened.'

'You know if you stay, you can work on that.' He gestures at the staff. 'They're serving drinks and clearing up the mess tonight, but these people are scientists, Amelia. Every one of them has been trained by Merryn. Every one of them has the capability to carry on the work. Well, almost . . .'

She looks around the room at the tired, pale faces. 'What do you mean, almost?'

'You hold the key now, Amelia. Merryn left strict instructions. You need to take her place. You need to authorise the research. If you don't, it has to be destroyed.'

She swallows. She doesn't want this responsibility. If all the things that Merryn claims to have developed are true, then there is a huge amount of good that could be done with her knowledge . . . and bad, of course.

'You don't have to decide now,' he says. 'There's a package for you. Take a look on the way home. Or when you get home. Think about it for a while. We've got enough to be going on with at the moment, sorting everything out here.'

'The police will help with that though, won't they?' she says.

Harvey shakes his head. 'We can't do that, I'm afraid. That's the one thing we do need to enforce. We can deal with it all, but you need to stick to the terms of the non-disclosure agreement. You can't tell anyone what happened here.'

'But . . . but . . . James? And Tiggy? And Giles and Lucy and Brenda and Scott . . . they didn't deserve this. You can't just make them disappear.'

Emily walks over to her, carrying a box. She holds it out to Amelia, gives her a smile. 'Thank you,' she whispers, then turns and walks away. She sits back on one of the sofas with the others, and none of them says any more.

Amelia looks down at the box. On top, written in beautiful calligraphic script, it says:

To My Friend, Anne. Always.

The small plane feels strange without the other seats occupied. She thinks back to what happened less than twenty-four hours before, seeing those people for the first time. Beautiful, fragile Tiggy and her pretty-boy boyfriend, Giles – the games designer, the one who could have helped them the most; he'd have been able to work it all out, Amelia is sure of it. Merryn probably knew that too, which is why he'd been removed from the action as early as possible. Brenda, with her powerful life lived at the expense of all others. Lucy, with her broken heart turned to stone. And Scott, desperately seeking a cure for his own loneliness. And then there was James . . . or Jago, as he once was. Broken by his childhood, then destroyed by his half-sister . . .

She'd had an intense day with these people, making and breaking bonds, every one of them having their lives laid bare. Now all of them are gone.

All because of that day, that summer, when she'd met *George* . . . Merryn. Damaged, abused and desperate for a friend. Amelia had shown her kindness, and Amelia had become the object of her misguided, desperate affections.

She opens the box.

Inside, there are a series of compartments containing small black cuboids, each with a name engraved on the top in white. She lifts out the first one, marked with her name – her real name, this time. It's a memory stick. Of course it is. She runs a finger across all the others. Everyone from the plane, all the friends she made and lost today. Then there's Harvey, and another five sticks with names she doesn't recognise – clearly they are the staff, who've been trapped there on the island, hiding from whatever they'd done that was so bad they felt they had no choice.

In the middle of the box, in a separate compartment, is a small mobile phone. She lifts it out, and underneath finds a folded piece of paper. She unfolds it and starts to read.

> *My Dearest Anne,*
> *I shall always call you this, as this is how I know you – in my heart. If you are reading this, then I'm deeply saddened to say that you've chosen Plan B. I'd so hoped you would choose me – Plan A. Plan 'Anne'. But I suppose I can't control your decisions. Not yet. Not ever, now – unless you allow the staff to continue with the programme.*
>
> *I'm sure you've worked out what they are all doing there. If you care to know more about their memories, you can slot the sticks into the phone and it will project them for you. I warn you now, some of those memories are not pretty.*

However, deep sins lead to deep loyalty – and in return for keeping them alive and out of prison, my staff were trained well and live in luxury – albeit on a small, isolated island. If you want to talk more, please call Harvey, and he will tell you everything that I can't capture in this one short letter. There is one contact programmed into the phone. Call it and he will answer, whenever you are ready. Right now, he is soothing the staff, helping them through the shock. They are good people, despite their sins and flaws.

You can keep them. They will be loyal to you, as they have been to me. You can continue the research, and you can have everything you ever imagined, and more. But as you know, the only way for it to continue is secretly, as it is now.

Just as Father and the Fathers before him kept their own family to themselves, this is what you must do now.

But . . .

You probably didn't expect a 'but', did you, my dear Anne?

There is another option.

Right now, the staff are busy dealing with what has happened today. They have their own instructions for this, and in time you will find out what these instructions are, and what the world will get to know about the tragedy of the 'Lost Six' and the host of the luxury party. Your name will never be mentioned. You are free to make your choice.

Your choice is simple. Take my place. Take my island. Continue my work.

Or . . . walk away. If you choose to walk away, you must do one last thing – for me, Anne. For my memory. Turn over the phone and press the red button on the back. As you guessed while on your way to the house, the caves lead to a network of tunnels. These were deliberately inaccessible to you and your group, due to the danger – but I wanted to show you just that one room. With a programme so secretive, it's always nice to be able to show off just a little of what I can do. The trackers, the projections, the asking for what you want and getting it – I wanted you to feel like there was something worth knowing about, just out of reach.

If you press the red button, fifty tonnes of dynamite will blow the island sky high. It will cause a tsunami that will hit the other island – the one where we met, all those years ago. An unfortunate side effect, I'll admit. I'd never want to cause such a tragedy. But once the water retreats, that island will be fine. Eventually. But Nirrik will be gone, and all of its secrets with it. Of course, it will still be up to you to destroy the memory sticks and the phone, but rest assured that once the hub is gone, the technology will no longer be accessible. I trust you to dispose of the contents of this box wisely.

So, my dear Anne – the choice is yours, and yours alone.

Choose well.

Your Loving Friend, your sister by blood,

George.

Amelia closes the box and her eyes. She sits quietly, barely noticing the whine of the plane's engine. She thinks back to the morning, when the pressure dropped and that lurch of turbulence had thrown everyone into a panic – and that turned out to be the least of their worries. But what's done is done.

And she knows how to fix it.

The plane lands smoothly and the engine is turned off. Harvey comes through into the cabin and unlatches the door. He folds the steps out and slides them from the plane. Then he turns to Amelia, offers a hand to help her out of her seat.

She smiles. 'I read the letter. I don't think I was meant to read it on the plane. You're meant to be back with the rest of the staff, helping them through this.'

'I'll be back there soon enough,' he says. 'Ready to go home?'

Amelia takes his hand. She leaves the box on the seat.

'Wait,' he says. 'You need to take it . . . she left you instructions.'

Amelia shakes her head. 'I'm in charge now. I'll decide what happens next.'

He looks her in the eyes, and she sees his face flash with fear. 'I understand. You don't owe us anything. Not after what we've all put you—'

'No.' She cuts him off. Gives him a careful smile. 'Here's what you're going to do. You're going to fly the plane back. Then you're going to get rid of the bodies. Take them out to sea. Dump them. Then sink the boat.'

He nods. 'But—'

She raises a hand, then points at the box. 'Take out the contents of the box. Smash all those memory sticks. Crush the phone. Rip the letter into a thousand pieces. Get everyone out of the big house. Then take all the candles from the centrepieces and move them as close as you can to the curtains. Let the place burn to the ground. Don't fly back here. Go further – anywhere you can land safely – and tell everyone to disperse. You'll need to sort out new lives for yourselves, but I'm sure you're all resourceful enough for that.'

He stands staring at her, open-mouthed.

'I'm setting you free, Harvey . . . and getting rid of that place the best way we can. I don't want to risk an explosion. I couldn't bear it if destroying that island led to any more deaths.'

'We'll need a cover story . . .'

'I'll deal with that.' She walks past him and out of the plane, down the steps.

The airfield is in darkness, apart from the runway lights, sparkling like diamonds in the inky night. She doesn't turn back. And after a moment, she hears the sound of the steps being retracted, the door closing.

She's not sure how she's going to get home from here. Her plan is to get to the main road and start walking. And whatever happens after that, she knows she'll be able to handle it. Tomorrow, wherever she ends up, she's going to call her parents – she needs to stay with them for a while. Get her head together and decide what to do next.

She's been gone for too long.

Epilogue

SIX DEAD IN BOAT PARTY TRAGEDY OFF CONDEMNED ISLAND

The Cornwall Coastguard has reported six dead after a party boat sunk off the island of Nirrik, on the Cornish coast.

Nirrik has been uninhabited and certified condemned since 1895, when the last settlers were evacuated. The island was removed from council jurisdiction and purchased by the Timeo Corporation, a technology company headquartered in St Helier, Jersey. No information about the CEO of Timeo or their links to the tragedy has been uncovered at this time.

The dead have been identified as Theresa 'Tiggy' Ramona (25), an Instagram influencer from Chelsea; her partner, Giles Horner (28), a games designer from Essex; celebrity gossip columnist Lucy De Marco (38); James Devlin (31), a photographer; Brenda Carter (62), a venture capitalist;

and Scott Williams (35), a nutraceuticals executive from Los Angeles. While it is not yet known why they were gathered on the island, an anonymous source, who alerted the coastguard, has suggested that a private party was underway.

The island's only building, a large, stone dwelling, has been burnt down, but it is not yet clear if the events are connected. Investigators have yet to access the island, as it is not known what type of contamination led to the island being abandoned many years ago.

Timeo has owned the island since 2010, according to the registrar general's office and the land registry, but it is still classified as uninhabitable amid concerns of a leaked biological agent.

The island was previously recorded under the name Father's Island, and local sources report stories of shipwrecks, drownings, extremist religious practices, child abuse, incest and more – although this is anecdotal and not officially recorded in either the parish notes or the council archives.

The families of the deceased have been informed.

ACKNOWLEDGMENTS

A few years ago, in an in-flight magazine, I read about the Swedish company Biohax International. Set up by a former body piercer, the company makes microchips that are inserted into the user's hand, just above their thumb. These chips are just like the ones used in any contactless technology – and they can be used for all the same purposes, such as paying for things, information transfer and replacing keys. I was fascinated by this, and the fact that the users are more than happy to be almost 'experimented' on, with an actual device under their skin. Being a crime writer, I immediately thought about how this could be exploited for nefarious means – hence the tracking device I invented for this book.

Next, I decided that I wanted to write something set on an uninhabited island. I was inspired by some of the tiny islands along the East Lothian coastline (where I grew up) and also by the Scilly Isles off the Cornish coast, which I visited to do research. It almost became a very different kind of book, when the *Scillonian* ferry broke down, leaving us stranded there for a few days longer than planned! Anyway, when I pitched this idea to Jack Butler at Thomas & Mercer, he was immediately intrigued and instantly came up with 'The Digital Age meets the Golden Age' – which sums the book up perfectly!

So the first thank you goes to my editor, Jack. Thank you for believing in me and my ideas, and for helping me shape the plot in its early stages into something that ended up being very fun to write. Thank you to my developmental editor, David, for making me pull it apart and dig deep into the darkest corners of my mind to make the book even better. And thank you to the copyediting, proofreading and production teams for whipping it into shape and polishing every last detail.

Huge thanks, as always, to my agent Phil Patterson, and all at Marjacq, for making this happen.

Thank you to my ever-present encouragement crew: Steph, Ed, Vicki, Lisa, Kat, Jenny and Amanda; and to my very good friend Colin Scott – who knows more than anyone else, about most things.

Big thanks, as always, to *you* – and if this is the first book of mine you've read, then I hope you'll read more! And to my faithful fans, who've been with me right from the start – thank you!

Without readers (and listeners!), bloggers and booksellers, there would be very little for me to do, except write for myself – so thank you all from the bottom of my heart, for letting me tell my stories to as many people as I can.

To my family and friends – thank you for always supporting me, for buying all my books, coming to my launches and being so proud of me, even when I struggle to make enough time to see you.

And finally, to JLOH, my travel companion, tea and toast maker, and the one who has to deal with me when writer's block turns me into a demon . . . you are the very best.

If you want to find out more about me, you can go to my website: www.susiholliday.com, or have a look here: linktr.ee/susiholliday for my social media links. I'd love to hear from you!

And of course, if you enjoyed my book, I would really appreciate it if you could leave a review . . .

Love, Susi

FREE *DARK HEARTS* BOX SET

Join Susi's readers' club and you'll get a free box set of stories: 'As Black as Snow', 'The Outhouse' and 'Pretty Woman'. You'll also receive occasional news updates and be entered into exclusive give-aways. It's all completely free, and you can opt out at any time.

Join here: sjihollidayblog.wordpress.com/sign-up-here

ABOUT THE AUTHOR

Susi Holliday grew up in East Lothian, Scotland. A life-long fan of crime and horror, her short stories have been published in various places, and she was shortlisted for the inaugural CWA Margery Allingham Prize. She is the author of seven novels, five of them written as SJI Holliday. You can find out more at her website, www.sjiholliday.com, on Facebook at www.facebook.com/SJIHolliday/ and on Twitter @SJIHolliday. She also provides coaching for new crime writers via www.crimefictioncoach.com.